Dedicated
to
my parents,
Robert and Edith Mignard,
who taught me the difference
between true and false religion.

NOVEMBER VEIL

Linda Hall

Published by
Bethel Publishing Company
1819 South Main Street
Elkhart, Indiana 46516

Cover Illustration by
Ed French

Editing and Typesetting by
Karen Berger

Printed in the United States of America

ISBN 0-934998-68-X

ACKNOWLEDGMENTS

The town of Chester, Alberta, Canada and all of its inhabitants exist only in the pages of this book. Also, the towns of St. Matthews, New Brunswick and Playa Brisa, Maine are fictitious as well.

Thank you to Sergeant Clint Dykeman of District 2, J Division of the Royal Canadian Mounted Police, New Brunswick, for answering my questions and offering advice.

A special thank you to Debbie Jespersen for loaning me newsletters and giving me a lot of information about an organization called Parentfinders.

And, to my husband, Rik, thank you for your continual support and faithfulness.

Summer 1971

"I confess before God and before this congregation of my...my...." The girl's voice was thin, unsteady. As she stood, her hands gripped the pew in front of her for support until her knuckles were white. Beside her, the mother was still, emotionless, her hands folded primly in her lap. The girl knew that her father was standing straight and stolid behind his pulpit, his body grim and hard. She did not look at him, but instead focused at the wooden cross which hung on the white wall behind him. Brown beams met in a small arch above it.

His words of that afternoon still echoed in her memory, *"You have disgraced me, child, utterly disgraced me! I am an anointed man of God and you have plunged my entire ministry into contempt."* His eyes were wild and feral, the eyes of a caged animal. She trembled in fear before them.

"I confess...." She began again, slowly, tentatively while a hundred pairs of eyes watched her and waited. Her mouth was dry. She swallowed. Her father had told her that the Bible commanded, "Confess your sins to one another." This was difficult. She also remembered the many Sunday evenings when she had sat right in this very pew while others stood and recited their misdeeds. Now it was her turn.

A small breeze fluttered from the hot night through an open window. One of the overhead lamps began to sway, covering the walls with slow moving shadows; dancing, dusky images on a pale canvas. Suddenly she felt nauseous and covered her mouth with her fist.

"Say it!" her father's voice thundered.

The girl, barely 16, looked up at this man who was her father, his purple and gold robes cascading around him like some garish costume left over from a grade school pageant. As she did, something in her died. She saw him looking ridiculous, stripped of his authority, and naked. The emperor without any clothes.

She stood tall. The nausea passed. Her voice was even as she said the words—*"I wish to confess before God and before this congregation that I have been promiscuous. I am with child."*

"With child." The words her mother had instructed her to say. Like it was holy or something. The congregation gasped. Heads turned. Whispers from behind cupped hands. Frowns. Smirks.

An hour later her father—sweat beading on his forehead and dropping onto the pulpit—was still howling down about fornication and adultery and God's inescapable judgment. Children fidgeted. Elderly ladies fanned themselves with folded up bulletins. Some glanced furtively in her direction, but she stared straight ahead at her father. Pleased with her new strength, she smiled slightly.

Finally, the communion tray was passed, the elders carefully avoiding her. She would not be allowed to partake until the church board decided on a suitable punishment for her. But she had already decided. She would never take it again.

Half an hour later the service was over, and the girl walked out of the church door without a backward glance. Once outside, she calmly walked next door to the backyard of the parsonage where she lived, and lay down on the lawn, her hands pillowing her head in the soft dark grass. She gazed out into the starry night. There was a place—there had to be—of security. Of love. She would find it.

In a few moments she smelled the perfumy, soap scent of her mother bending over her.

"Come inside. Father will be back soon." The mother's voice was strained; her eyes red.

"Father will be back soon." The mother was a victim,

too, just as powerless against him as she had been. Somehow, she had known this all along.

Her father had what they call "charisma," a presence that draws people. Pew sitters thrived on his fist-pounding, nostril-flaring, finger-pointing, pious-looks-toward-heaven sermons. She had seen them arrive by the busloads from neighboring Montana towns. She had watched as they filed into the little church overfilling it, all the while smiling to each other as they talked about miracles and the power of faith. She had overheard women whisper how handsome he is. This surprised her the most. To her, he was horribly ugly, a caricature really; his face a Halloween mask, blotched and warted.

The girl rose. *"Yes, we better not let father catch us out here, or we'll both be in trouble."* She even surprised herself with this new boldness. Her mother looked at her sharply but said nothing.

That night the girl laid on her bed and cried. Her tears enraged her. She had vowed not to cry, yet her pillow was damp with them and she was powerless to stop. She clutched her abdomen, already beginning to swell under her thin summer nightgown. Her one triumph was that she was not crying for her father, but she was thinking of Sammy, and a brief moment of comfort, of love. And then he was gone. Laughing, like a clown in a parade who passes out balloons and candies. You think you are the only one, the truly special one, but when you turn around he is up the street, and other children are receiving his special favors. The parade has moved on.

Four and a half months later on December 12, her baby was born. She named him Sean, but her father called him Ichabod.

The delivery had been difficult for her, so she stayed in the hospital for six days. The nurses were kind to her, but when she begged, *"Please, please, please let me hold my baby,"* they avoided her eyes. *"Your father has left strict orders,"* they said, fiddling with her water pitcher or the curtain clasps surrounding her bed.

But on the fifth night, a nurse quietly opened the door with a finger to her lips. She placed baby Sean in the girl's arms. He was wrapped in soft white cloths, a tiny bundle, no larger than a doll. His face was pink, his nose a tiny, pale button. His eyes were shut and his mouth moved slightly. He was the most beautiful little thing she had ever seen.

The nurse whispered to her, *"They'll have my head if they see. But you take him. I have five children of my own. This is barbaric, this not letting the mother see the baby. I don't care if he is going out for adoption. It's just not right. I'll be back in about twenty minutes."*

Despite the girl's persistence, Sean did not awaken. She held him, cuddled him to her neck, touched his smooth, dimpled cheek, outlined his face with her finger. For the next few moments in a cheerless hospital room in the middle of the night, she had to stash away enough memories to last a lifetime. In a sudden moment of inspiration she reached beside her for the small hospital menu card, turned it over and scrawled, "Baby Sean, I will love you always, from your mother Marylouise." Then she unclasped her grandmother's gold chain and cross, took it from around her neck, placed it inside the folded note and tucked them both within his blankets.

Fifteen minutes later the nurse was back. The girl's last memory was a flick of a tiny pink tongue and a reaching, a flexing of a small fist toward her.

A week later Sean was gone. *"But don't worry,"* her mother told her, *"he has been adopted into a good Christian family."* The girl looked away.

Eight months later, the girl left with her birth certificate and $2,134.47 in cash. Cleverly, she had picked up unnoticed bits of household change and tucked them in a small brown paper bag behind some old books in the back of her closet.

Her father's desk at church was a gold mine. Often late Sunday night there were five or six hundred dollars, some stuffed in tiny, white offering envelopes, some in letters addressed to him. He had begun a weekly radio show and people sent him money. *"Stupid people,"* she thought, *"why do they so blindly follow him? Can't they see how he really is?"* A twenty here, a ten there. He wouldn't miss them. He wouldn't suspect. She had become the perfectly obedient daughter. Compliant. Quiet. "Yes, ma'am. Thank you, sir."

One Wednesday night while her parents were next door at prayer meeting she walked out the back door, headed to town, boarded the Greyhound and rode two days and two nights until she reached Calgary, Alberta, Canada. She has never been to Canada, but it was about as far away as she could imagine.

Seven years later she graduated from the University of Calgary with a degree in education. During this time she became convinced that her father had lied to her. The church had lied to her. There was no God. There were no miracles. Religion was a man-made crutch for the unenlightened, the weak. She had become one of the strong.

CHAPTER 1

On November 15, 1996 the fragile, fictional world of Mary Louise Jones came close to crumbling.

Mary Louise lived alone except for a nine-year-old Himalayan cat named Piaget (PJ for short) in a small, square pale yellow bungalow in the downtown section of the rural farming community of Chester, Alberta, population 5,600. For 15 years she had taught at the Chester Elementary School, and for the past seven of that she had been the principal. Her house had four rooms; a living room, kitchen and two bedrooms. Small but home, it offered her solitude and comfort. In the dozen years she had owned the place she had completely gutted and remodeled three of the four rooms and had added a large wooden deck onto her kitchen. The deck ringed with perennials, planned so there was color all summer. The row of hedges she had planted around the perimeter of her property now plunged her back yard into privacy. Two summers ago she had constructed an enclosed gazebo in her wide back yard. A little room within the grounds, it was a place for quiet meditation, a place for relaxation and reading. In the winter it was shuttered and locked. It was that way today.

Through the years she had filled her rooms with expensive furniture and had clothed her walls in warm woods. Her entire small home was a study in woods; rich mahogany in the living room; pale oak in the kitchen; and in her dining room, which also doubled as her office, a heavy, antique, dark oak table with four chairs gave the place a medieval look. Friends had occasionally commented that she was putting so much money into a small place. "You've got the money, wouldn't you rather get a bigger house?"

"Why?" she would respond. "When it's just me?"

But in truth Mary Louise liked the smallness of her space, the richness of it. It was her own. She felt safe there.

She had never quite got around to moving her office into the second bedroom, which now served as her storage room. It was on her list of things to do next summer. Instead, her papers, educational journals, computer, printer and modem took up the lion's share of the space on her oak table. In her own bedroom, which looked out over her back garden, she slept on a single four poster bed with a good mattress. Against one wall was an antique dressing table with an enormous mirror. She had no guest room, no second bed, but Mary Louise couldn't remember ever having overnight guests.

Her newest acquisition was what the salesperson in Calgary had described as a "state of the art entertainment center"—stereo, VCR, big screen TV, five disc CD player—all accessible via remote control. Mary Louise would never have to leave her couch. Unfortunately, the only time Mary Louise sat on her couch was in the early evening when she would fix a sandwich or heat up a bowl of soup and curl up in the overstuffed couch to watch the news.

Usually by 7:30 in the evening, Mary Louise had loaded her CD player with Vivaldi, Bach and Beethoven, and was seated at her dining room table, her journals and her papers spread open in front of her. To complete her doctorate in education all that was left was her dissertation and a year's residency at the University of Alberta in Edmonton. By 10:30 p.m. Mary Louise was usually in bed.

If her evenings were routine, her mornings were even more so. At 6 a.m. Mary Louise wakened to the voices from her kitchen clock radio. After showering, she would wrap herself in a thick terry robe, grab a mug of coffee from the pot which was on automatic timer, pick up the Calgary Herald from her door step and stack her previous evening's notes into neat piles before spreading out the newspaper on the table. Mornings for her were the quiet before the storm, a time of solitude before the daily deluge of administrative problems. The paper read, she would fix herself a bowl of hot oatmeal, cooked on her stove in a double boiler, and pour herself a second cup of coffee. Then she would fix a small lunch to take with her—a piece of fruit, a sandwich, maybe some soup in a thermos. Finally, she would dress, run a comb though her short, no-fuss hair and leave for school in her Honda Prelude.

At 3:23 on the morning of November 15, the day her life would change forever, Mary Louise awoke to the desolate sound of wind gusting against her house, tree branches crackling against each other; a sinister sound that made her think of black-robed witches riding broomsticks across the moon. She pulled her feather quilt to her chin and reached for PJ. He was not in his usual place at the foot of her bed. "Probably roaming around the house," she thought, "or outside through his 'cat' door."

In the full moonlight, the shadows of tree branches danced across her ceiling, swaying and singing and chanting, urged on by the outside wind. In the distance the siren of a police car added to the foreboding chorus. She felt cold; impossibly chilled. It was as if winter were seeping through her walls, and was now gaining entrance through her skin. She slept only fitfully for the rest of the night with dark thoughts invading her dreams.

At 6:00 a.m. the radio jangled her awake with its news that the temperature was plummeting. Unseasonable. Snow by noon, possibly earlier. "Don't forget your boots and your windshield scraper," the voices said cheerfully. "Button up your coat and bring in the cat." She switched off the radio and sat on the edge of her bed. PJ was meowing around her legs; absently she scratched his ears. On her way to the shower, Mary Louise flicked on light after light in the dark house.

After her shower she towel dried her hair in the mirror and frowned slightly. Here and there her hair was turning gray. At forty-one she felt she was too young, but maybe the gray would give her a measure of distinguishment as she aimed for her doctorate, and then maybe, just maybe, a professorship with the Faculty of Education. She hated to admit it but she was wearying of the children with their hundreds of sticky-faced questions and pouty-mouthed requests. And it seemed she couldn't walk down the streets of Chester without a dozen little children sing-songing, "Hi, Mrs. Jones." She was tired of reminding them that it was "Ms. Jones." Maybe a year in Edmonton would do her good. She planned to talk to the superintendent later this week about taking next year off for her residency.

The smell of the coffee beckoned her. She filled a cup and grabbed the Calgary Herald from the porch. When she opened up the paper, the first thing she saw was a large, color photo of his face. Momentarily it startled her until she remembered. Of course, he was in Calgary (she had known that) for a week of healing meetings at the Saddledome. She peered closely at his face. It was a publicity photo taken no doubt by a professional photographer. Only a pro could capture that confident glint, that smile, the small cleft in the chin, the strong jaw line, the deep set eyes. She read the caption: "Dr. Sterling Jonas." "Dr." What a joke. What a slap in the face to someone like her who had labored for everything she had. Cradling the warm mug of coffee in both hands she saw, for the first time, the headline. How could she have missed it? — "Evangelist Dead."

Shivering, shaking she sat down at the table and forced herself to read on:

"The body of Dr. Sterling Jonas, 62, was found shot to death early last evening in a hotel room in Chester, Alberta. Dr. Jonas, a well-known evangelist and founder of the Portland, Oregon, based Disciples of Grace Church had just finished a week of meetings in Calgary. It is not immediately known why he was in Chester...."

Her hands shook, the coffee spilled, rivulets of it spoiling the face—a dark blotch running down the forehead to the nose and onto the cleft chin, blurring the edges. Trembling, Mary wondered how long before someone would come to her door.

CHAPTER 2

By noon the two extra-strength Tylenols she had taken at 10:00 were already wearing off. Mary Louise paused, pressed the fingers of both hands into her forehead and stared at the computer screen. How she longed for a cup of tea and her comfortable couch.

The day had started badly. Not five minutes before the 8:45 bell rang a little first grader, Jacob Fletcher, was throwing up in the hall. Mary Louise and Ed Thiessen, the assistant principal, were down on their hands and knees with scrub buckets and mops. Little Jake lay on a cot in the office crying while Jennifer, the school secretary, tried to locate his parents. No answer at home. A check of his father's work informed her that Jake's dad was out of town on business. His mother's work place reported this was her day off. Finally, an aunt was located and arrived 45 minutes later, frowzy and bad-tempered. It turned out that Jacob's mother had gone to Calgary to do some pre-Christmas shopping. The aunt, who had just gotten off the night shift at Tim Horton's Donuts on Highway 2, did not appreciate being called to come for her sister's sick kid, and she let them know it.

That was number one. At nine-thirty she had to deal with two fourth graders who were caught smoking in the boys' room. She shook her head as she led them by their shirt collars into the office.

Mary Louise stared at the computer screen trying to make sense out of the memo she was putting together. Suddenly the words on her screen began to dance, to swirl until they were no longer words, but a face—his newspaper face. And then his motionless publicity-photo face became animated; he was laughing, preaching, sneering—the way he was when she would accidentally tune into his TV program. She was always mesmerized by his theatrics—back and forth across the stage, hands waving, strutting in his thousand dollar suits. She remembered thinking that somewhere along the way—it certainly wasn't from his northern Montana home—he had acquired a southern accent.

She closed her eyes and rubbed her forehead. When she opened them again her computer screen was again a computer screen with a half-written memo to the superintendent. It was now nearly 12:20 p.m. There was precious little time to get this finished, eat her lunch and make it to her class of fifth graders by 1:00. Three afternoons a week she taught. Administrative work in the mornings, teach in the afternoons. "A heavy schedule," she thought. She shook her head at her choice of words. Until today she had preferred to call it "challenging."

She pulled her cloth lunch bag from her bottom drawer. The sandwich was unappetizingly limp, and the coffee she had poured for herself an hour ago was cold. She was avoiding the staff room today. Normally she liked to mix, but today the only topic of conversation seemed to be the murder. There weren't many murders in Chester and especially none so significant. Everybody, it seemed, had an opinion and a theory on why the infamous Dr. Sterling Jonas had ended up meeting his demise in a small, rural Canadian town. Roy Staves, the Physical Education teacher, said it was probably a clandestine meeting of his organization. "He was probably into selling drugs, that sort of thing." Monique Dubois, who taught in the French Immersion program, said that he was meeting a lover; and Georgia Smythe, the grade two teacher, was convinced it was theft. "Let's face it," she said pushing her heavy horn rims up on her pudgy nose, "the guy has money. He drives into a little town like this in his Jaguar and every entrepreneurial thief within five miles is gonna sit up and take notice. It just got out of hand."

At 12:35 Jennifer poked her head in and Mary Louise regarded her over the top of her reading glasses.

"Yes?"

"This came today," Jennifer said wagging a legal size envelope back and forth. "We think it's for you, at least Ed does." She placed the envelope down on the desk in front of Mary Louise. "As you can see it's been all over the globe. But I didn't know your middle name was Louise."

Mary Louise picked it up. The envelope was criss-crossed with addresses marked off and rewritten. It was from someone named David Brackett from Colville, Washington. Jennifer was right. It had gone all over the globe. It looked like it was first mailed to her on August 11 in care of the Edmonton School Division. Someone in the office must have known that Mary Louise was enrolled at the University, because it was then forwarded over to the Faculty of Education. From there it sailed down to the Calgary school division which had sent it east to Chester. "Good thing you're so famous. Everyone knows you," said Jennifer.

"Probably a former student," thought Mary Louise as she placed the envelope on the top of her "in" box.

Three hours later she was back in her office, her day nearly over. Too bad her headache wasn't. Through her closed office door she could hear other staff members collecting their things and saying their good-byes and see-you-tomorrows and have-a-nice-evening and be-careful-in-that-snow-out-there. She decided that she, too, would leave although by the stack of things in her "in" basket she could easily camp out here.

Jennifer poked her head around the door. "I'm on my way now. Anything else you need?"

"Nothing, no, I'm fine. I'm going to pack it in early today."

"You?"

"A bit of a headache," said Mary Louise stuffing the contents of her "in" basket into her briefcase. She'd take care of all of this at home. At least at home she could wander around in her sweats and wool socks.

To get to the hallway from her office Mary Louise had to pass through the staff room. A few teachers were still there.

"Whoa," said Roy making a dramatic gesture of looking at her and then his watch and then back at her again. "Mary Jones, you're leaving early. Is this some kind of record?"

"Not feeling well," said Mary Louise grabbing her coat. "Bit of a headache."

"Then you go home and make yourself a nice cup of hot lemon tea." This was from Marsha Friedmont who taught fourth grade.

"No, not tea," said Roy rinsing out his coffee mug in the sink. "Get yourself some boiling water, add a squeeze of lemon, some honey and a couple shots of Irish Whiskey. Much better than tea for the old flu!"

"Who said anything about flu?" said Mary Louise smiling. "It's just a headache."

"Well, you take care of yourself. There's a lot of flu going around," said Marsha. "We don't need your getting sick on us."

"Flu and murder," said Nick Utley, another fifth grade teacher, with his nose in the daily paper. Mary Louise buttoned up her coat and pulled on her gloves. As she walked out the door she heard Roy say, "What I'd like to know is what was he doing in Chester?"

CHAPTER 3

"What was he doing in Chester?" asked Corporal Roger Sheppard of the Chester detachment of the Royal Canadian Mounted Police. A warmish can of almost empty Diet Coke in hand, he stood facing Constable Clayton Lavoir who was leaning against the wall in Roger's office skimming through the reports filed by the constables on the scene.

Roger continued, "Why would a well-known TV evangelist get in his car, drive 20 miles east of Calgary, check into a second rate hotel and promptly get shot? Did he know someone here? Was he meeting someone?"

Clayton shook his head and said nothing, still reading.

For most of the day Roger had puzzled over this. Jonas and his entourage, which included his wife, some board members of the Disciples of Grace Church, and a large crew of techies had rented the entire premiere wing of the ninth floor at the Four Seasons Hotel in downtown Calgary. Late yesterday afternoon, Sterling Jonas had apparently driven his car to Chester where he checked into the Chester Inn. The Calgary police force had spent the day questioning, and re-questioning, most of the members of Jonas' crew.

All day Roger had intended to drive over to Calgary to meet with the officers there and talk to Jonas' people, but one thing or another had kept him in Chester. He would be ready to grab his coat and then Adele, the detachment receptionist, would poke her head into his office, "Call on line one." He would be delayed again another half hour or so.

Earlier he had met with Sergeant Roy Laird and together they were working on a public relations plan. Theirs was a small, rural detachment with no public relations officer. So far, if the media called (and the media was becoming relentless), it was up to whoever answered the phone to come up with an answer. Laird and he had written one "official statement" and under pressure of some of the bigger media were in the process of scheduling a press conference.

Clayton sat down on a wooden chair and was leaning back against the wall the with file in his hand. Roger turned, frowned, took the last warm gulp from his Diet Coke and said again, "What was he doing in Chester?"

Clayton grunted. "According to the reports, Denise Jonas, the wife, didn't even know he was missing. It looks like the media got the news of his demise before she did."

"So her husband takes off, is gone all night and she doesn't even know he's gone."

Clayton said, "These people lead different lives than you and I, Corp. The reports say that they were checked into adjoining suites. She says, 'It's so he can pray.' But if you ask me, all was not bliss in blissville."

Roger frowned. "But why Chester?"

Clayton shrugged his shoulders. When he shrugged his shoulders, his whole body shrugged, right down to his belly which strained against the buttons of his uniform shirt. Clayton's wife, Marge, had recently opened her own bakery in Chester where she specialized in home baked pies and donuts. Roger guessed it was difficult for Clayton to resist eating the bakery goodies. Clayton said, "In my opinion, I think we got around four possibilities here."

"I'm listening."

"Possibility number one," said Clayton raising his forefinger. "It was completely random. The poor fellow just happened to be in the wrong place at the wrong time."

"Doesn't happen very often."

"Right, so we scratch that one. Two," he said raising two

fingers, "it was a bungled burglary attempt."

"Except he's found with more than four hundred bucks in his wallet, his Jag is still in the parking lot. Plus," said Roger tapping the topmost police photo which was on his desk, "burglars don't mutilate bodies. Typically they're surprised, and if they shoot, they just shoot and run. Whoever did this was in a rage." Roger studied one of the photos. The body of Sterling Jonas was naked except curiously for a dress shirt and tie. He was lying face down on the hotel bed, his feet bound together with his belt, and his hands tied together behind him with the electrical cord from the lamp. But that wasn't what had killed him. Six bullets had. Blood had spattered on the floor, on the rug, on the walls. It was a grisly sight, and Roger felt for the bell hop who the evening before had found the body.

"Okay, rule out two. Here's three," said Clayton. "It was a prostitute, a thwarted lover, something along that line."

"Could be, but I don't think a woman could have overpowered him like that. He's a big man."

Clayton gave him a look. "Who said anything about a woman?"

Roger shook his head and frowned.

"Here's four. It had something to do with his church, some sort of a power struggle within his organization, someone with a grudge."

"Who just happened to see him get in his car and then followed him all the way to Chester?"

"An awful lot easier than killing him in his armed fortress in Oregon."

"Armed fortress?"

"Mansion. Big house. I saw it on TV once, on Lives of the Famous and Rich or something like that. Electrified fence and dogs that would rip your heart out on command."

"So," said Roger, "maybe someone is out to get him. They follow him all around the country. Finally they get their opportunity when he leaves his group, tells no one and drives out to Chester. They watch him check into a ground floor hotel with not a whole lot of security, and then climb through the window and shoot him."

"Can you come up with anything better?"

"Maybe someone lured him to Chester."

Roger picked up his Coke, realized he had finished it and tossed it in the trash. "Maybe the someone who lured him to Chester wasn't from Chester at all. Maybe the perp is from Oregon. He follows Jonas to Calgary and then he himself goes to Chester. Calls Jonas, tells him to meet him here. Jonas goes and gets murdered."

"You're still assuming the murderer is a guy."

"I'm using 'he' in the generic sense."

"You can't do that. It's not politically correct. You can't put that on reports."

"So what do we say instead?"

"'He-she.' 'They.' Don't ask me." Clayton smiled. "I just work here."

"Maybe he came to Chester because he wanted to start a branch church or something," Roger said, absently picking up the computer print out reports from the corner of his desk.

"Lucky us. The Reverend Doctor Sterling Jonas." said Clayton rising. "Did you ever happen to catch his act on TV?"

"Can't say that I've ever had the privilege," said Roger skimming the reports again.

"Sometimes Marge and I watch it for a laugh. Wonder what they'll have on this Sunday. You ought to tune it in."

"When's it on?" asked Roger.

The hotel clerk at the Chester Inn had seen no one enter or leave, and the special RCMP Ident crew from Calgary determined that the murderer had presumably entered the room by the door, but had broken the window, probably with the gun, and had exited that way. There were prints all over the place, but none of them matched any of the RCMP files in their computers. So the guy didn't have a record.

"Sunday, 10 a.m., on cable."

"What?"

Clayton looked up at him. "You wanted to know when Sterling Jonas was on."

"I'm in church on Sunday mornings. Besides we don't have cable."

"No cable? How can you live?"

"We canceled it. Becky was becoming mesmerized by the rock music station. That we didn't need."

Clayton grunted. Then he spread his hands behind his head and stretched. "Don't think I could stand not having the sports," he said.

"You get used to it."

Only occasionally, and by extreme accident, had Roger ever seen the Reverend Dr. Sterling Jonas in action. Although, there was a time when his books had been prominently displayed on the shelves of every Christian bookstore. Roger tried to extract from his memory bits of information about the man. He was a popular, prolific author who wrote dozens of books on healing, faith, grace. Then there was some kind of scandal. Roger hadn't paid too much attention at the time. Maybe his wife Kate would remember. She was a bit more up on these things; but whatever the reason, his books were pulled from the bookstore shelves. Jonas called it "persecution" and began offering his books on Cable TV via a 1-900 number where the caller would pay for the call, get a "prayer for the day," and for a small donation Jonas send a copy of his latest drivel as well as a promise that he would "pray over" the call. Roger remembered that much.

Clayton said, "Do we know anything about this guy? I mean before he became what he is today?"

"Roberta is starting a background check to see what she can dig up about things like potential enemies from a long time ago."

Roger knew Constable Roberta St. Marie to be quick and efficient. He said, "Can you get me some videos of his programs? The ones from last week in the Saddledome? Call down to the networks and see what they have. If the networks get sticky, which I can't see happening, get a warrant. I'm especially interested in pans of the audience."

"You gonna be around to see this thing through?" asked

Clayton.

Roger managed a smile. "I have no idea," was what he finally said.

"Would he be around to see the end of this case?" The suddenness of this murder was allowing him a small reprieve from the thing that had captured most of his attention for the past month, the past two months. For it had been two months ago when Sergeant Laird had walked into Roger's office, shut the door and said in his blunt manner, "Roger, you did outstanding on the Sergeant's test. They want to know if you'll consider a promotion."

Consider a promotion? Wasn't that the reason he had written the exam in the first place?

"It would mean a move east...." Laird was saying.

East? Saskatoon? Winnipeg? Regina?

"To a town in New Brunswick, St. Matthews. It's on the border with Maine, population 6,000...."

New Brunswick!! His wife's family lived just outside of Toronto. That was about as far east as he had ever been in his life.

"A lot of small towns out there have their own police forces. It's sort of a historical thing. They were policing towns even before anyone thought of the RCMP, but now some of these towns are facing the money crunch. So the RCMP is taking over the policing duties of some of these little towns. St. Matthews is one of them."

New Brunswick!! Finding his voice he managed to say, "How does the community, uh, St. Matthews feel about the RCMP coming in?"

"That's why we're thinking of you."

"Meaning what?"

"Your people skills are high. A lot of townspeople naturally feel they're going to lose the personal touch. At first, there might be a bit of resentment."

"Oh great, so they bring someone in from the west, someone who's never even been to New Brunswick...."

"That's the thinking, yes. And that's why I'm recommending you. You've got a soft touch, good community spirit, a stable family life..."

"I don't know how stable it will be after I tell them this."

"Trust me in this, Roger. I think you'd be perfect for St. Matthews."

New Brunswick!

"With the new emphasis on community-based policing you won't be stuck behind a desk either. You'll be out in the community, giving the newer members the value of your experience. Plus, you'll love it there. St. Matthews is right on an inlet of the Bay of Fundy...."

New Brunswick!

"...it's right on the border with Playa Brisa, Maine...."

New Brunswick!

"So, you'd be working a lot with the Maine police department and customs. I'm also recommending that you take some training offered by the FBI for RCMP officers. It's a promotion plus an exciting opportunity."

Trying to find his way back to reality, Roger had said, "Won't that leave the detachment in a bind, what with Roberta and my being transferred at the same time?"

Roberta was being transferred to a small, rural outpost in the Northwest Territories, a transfer she had requested. She would be one of only two police officers there, so in a sense this was a promotion for her as well.

"No," Laird had answered. "We've known about that one for a while. They want a female up there. We're already working on a couple of replacements for here...."

Kate, when Roger told her, had seemed genuinely pleased. "We'd be so much closer to my family, my parents and sisters."

Sara, his 18 year old daughter had beamed. "Dad, that's so great, congratulations!"

But Becky, his 14 year old had shrugged her shoulders and said, "That's nice for you, Dad. I think that I'm going to stay here."

He had said, "Yes." He would go. Whenever the town

police pulled out and the RCMP moved in, he would be on the next plane. That could be a month. That could be two months. That could be two weeks. Kate and he decided she and the girls would stay in Chester until the end of the school year.

But for right now, he would work on the case until he got the call. Maybe it would give his mind a bit of a breather.

CHAPTER 4

On her way home from school Mary Louise found herself driving beside the Chester Inn, not her usual route. It had been snowing since around ten that morning and the roads were slushy and slippery. Several times she had to hang on to the steering wheel as her Honda skidded around a corner or protested at a stop sign. The car's heater was on the high setting, the fan screaming warm air into the car, yet she shivered inside her zipped coat. Outside, pedestrians held their jackets tightly around them as they struggled against the wind. Next to the Inn there were three police cars, two television vans and an assortment of cars parked jaggedly around the building. She guessed that the Chester Inn had not had this much business since the 1988 Winter Olympics. She drove by slowly and then turned left at the light and headed up the street that would take her into her own neighborhood. She turned the radio on—just in time for the news—the Sterling Jonas murder, what else? She switched it off. Silence was better.

It had been relatively easy, she remembered, to change her name to Jones. Jones was more logical, more common, made more sense. A "typo" she laughed at the Motor Vehicles Division, and they smiled back and made the correction on her license. No one questioned the well-dressed professional lady school teacher with two degrees and an impeccable driving record. She had also changed her first name from Marylouise, all-run-together to two words, Mary and Louise. But most people simply knew her as Mary. When she had come to

Canada twenty-five years ago, getting a student visa was relatively easy. She had paid cash in advance for her first semester at the University of Calgary and registered as a foreign student. If she lived frugally, she had enough to get by. Six months later she was granted landed immigrant status, applied for and received her Social Insurance Number as Mary Louise Jones. Then she got her first job in Canada—working in a department store selling children's shoes. All of her Canadian papers, her driver's license, her Canadian Social Insurance Card, her Alberta Health Card read Mary Louise Jones. Thirteen years ago she had taken out citizenship in Canada. Her ties with the United States and with Montana were completely severed.

Up ahead on her right, her little bungalow looked dark and unwelcome. Cold. She pulled the Honda under the carport, got out and locked it up. Inside, she turned up the furnace and sat down on her couch, her coat still zipped to her chin, her briefcase in her lap. For several minutes she sat there in the darkness. The fictions she had established—that her parents had died in a car accident when she was 16 and she had no other living relatives—had served her well through the years. She had recited them so often she herself almost believed them.

The closest thing she had to family—to a sister, was Perry who lived across the backyard. She spent every Christmas, every Thanksgiving, every birthday with Perry, Perry's husband Edwin and their daughter Johanna. She had watched Johanna grow from a gangly tomboy climbing her trees to a young woman studying computer science at the university in Calgary. Mary Louise took as much care to find the perfect Christmas gift for Johanna as she would for her own flesh and blood.

Finally, the house was heated up enough for Mary Louise to take off her coat, flick on all the lights and put the kettle on for tea. "Keep busy," she told herself. Careful to keep the radio or TV off, she loaded up her CD player and dumped the contents of her briefcase onto her cluttered table.

On the top of the stack was the letter that had "gone around the globe." She picked it up. Sometimes she did get letters from former students. She fingered the letter and then gasped and dropped it as if it had stung her. She peered at it again, afraid to touch it. Marylouise Jonas. It was addressed to Marylouise Jonas! How had she not seen that before? How had no one seen that before? Louise—she should have dropped that name entirely from all her papers. Why hadn't she? But deep within she knew the reason. It was the only vestige of "family" that she cared to hold onto. She was named after her maternal grandmother who had died when Mary Louise was 13. It was this grandmother who read Bible stories to her, and together they memorized long sections of the Bible. Even though she no longer held the Bible to be anything more than religious literature, her grandmother represented warmth and love. Also, it was surprising and a bit annoying that remembered fragments of the Bible popped into her mind at the most inopportune times. "For God so loved the world that He gave His only begotten Son....The Lord is my shepherd I shall not want, He maketh me to lie down...."

It was her grandmother who had also given Mary Louise a gold chain with a cross which she wore continually when she was young, a cross engraved with her grandmother's name, Marylouise Isaacs.

Trembling, she sat down at the table and slipped her thumb under the flap. Slowly, carefully she extracted one sheet from a lined yellow legal pad. It was handwritten. And in some far away corner of her mind she knew immediately who it was from.

Dear Marylouise,

I think I may know you from Great Falls, Montana. And the date that I may know you from is December 12, 1971. If you want to get in touch with me my phone number is (509) 555-0012. I have a gold chain and a cross that I think may belong to you.

If you don't wish to contact me, I will understand.

Sincerely and with much love,

David Brackett —"Sean"

She read it again. She touched the letter, running her fingers along each line. Several times she reached for the phone and then hesitated. What do you say? "Hi there, David. I'm your long lost mother—I'm sorry that I wasn't there for you? I'm sorry I wasn't there to walk you to kindergarten and to drive you to hockey and piano lessons? I'm sorry I wasn't there to sign your grade cards and help you study for math? I'm sorry I wasn't there to bake birthday cakes for you? I'm sorry that I never looked for you. I wanted to. I really did, but so many things got in the way. But I thought of you. Every single day I would think of you. And on your birthday, every year on your birthday I would buy a single flower and place it in a vase for you. And when I would choose with care a present for Johanna, I would think about you and hope fervently that someone were buying presents for you."

She pulled the phone toward her, cradling it gently in her hands, and then she realized with a kind of horror that it was too late; the time for contact was way past. Because of the murder, he cannot know who his grandfather is. He must be protected from that, at least. Or was she protecting herself?

As darkness descended on the town and the snow-borne wind whipped around her little house, Mary Louise held the letter to her cheek wetting it with her tears, oblivious to the harsh whistling of the kettle on the stove and the meowing of PJ at her feet.

CHAPTER 5

Before heading out on the highway toward Calgary, Roger stopped at a convenience store and poured for himself an extra large coffee with double sugar, double cream.

"It's crazy out there," said the large balding man behind the counter.

"Yeah, the snow's not supposed to let up for a couple of days," said Roger.

The man shook his head. "It's got to be this greenhouse ozone thing," he said. "We never before had snow so early and so much."

Roger smiled and left. Back in the car he punched his home number into the car phone.

"Hi, it's me," said Roger when Kate answered. "I might be late. I'm heading into the city to talk to some of Jonas' people. Don't wait for supper."

"Is it a madhouse yet?"

"The highway's getting crazy, yeah. This stupid snow. No one has their snow tires on yet."

"Not the roads, silly, this case. It's all over the TV and radio—on every station."

"Great. Just what we need. What are the girls up to?"

"Sara's in her room studying and Becky's at Jody's. Gladys will be driving her home soon before the roads get really bad."

"They already are really bad. How's Becky? Any better?"

They were talking about their daughter's steadfast refusal

to have anything to do with the move to New Brunswick.

"She still plans on moving in with Jody."

"Yeah? What does Gladys say?"

"I haven't talked with her, but I'm sure this is something the girls have concocted."

Roger detected a note of strain in Kate's voice. The move would be hard on her, too, and having a daughter who was becoming increasingly uncommunicative was even more of a worry. Together they prayed about it, but many nights he would wake up in the middle of the night to find Kate awake and sitting on the living room couch. "Becky's not the only one who's going to miss it here," she had told him a few days ago.

"Hang in there, Kate," he said gently.

Nearing downtown Calgary, it was as Kate had said—a madhouse. Lining the streets on all three sides of the hotel were TV vans, cars parked at odd angles, newspaper people scurrying along with cameras and notebooks through the wind and snow. He drove through the congestion and pulled up at the front of the Four Seasons. There's not a lot of room at the front entrance of the Four Seasons at the best of times. And this wasn't was one of the best of times. A city police constable who was directing traffic in front of the hotel pointed him toward the side of the building. Roger complied. Next to the Four Seasons the one way street had been closed to traffic, roped off and was being used for parking. Roger pulled into a space beside a large yellow and black sign which read, "OFFICIAL POLICE PARKING ONLY. ALL OTHERS WILL BE TOWED AWAY. NO EXCEPTIONS." "NO EXCEPTIONS" was underlined.

Inside the large crowded lobby Roger spotted Mick Michalski chatting with the valet. Roger made his way through the crowd toward him.

"Is this nuts or what?" said Mick gesturing to the melee in the lobby. As Mick led Roger toward the elevators, he said, "All this and the San Jose Sharks are in town tonight to play the Flames at the Saddledome. What a zoo! We're thinking of hiring a couple of PR people just to handle all of this. Except

we don't have the budget. Cutbacks. We have a quick pro-
posal in to the mayor's office, anyway. Can't hurt. We're
trying to appeal to the fact that all these—CNN, ABC, NBC,
not to mention the CBC and CTV types—will be bringing in a
lot of money to the city. I can just see the fast food merchants
within twenty miles of this place rubbing their hands together
in glee."

Roger made a sound of agreement and looked over at Mick
as they stood beside the elevators. He had worked with Mick
on a few minor things; B & E's, a runaway thirteen year old
kid from Chester who was caught stealing cars in Calgary. For
serious crimes, such as drugs and homicide within Calgary,
the RCMP, who were sort of like the Canadian equivalent to
the FBI, worked with the local police forces. But unlike the
FBI, in small rural towns in Canada, especially in the west, the
RCMP was often the only police force.

Mick was still talking. Roger knew Mick to be a bit of a
loud mouth, maybe a bit blunt, always speaking his mind. He
was slightly overweight, shorter than Roger with a ruddy, pit-
ted complexion, remnants of an acne-filled adolescence.

"I want your opinion of Denise," said Mick as they boarded
the elevator.

A few minutes later the door of Denise Jonas' room was
answered, not by the woman, but by a small, fine boned man
who scowled at them and squinted through wire-rimmed
glasses. His lined, very tan face bore deeply embedded permanent scowl marks. His face looked oddly like the wooden face
of a ventriloquist's dummy. The man sighed. "What do you
people want now?" he said.

Mick said, "We'd like to talk to you, Mr. Soames. Actually to Mrs. Jonas."

"You already talked to her. There's nothing more to say.
He began to close the door. Mick grabbed the side of the door.
Roger was afraid that Mick was going to push the door open,
shoving the man back into the room. That's all they would
need, a charge of police brutality. Instead, Mick said gently,
"Jud Soames, chairman of the board of Jonas' Church, I'd like

you to meet Corporal Roger Sheppard of the Royal Canadian Mounted Police in Chester. He'd like to speak for a moment with Mrs. Jonas."

"It's the Disciples of Grace Church, not Jonas' church." said Jud stiffly.

"May we come in?" asked Mick politely.

"Fine. Come in. Stay all night. Camp out if you wish," he said flinging the door wide. "Invade our lives. It's just religious persecution. That's all it is."

Mick was getting angry. Roger could tell that he was doing everything he could to stay calm. "Religious persecution? We're trying to solve a murder here."

There were large white suitcases on the bed, and laying across the chair was a white leather garment bag. Women's clothing was in various stages of being folded and placed in the suitcase.

In a far corner of the room a woman sat on a chair, her face bowed low into her hands. Her brown hair, long and straight covered her shoulders like a shawl. She wore a monotone beige outfit, slacks and sweater in some matching cashmere fabric. She wore lots of bracelets, Roger noted, and rings on every finger. She did not look up. Ignoring the two police officers, Jud went back to placing the mounds of folded clothing neatly into the suitcases.

"What do you think you are doing?" asked Mick calmly.

"We're packing. We've got a plane to catch."

"I see you packing, Mr. Soames. I don't see a 'we' involved here.

The woman looked up. It was a young face, a delicately featured, clear complexioned face, a frightened face. Her eyes darted nervously here and there, to Jud, to the window, back to her hands which were now clutched in her lap. She looked not much older than his own daughter Sara thought Roger. Instead of enhancing her appearance, her clothing and jewelry only served to diminish her, as if everything she wore was too big for her. A scared little girl dressed up in her mother's clothes.

"Meet Mrs. Jonas," said Mick triumphantly. "Are you going to talk now, Mrs. Jonas?" Roger noticed a note of sarcasm in his voice.

Roger moved toward her extending his hand. She looked down. He said, "Mrs. Jonas, I want to say first of all how sorry I am about what has happened to your husband."

She looked up, nervous. brief momentary eye contact, and then back again to her lap.

"I think you should leave her alone, and I think you should go. She's had a terrible shock." This was from Jud who had put down a pile of folded blouses and was striding toward them.

Roger ignored him and pulled a chair closer to Denise. He reached inside his jacket pocket and pulled out his small notebook.

"I know this has been difficult for you, but if I could talk to you for a few minutes."

She nodded. Still no eye contact.

"Mrs. Jonas, I know you have talked to a lot of police officers and some of my questions may be repeats, but please try to answer them as carefully as you can."

She looked at a spot on the floor between them and said hoarsely, "Okay."

From beside the bed Jud scowled.

"Yesterday afternoon your husband left his room and apparently drove to Chester by himself. Do you have any idea why he did that?"

"No."

Mick said, "Your husband was gone the whole night and you didn't even know he was gone? I find that remarkable."

After a long pause her voice barely above a whisper, she said, "I think he went....I don't know."

"You think he went where?"

"I don't know. To pray, I think."

"Did he often leave you to go and pray?" Roger tried to make his voice as fatherly as he could.

Mick's voice dripped with sarcasm when he said, "I'm sure Jonas went off to pray."

Jud could contain himself no longer and blurted out, "An un-Christian and totally pagan police force from Canada could not be expected to understand the ways of God—that true men of God, real Christians sometimes go away to pray by themselves!"

Roger turned to him, "Mr. Soames, I am a Christian, a *real* Christian, but if I were to go off to pray by myself I would still leave my family a note."

Jud backed away, startled and then sat down on the bed between the two mounds of folded dress shirts.

"Now," he said turning back to Denise, "your husband left and you did not know where he was or whom he was with?"

She shook her head and looked down.

Feeling as though he was having about as much success as a mosquito on a lead pipe, he tried a different tack. "Okay then, I'm going to ask you if you know of anyone who might want to do this to your husband. Did he have any enemies that you knew about?"

Jud was on his feet again. "Enemies! Of course he had enemies! He was an anointed man of God. God's prophets always have enemies.

"Who?"

"Many people. Any number of people. Enemies of God...."

"Name one," said Roger, his pen poised over his notebook.

Jud clamped his mouth and said nothing.

Roger turned back to Denise. "I want you to think hard."

"I...don't...know." She pronounced each word slowly, as if she were learning the language for the first time.

Reluctantly Roger moved his questioning to Jud who continued to tell them in no uncertain terms that he saw nothing, knew nothing and no, he didn't notice anything different in Jonas' demeanor yesterday. But Jud made sure that the two police officers knew that he had been involved all evening, that was "*all* evening, gentlemen," in a Disciples of Grace board meeting. Denise was there, too. They could vouch for each other. So could all of the other board members.

"Well, bully for them," said Mick later as they walked down the hall to where more Disciples of Grace staff people were lodged.

Phil Kolanchuk, the head sound man, was a large, well-muscled man in his mid-thirties who told them he had worked in Hollywood before coming on with the Disciples of Grace. "Hey, it was a steady job. Hollywood's so hit and miss," he said as the two entered his room. He was clearly not packing, as Jud and Denise were. Instead, clothes were strewn around the room in a haphazard way, along with empty pizza cartons and beer cans. The TV was tuned into the all-rock music station and figures on the TV gyrated in time to the sounds. He turned down the volume and said, "You want a beer?"

"No thanks."

"Well, I'm having one. I'm on vacation—officially on vacation now that my boss has kicked the bucket." He winked at them.

Mick said, "You're not leaving?"

"Me, nah, no. I'm gonna stay and enjoy the sights and sounds of Calgary for a while. Maybe go to a hockey game. They got the ice back in the Saddledome, I hear, and I got some money saved. So shoot, what do you wanna know?"

Roger began, "What exactly did you do for Mr. Jonas?"

"*Doctor* Jonas," he said pointing the can of beer toward them. "We all had to call him Doctor Jonas and don't you forget it." Then he laughed, a deep belly laugh. "What didn't I do? Let's see, lighting, sound, sound effects, smoke. I even got to be 'Mr. Wheelchair' on occasions."

"Mr. Wheelchair?"

"Yeah, when he came to the healing part, one of us would come wheeling down the aisle, then *Doctor* Jonas would put his hand on our foreheads and say 'be healed!' Next thing we know we're stumbling across the stage yelling, 'I'm healed, I'm healed, praise the Lord!!'" He told the story complete with all the theatrics; the waving of arms, the rolling of eyes.

"He actually did that?" Roger thought that was incredulous.

"He actually did that," Phil said mimicking the naiveté in Roger's voice. "Do you actually think any of that is real? I look at it this way—it's sort of like big time wrestling. I mean, you know it's fake, but you enjoy it anyway." Phil belched lightly, then continued describing his part in making a Sterling Jonas Crusade, a truly memorable experience. "You gotta hear this," he said leaning forward and gesturing with his beer can. "My favorite part was the angels. Angels are a big thing now, you know, and since we always aim to please, every so often when the time was right I'd give 'em a dose of angels."

Roger wasn't sure he even wanted to know about the angels, but was sure he was going to be given the story anyway.

"It was during the singing. It could only happen during the singing. I mean imagine this—the singing is rising to a fever pitch, right? And so all of a sudden I dub in these angel sounds. Actually it's a synthesizer sound of a lot of people falsettoing 'ahh, ahh, ahh.' Well, the crowd thought they were about to be transported! They were falling all over the floor. I about died laughing!"

Aside from these interesting tidbits and insights into the ministry of the Disciples of Grace, Mick and Roger did pick up a few useful things. It turned out that Sterling hadn't been his usual self lately and that all was not sweetness and light between Jud and Sterling.

"It was the first meeting of the crusade here," said Phil, who was now into his second beer. "And Doctor Jonas comes up to me and goes, 'no angels tonight, Phil.' I say, 'Why not?' and he goes, 'just do what I say, and if Jud comes up and says to do the angels you tell him no. You got me?' And so I say, 'Well, you're the boss,' or something like that. And he goes, 'Yeah, and don't you forget it!' Later just before the meeting I seen him and Jud arguing. They didn't see me and I was too far away to hear what they were fighting about, but I did hear Jonas saying something like, 'I'm sick of it, all of it.' I didn't hear nothing else. I try to keep my nose outta those kind of things."

"Was this behavior different than his usual behavior?"

asked Roger.

"Yeah. No doubt. Him and Jud used to be like this." He crossed his fingers, "And now they hardly speak. I mean I don't know what's with Jonas lately. The guy's a millionaire, you know? He shouldn't have a care in the world. But lately he's all teary-eyed. And it wasn't the fake teary-eyed stuff he'd do for the show. Couple times I seen him in his dressing room down on his knees crying. I don't know, man. I think it was like mid-life crisis or something. He had all the broads he wanted. All the cars. What more is there?"

Next they spoke with Andrea Macintosh, one of Jonas' publicity people. A large, square-bodied girl in a plain cotton dress; she answered their questions with as few words as possible.

"Did you ever witness any arguments between Mr. Soames and Doctor Jonas?"

"No. They were good friends. They were like brothers." There was no inflection in her voice. It was as if she had memorized a part and wasn't a very good actor.

"We have heard otherwise, that lately they did not get along."

"No. They were like brothers."

"Do you know why Dr. Jonas went to Chester?"

"No."

"Did Dr. Jonas seem any different to you during the past few weeks?"

She shook her head.

"Thank you, Miss Macintosh."

Roger sighed and gave her his card with his usual spiel about contacting him if she should remember anything. She took his card and nodded mechanically.

They spoke with other board members who were still at the hotel; Marion Sharpe, Corrine Matthews, Arnold Blackfield, John Dracobee. None of them knew, or would admit to knowing why Jonas had driven to Chester. And, no, none of them knew anything about any so-called arguments between Jonas and Soames. The two were the best of friends. Like brothers.

Marion, secretary to the board of directors, was a lot like Andrea. Although Marion was smartly dressed in jeans and a cropped black jacket, she avoided their eyes when she said, "They were like brothers."

Corrine, a striking blonde with classic cheekbones, tall, lithe, model-like, worked as Jonas' press secretary. That was a fancy title for someone who regularly wrote up the events of each of Jonas' crusade meetings—how many healings, what Jonas spoke about—and then took them to the local papers which promptly deep-sixed them and wrote what they wanted to anyway. Roger thought Sterling probably kept Corrine around for window dressing. He read one of her press releases. It wasn't very good. She said it, too: "They were like brothers."

Mick said in disgust, "What's with you people? Doesn't anyone have a brain around here? Are you all blind?"

She looked at him blankly as through a veil.

Arnold Blackfield, owner and manager of a large car dealership in Portland and member-at-large on Jonas' board warned them about Phil Kolanchuk. "I would take anything he says with a grain of salt. He has a drinking problem. I told Sterling that Phil was a liability, but Sterling didn't agree."

When they approached Jud again he denied arguing with Jonas. "We were like David and Jonathan. I loved that man, " he said, his voice breaking.

Much later Roger and Mick were sitting at a corner table in the restaurant on the second floor of the hotel trying to get some supper. A room on the third floor of the hotel was being used as a temporary investigations office, but with officers coming and going it was too noisy. Mick and Roger had talked to scores of Disciples of Grace staff, none of whom, thought Roger, showed any emotion at Jonas' passing. All except Phil. And he seemed quite pleased about it.

Mick looked up at Roger after they had ordered suppers and a pot of coffee. He said, "That was a neat ploy earlier, telling Soames that you are a *real* Christian. A new twist on the old good cop/bad cop routine."

"Mick?"

"Yeah?"

"That wasn't a ploy."

CHAPTER 6

He had never meant to kill him. It was an accident. He had taken the gun just to threaten him. He was only going to wave it around in his face, scare him, maybe. But kill him? He had no idea that old gun of his father's was even loaded!

But he couldn't be blamed, really. It wasn't his fault. In the hotel room when he had stood in front of the great and famous and powerful Doctor Sterling Jonas and Jonas had sneered at him and said, "I don't know what you're talking about, man, you are crazy!" something in him had snapped. And then he shot him and shot him and shot him. Afterwards he had carefully pulled off the man's shoes and socks and pants, and tied his feet together with his belt and his hands behind his back with a cord from the lamp. Now he would never get away. Never. Never. Never!

His basement apartment was getting darker. He sat on the edge of his cot hugging his arms, rocking gently forward and backward. How long had he been sitting like this? He didn't know for sure. Had he been sitting here all night? Had he slept at all? He couldn't remember.

When he had arrived back, he had carefully, very carefully wiped the blood off of himself and the gun. Then he bundled up his clothing and took them to the washer and dryer in the laundry room across the hall. Everything was clean now. Clean and dry. He rubbed his sore knees. His stomach lurched again. He was probably hungry, but he couldn't eat. If he ate anything, he knew he would throw up again. Lately there was less and less that he could eat without getting sick.

In front of him on a rickety wooden cabinet the TV flickered blue light into the dusky room. The volume was down, but he could see that Jonas was on it again. Every channel. He brightened somewhat. To think that he was the one who had caused all of this. The one!

Finding out about the daughter had been a stroke of luck. Luck? No, a stroke of genius! Imagine, that teacher person hiding all these years, all these years in the same town that he lived in. But people don't stay hidden forever. He had found her. And then written and sent that phony letter to Jonas. The letter was crumpled up in his pocket. He pulled it out and flattened it on his bed.

My dearest father, (he knew that would get to him.)

I am your long-lost daughter Marylouise. I live in Chester now. I am a teacher.

Come to meet me on November 14 at the Chester Motel in room 114 and bring this letter.

With great love,

Marylouise

Two weeks ago he had called the hotel from the pay phone down the street. He didn't have a phone in his own apartment, and using one of his voices, he reserved room 114 for November 14. Thinking back he was glad he hadn't used his own voice when making the call. He was just about as smart as they come. He prided himself, too, that he knew everything there was to know about Dr. Sterling Jonas. Everything. He could write a book. He had devoted his entire life—ever since Paula died—to knowing this man inside out. He drew his knees up under him. That felt better.

He folded the letter in quarters and put it back in his pocket. Tomorrow when he went to work at the church, he would add it, plus the gun to the black trunk with the big gold claps which was hidden in a small closet in the basement boiler room where no one would ever find it. The trunk contained his life's work:

scrapbooks—dozens of them, hundreds maybe—all about the life of Dr. Sterling Jonas; pictures, articles, magazine stories, news clippings. And then there were his "research notes," he called them, which were tape recordings of phone conversations of people who knew him a long time ago. He knew just the right questions to ask, just the right voice to use, pretending he was a reporter, a "concerned" minister, someone from the IRS or the government. He used to keep his collection in a cardboard box in his closet, but when the collection outgrew the space, he had to find a new place. So he pulled out the trunk from his closet and unloaded its contents—a dozen or more puppets and marionettes and sat them on the chairs and tables all around his apartment and then he put his notes in the large black trunk. Almost a year ago now he had hired a cab to take him and the trunk to the church. He didn't trust that nosy Mrs. Philpott. It would be just like her to come snooping into his apartment and go through the trunk. But she had no quarrel with him. He always paid his rent on time. Still, he didn't trust her. She was nosy and crabby and always looked at him like he was nothing but a speck of dirt. "I hate walking in that place," he would hear her say to Mrs. Swanson who lived down the street. "All those eyes staring at you—those dolls. It's eerie, the work of the Devil himself."

But they weren't dolls, he would smile to himself. They were puppets. Dolls just sat there and did nothing. Puppets did and said what you told them to.

The little bit of money he earned as the church janitor, plus his disability pension was enough to pay the rent on this measly place and buy some food. The rest went for supplies; scrapbooks, tapes, film for his camera and paper.

All of this he had done for Paula. The thought of her almost made him stop breathing. He scrunched up his eyes and hugged himself, moaning slightly. It was getting harder and harder to remember her face. What if he forgot what she looked like entirely? He reached for the gilt-framed 5" X 7" photo of her from beside his bed and stared at it for a long time. She was smiling in there, her long red hair blown back from around

her face. She was kneeling, with one arm around her dog—
their dog—a golden retriever named Walter. Dead now, too.
The puppets were Paula's. She was always really good with
the puppets. She had taught him about being a puppetmaster.
That's where he learned all of his voices. He ran his finger
around her framed face. This was the only picture he had of
her. After he got out of the hospital all of her pictures were
gone. They told him that he was the one who had ripped them
up. Imagine!

He laid her picture face down on the bed and began to
think about the daughter. Jonas' first wife Helene had died a
long time ago. God, Himself, had punished her. Good. And
now Sterling was dead, too. But there remained this daughter,
this new found daughter. She must be punished, threatened,
tortured, made to pay. The sins of the fathers....

He groaned, stumbled into his bathroom and retched again
and again. A few minutes later he was back on his bed, shivering under a threadbare spread and making his plans about the
daughter while from around his small room the puppets watched
him.

CHAPTER 7

An hour and a half later Mick and Roger were still in the hotel dining room going over notes. The restaurant was full, groups of people glanced over at them, faces grim talked in whispers. Outside, snow whirled in the blackness. Roger looked down at his watch; almost quarter to eight. He really wanted to get home tonight. It seemed like forever since he'd been called out, forever since he'd seen Kate.

On the table between them were the remains of their supper, New York steak for Mick, and lasagna and garlic bread for Roger. They were still drinking coffee poured from a silver hotel coffee pitcher. They'd gone through two of these pitchers already, and were due for a third.

Mick brought him back to reality. "So what did you think of Denise?"

Roger said, "She's scared—a child, really. That's my impression."

"A zombie," said Mick. "That's what she is. There's a religion down somewhere—they turn people into zombies. That's what I heard. Maybe this is the same thing."

"You've seen too many episodes of Unsolved Mysteries," said Roger spooning sugar into his recently poured cup of coffee—three teaspoons of the stuff to keep him awake.

"No, but I'm a little serious here, Roger, hear me out. All of them, all except drunken Phil, looked like they've been brainwashed or on drugs or something."

Roger mulled that over in his mind. He knew there were

religious cults that had done just that, but the Disciples of Grace? Were they a cult? He closed his eyes briefly and leaned against the back of his chair. Sure, Sterling Jonas had some strange ideas, and if everything Phil said was true, then the guy was a charlatan as well, but a brainwashing cult?

"How old is Denise?" Roger finally asked.

"Twenty-six."

"How long have Jonas and she been married?"

"Four years. I got that much out of Jud. Classic case of the boss marrying his secretary. She was the church secretary."

"Oh?"

Mick grunted. "I know what you're thinking, but it all seems to be on the up and up. His first wife died of pneumonia in 1989, the death certificate says. He had a proper time of mourning and then he married again."

"Any children?"

"None. We know that for sure. In his books he talks about how God *chose* to give him no children. That was a big thing with him. No children. Don't ask me why."

"I never read any of his books, although Roberta in our detachment, you know Roberta, is skimming through them. You never know what names will come up. What about Jud? Where does he hail from?"

"Oregon," answered Mick. "He joined forces with Jonas about a dozen years ago. He seems to be the brains behind the operation."

"I'm interested in the relationship between Jud and Denise...."

"Yeah, that's one for the books, isn't it?" said Mick.

"What about finances? He holds the purse strings, doesn't he?"

"The IRS is running a full scale investigation of the Disciples of Grace as we speak. This was launched a few months back. Jud's been front and center of that audit."

"Which could account for the less than amiable behavior between him and Soames. 'I'm sick of it, all of it,' could refer to the investigation."

"Could be," said Mick tapping his coffee mug with his fleshy thumb. "My gut tells me Soames is involved."

"Except he was at that Disciples of Grace meeting all evening," said Roger.

"I know, and his car never left the parking garage. We have the valet's word for that." "Even Phil vouches for him, that he was there all evening."

"Phil, our breath of fresh air, among the zombies."

Roger said, "We're only beginning to scratch the surface here. He could have hired someone."

CHAPTER 8

It was close to midnight when Roger pulled into his drive-way. It was still snowing, and the drive home had been a killer.

Kate's bedside lamp was on but she was asleep, a thick book face down on her lap. "Real Estate Accounting Prin-ciples," he read. No wonder she fell asleep. Kate worked as a receptionist two days a week and every other Saturday morn-ing at a local real estate office. Lately she was thinking about getting her real estate license and becoming a broker. He turned out her light, put away the book and slid into the bed beside her.

"Are you home?" she said groggily, her voice full of sleep.

"No, I'm still out there."

She mumbled something and turned over.

The next morning over toast and coffee Kate asked him about the investigation; and he told her what he knew, which wasn't a whole lot.

He shook his head, "I don't know. I would pray for a quick end to this one, but I have a feeling it's going to be a long one." Roger got up and placed his coffee mug and cereal bowl in the dishwasher and said, "The whole crew of them seemed strange, odd. I mean, I know people grieve in differ-ent ways, but those people didn't even seem normal."

"Not normal, how?"

Roger leaned with his back against the sink. "Mick called them a bunch of zombies. He wasn't far off the mark."

"Jud Soames was like that, too?"

"Jud? No, not so much. He seemed very angry, full of rage. I kept wanting to say, 'What *is* your problem? We're trying to investigate the death of your friend here.'"

From the living room they heard the sound of the TV being flicked on. Sara appeared in the doorway wearing a t-shirt and plaid flannel boxer shorts in which she'd obviously slept. "Sara," said Kate. "I thought you'd be at the university by now."

"Don't have a class till ten," she said yawning and opening the fridge door. She poured herself a large glass of orange juice. Her short hair was disheveled and she was wearing her glasses. A sure sign she hadn't woken up yet. The first thing she usually took care of were her contact lenses.

"You look tired," said her mother.

"Was up till three working on a paper."

"Got it finished?" asked Roger.

"Yeah, but I'm not happy with it."

"But you'll probably ace it like everything else you do." This was from Becky who had entered the kitchen clad in her grade nine school uniform which consisted of faded jeans, frayed at the knees topped by a flannel lumber jacket, and her back pack slung over her shoulders.

"Hey Becks, what's up?" asked Sara.

"I don't know how you can be so happy, Sara. You know we're going to move. Aren't you going to miss your friends?"

Kate looked down and Roger put his hand on her shoulder.

"Sure I am, but the Bay of Fundy has the highest tides in the world," said Sara pouring herself a full bowl of Cheerios. "And I always wanted to live in a place where the tides are awesome."

Becky rolled her eyes.

From the living room a morning TV news program was featuring something about fringe religious cults and the type of people who joined them.

"You are so weird, sometimes, Sara. And what about Mark?"

Mark was Sara's newest boyfriend, a fellow student at the University, a percussionist and music major who came from a well-known musical family. His father was a violinist in the Calgary Philharmonic Orchestra, and his mother was a soprano who was often the soloist in Calgary Philharmonic Orchestra's annual presentation of the Messiah. Mark himself apparently played percussion in a small orchestra. The Sheppards hadn't met Mark yet. Supper at the Sheppards next Tuesday was the big day.

"I'll survive. If our love is meant to be, it will be," she sang and still holding the milk carton in her hand she danced around the kitchen. "Whatever will be will be...."

"Must be love," thought Roger.

Becky, however, did not look amused. She turned and stormed out of the house. "Yeah, well no one asked me what I thought about this stupid move!" The door slammed behind her.

Kate rose. Roger said, "Let her go. She needs time. This will take time."

Suddenly serious, Sara sat down again. "Don't worry about her, Mom. I think she'll be okay. I've really been praying for her."

"Thanks, Sara. So have we."

"I told her I was praying for her and she got mad at me; said that she didn't want people praying for her like she was a mental case and to mind my own business. I said, 'Too bad, I'm going to pray for you anyway.'"

"Do you think you're being a little overbearing, Sara?" asked Roger.

"Me?" she said opening her eyes wide. Ever since Sara had gotten back from a summer working with a mission group in Spain, she was a changed person. Alive. Eager. Which only made the difference between his two daughters more pronounced than ever. How do you tell your vibrant, on-fire 18 year old daughter to please be a little less so around her 14 year old sister?

CHAPTER 9

When Mary Louise arrived at school that morning there was a large paper bag on her desk. Jennifer wasn't in yet and the other teachers were just beginning to arrive. She could hear their loud chatter in the staff room—Georgia saying something about seeing Dan Rather at the KFC and Nick's reply in low tones. Yesterday one of the teachers had brought in a small portable television, which was usually turned on and turned into the all-news channel just as soon as any teacher entered the staff room. Mary Louise was just about to take the bag out into the staff room with a cheery, "Somebody forget their lunch," when she heard the sound of the TV being flicked on. "RCMP still have no leads in the brutal slaying Monday night of popular television evangelist Dr. Sterling...."

"No thank you," she thought. She went into her office and shut the door.

The bag on her desk was an old bag, crinkly and dusty, with a faint musty odor about it, as if it had been in a closet for a long time. It was dirty too and her fingers were smudgy from touching it. She wiped them on a Kleenex. There was no name on the bag, so she unfolded the top. Inside, two eyes stared up at her—sad eyes, plaintive eyes with the beginnings of traced tears painted carefully at their corners. A doll? Most likely a student had left it. She lifted it out of the bag—not a doll, a puppet, a small hand puppet, the kind used to entertain children from behind a counter. It was a well-made puppet with porcelain painted face and cloth body. The clown face was frowning softly, it's painted lips almost pleading. She put it on her hand and walked into the staff room.

"This belong to anybody?" she asked.

Heads shook in synch.

"You got a new friend?" asked Monique pointing to the clown.

"Who's doing a unit on drama?" she asked absently. Again, there was no response. She held the puppet-clad hand high, but the teachers were intent on the TV.

"Well, if anyone hears of anyone missing a puppet, here it is." And she took it off and placed it on the coffee table.

CHAPTER 10

His parents had told him not to come. His pastor had told him not to come. His search consultant at Parentfinders had told him not to come. "You've sent the letter, David," the woman from Parentfinders had told him one morning a little more than a week ago. They were squeezed into a small booth at a crowded and smoky Dunkin' Donuts in the south end of Spokane, Washington. He was munching on a cornmeal muffin. She was sipping a large coffee, the plastic lid still on.

She said, "You can't just turn up on her doorstep. Your birth mother could have a husband and a family and a career. You don't know what upsets you may cause by just showing up at her door. She may have told no one about you."

"But what if she didn't understand what I'm talking about in my letter?"

"She'll know," said the woman placing her coffee down on the table. "Believe me, she knows exactly who that letter came from."

"But she hasn't called me," he protested.

"Give her time."

"But what if she never does call?"

"Then you have to accept that, too. We talked about that, remember?"

"But I just want to go there, find out what she looks like..."

"You mean stand outside her house and look in her windows?"

"No. Of course nothing like that."

"Oh, let's see, park outside where she works..."

"No! Yes! I don't know...."

"That's called harassment, David and it's against the law." She reached across the table and touched David's arm. "Believe me, David. This isn't easy for her. She could have other children...."

"But she's not married. She goes by the name of Jonas."

"The fact that she goes by the name on her birth certificate is no indication of anything. Lots of married women keep their names."

"Well, then I may have brothers and sisters. It would be unfair if I can't meet them."

"No one said life was fair." She paused. "I know this is tough, but let her handle it in her own way. I think she'll call. Most birth mothers do. But it may take her a while."

"But I don't have a while." He ran a shaky hand through his hair. " I have only this year. I leave for Israel in four months, then I'll be gone a whole year. I wanted to meet her before I left."

"A year isn't a long time, David. I'm asking you, begging you, please, *please* don't drive up to Canada."

But he hadn't listened. A few hours after he met with his Parentfinders counselor he had thrown a few things into a duffel bag, said good-bye to his parents—who had also begged him not to go—got into his blue Datsun and headed north. He had driven first up to Edmonton and to the University of Alberta, then getting the run around until some one in the registrar's office thought that Marylouise Jonas might be the one who was studying in the graduate school. She looked up the name for him. "No, sorry. That was Mary Louise Jones, the principal of Chester Elementary School." Jones? That got him thinking. Had he been wrong all along? Maybe this Mary Louise Jones who was working on a Ph.D. in education wasn't the Marylouise Jonas he'd been looking for. Maybe that was why she hadn't responded to his letter. Maybe she thought he was some kind of crank. If this wasn't his mother, he'd have to go home and start all over again—call up his search consultant at Parentfinders. But the thought of starting all over again gave him a hollow feeling which began right in the pit of his stomach. But this teacher's name was Mary Louise—how many Mary Louise Jonases or Joneses could there be? Now Mary Jones, that would be a different story, but *Mary Louise*? Maybe it'd be worth his while to head into Chester and find out.

And so, here he was, sitting on the edge of a neatly made bed in the middle of the morning in the Whispering Pines Motel on Highway 1 just outside the Chester town limits. About an hour earlier he had checked in. David Brackett from Colville, Washington, car license, home phone and address. A small color TV was perched on the counter and as he filled out the form, the newscaster was talking about how there were still no suspects in some murder case. David opened his wallet and took out the appropriate amount.

"The streets aren't safe," said the hotel clerk as he exchanged David's American money into Canadian.

"You're telling me," said David.

"Good thing you're not trying to check into the Chester Inn tonight."

"Yeah, why's that?"

"That murder," and he pointed to the TV.

"What murder's that?" asked David.

"Can't believe you haven't heard about it—that bigshot TV preacher. Right here in Chester."

"No kidding." David had no idea who the man was talking about, nor did he particularly care at this point.

"Shot to death. No one's safe anymore. The streets aren't safe. Used to be you didn't even have to lock your doors," said the manager handing David the key to room 23. "Have a nice stay, Mr. Brackett. You're lucky you got in early. We're all bracing ourselves for a ton of reporter types. I'm going to spend the rest of the day making the beds and turning on the heat in a whole bunch of other rooms."

"So who was this guy that was killed anyway?" asked David.

"Jonas what-his-face. One of those TV preachers."

"Sterling Jonas?" David was interested now. "Murdered, are you sure?"

"Yup" He shoved the morning's paper across the counter proudly. David scanned it. Sure enough Sterling Jonas had been murdered at the Chester Inn the night before last.

Sterling Jonas. David knew him as the preacher who first of all said that no Christian should ever be poor. And that if you were suffering financially you were out of God's will. That was a few years ago. Now he was saying that grace covered all your sins. He remembered Jonas creating quite a stir in David's own church with that one. Yes, David's pastor patiently explained, we *are* under grace, and yes, Christ's righteousness covers us to the point where God doesn't see our sin, but that doesn't give us license to go out and sin. Just because we *can* doesn't mean we *should*. And there *is* something called true repentance. Still, many in David's own church had been led astray by Jonas' teachings, had even left, in fact. It was quite an attractive theology when you thought about it—nothing you can do can take you out of God's will and nothing you can do can strip the righteousness of God from you. He plunked down two quarters and took the paper with him.

He read through the entire front page story. He flicked on the TV, the all-news stations, both Newsworld in Canada and CNN in the U.S. seemed to be carrying nothing but the Jonas story. How could he have missed it driving down from Edmonton? But then, thinking about it, he had spent the three-hour trip singing along to a couple of new praise tapes he had bought at a Christian bookstore there near the West Edmonton Mall.

CHAPTER 11

Flanked by potted mums and portable green silk trees, Dr. Sterling Jonas strode confidently across the stage, FM microphone in his left hand.

"You are covered, covered, COVERED in Christ's righteousness!!" he bellowed. "Do you know what that means?" He paused and gazed out into the large crowd seated down in front of him and up along the sides at the Saddledome. Every seat was filled. Roger had been to NHL hockey games in that same arena which saw less enthusiastic crowds than this one. Roger, along with Constables Roberta St. Marie and Dennis Mayweather, Clayton Lavoir, plus Sergeant Roy Laird , were viewing the entire week-long Sterling Jonas crusade on video. They had gone through two of the tapes, studying the faces, pausing the VCR every so often when the camera panned the audience.

Jonas said it again, "Do you know what that means? DO YOU KNOW WHAT THAT MEANS?"

"Yes," came the reply from the crowd.

"I can't hear you...."

"Yes! Yes!" they shouted.

"I *still* can't hear you...."

"Yes, YES, PRAISE THE LORD," they shouted.

"Amen. Amen! That's more like it!" And then Jonas did a bit of a skip and dance before he continued.

"That means no matter what you do—NO MATTER WHAT YOU DO—Christ Jesus will forgive you. Yes, He will.

Praise the Lord. Praise God."

"Praise the Lord," came the reply from the auditorium.

"And do you know why He will forgive you? Because He HAS to. HE HAS NO CHOICE!!! His death on the cross sealed that choice for Him forever. He has NO CHOICE but to love you and forgive you no matter what you've done."

Roger, who had been studying a face in the front row, suddenly jerked his thoughts back to what the man was saying. "No choice?"

"Christ Jesus is bound by the New Covenant—BOUND by it, friends, and that's a fact we can count on, brothers and sisters. He HAS to forgive us because of the cross. Now you and I," he strutted across the stage, "you and I, we look at each other and we can see sin. If you lie to me and I find out I can see that you're a liar. And I say—'hey you're a liar,' and you can say, 'how do you know I'm a liar?' I can say, 'Because I can see the evidence.' But you know what, brothers and sisters? Jesus doesn't see the evidence. He can't, he CAN'T see our sin and you know why He can't? It's because of the cross, the New Covenant..."

"Weird," muttered Roger under his breath.

"You're telling me he's weird." Dennis Mayweather turned to Roger, "You're religious...You have any idea what he's talking about here?"

"Not really," said Roger. The others on the force knew Roger was a Christian, he made no pretense of hiding it. It was what he was. Often he would ask God to guide him when he stepped into a potentially dicey or dangerous situation. And he knew that Jesus Christ was with him. That wasn't to say that everything turned out wonderfully for him; nor did it give him a license to become careless in his work.

But he sometimes struggled with his lack of biblical education. After high school he worked for a whole bunch of unhappy years in his dad's hardware store. Then he attended one semester of Bible school where he'd met Kate, before dropping out to follow his dream of becoming a police officer with the Royal Canadian Mounted Police. Kate had graduated with her diploma in theology; interesting, he mused for someone who worked in a real estate office; but nevertheless she was the one he went to with his biblical questions. She was urging him to take a Bible correspondence course, but his work schedule left him little time. Still, he thought about it from time to time. He even had the application forms and a listing of course offerings on top of his dresser at home. Maybe when they were settled in their new home....

"There he goes again," said Tim. And indeed Jonas had struck a pose that they had seen him go into about once every ten minutes or so. He would stand completely still. As if on cue, the room would become hushed. Then he would cross both arms on his chest and eyes closed he would lift his face toward the ceiling, nose upturned. To the pious he looked as if he were gaining strength from a higher being, but to Roger, and no doubt to the others in the detachment room, the pose looked as if some director with a megaphone had choreographed it. *That's right, nose just a little higher. Look up; now close those eyes. Move your lips a little. There, that it. Hold that pose. Perfect!*

Roger leaned forward and stared into the eyes of Dr. Sterling Jonas. For a moment Roger could see—no, could sense—within the evangelist, some deep anguish, a pain, almost. He grabbed the remote and rewound it, and watched it again. It was definitely there.

"What is it Corporal?" asked Roberta.

"I'm not sure. Look at his eyes."

"What about his eyes?"

"See the way his eyes have scrunched up, sort of. There's some pain there, something," said Roger, his voice trailing off.

"Probably heartburn," said Dennis.

A few moments later Jonas was back ranting and raving across the stage, shouting down that Christ would forgive them, shouting down that Christ had no choice but to forgive them, shouting down that if Christ had no choice but to forgive them, He also had no choice but to heal them from all their physical ailments and provide them with material wealth.

Amens were heard throughout.

"Yeah, go on," said Dennis sarcastically. Roger felt suddenly very angry at people like Jonas who took his precious faith and turned it into a mockery, a way to gain power, a way to get rich. Big Time Wrestling—for the Sunday morning crowd. Ever since the people lined up for healing and bread in the New Testament, people have been waiting in line to get things from God, he thought. The great Santa Claus in the sky.

"Anyone for popcorn?" Adele stuck her head in the door. "I heard you guys were watching movies instead of working, so I made popcorn." The mood was suddenly lightened as she placed a steaming bag of microwaved popcorn on the table in the room. All of them helped themselves to handfuls as the remainder of the video ran.

It had taken them three hours to watch two hours of videotape. All of them without exception were rubbing their eyes, stretching and yawning. Every time the camera panned the crowd, they would lean forward and painstakingly examine every face, pressing the pause button or the slow forward button. It wasn't impossible, in fact it was highly probable, that the murderer could have attended the Calgary crusade. He or she could easily be seated in the front row, shouting "amen" or standing with his arms raised, or lying prone on the floor of the arena, shaking, sobbing.

"One thing you can say about Jonas," said Laird, "he sure does have the power to bring on the emotions. How does he do it?"

"Maybe you just have to be there," said Roberta.

Objectively watching the crowds in the arena display a range of emotions from tears to laughter reminded Roger of the times he had attended the funeral of a murder victim—not as a mourner but as a police officer, standing in the back, apart from the grief, watching, looking for that one person who didn't belong there. He felt like that now—invasive, intrusive, analyzing each individual's tears. And he found himself silently praying that these masses of people will find the God they are looking for, and shaking his head because he's not sure that

Dr. Sterling Jonas can lead them there.

When the video finally ended, and Laird suggested a 15-minute break before the next one, the entire party rose with mutters of "best suggestion I've heard all day" and "I've heard enough of that jerk for one day" and "how can people really believe in that bull" and "I've got to get some fresh air."

Roger retreated to his own office and looked at his watch—2 p.m. The detachment was being flooded with calls. Adele was having trouble dealing with them all. Laird and Roger decided they needed a spokesperson. Laird had suggested Roger, Roger who was so good with the public. Roger had balked and said he'd think about it. In the end he had said, "Yes." Laird had scheduled a press conference at the Chester Elementary School for 4 p.m. Because of the enormous number of reporters and TV crews, a large room would be needed and Laird chose the school gym.

He shook his head and for lack of anything better to do right now, he picked up, for the umpteenth time, the complete printouts of the crime scene interviews.

More than a week prior to Jonas' arriving, a reservations clerk named Penny Peters had received a call reserving room 114. The caller said his name was "S. Jonas" and said he would check in before six. Therefore the hotel did not record a credit card number. He did not arrive by six, reported the reservations clerk, but since they were almost empty, the room was not let out to anyone else. She did not recognize him as Dr. Sterling Jonas, the evangelist, when he checked in.

After checking in at 9:04 p.m. and paying in cash, Sterling Jonas had called to room service and ordered the special—Alberta prime rib, baked potato and Caesar salad. At 9:35 p.m., the room service waiter had knocked on the door but received no answer. He knocked again. He left the tray on the floor outside the door. At 10:15 p.m. the waiter was walking by Jonas' room on his way to deliver an iron and an ironing board to another guest and saw that the food tray was on the floor, still untouched. After delivering the iron he walked back to Jonas' room and knocked several times, calling his name.

He was sure he heard the television. He went down to the desk and phoned Jonas' room. Still no answer. Thinking that perhaps Jonas was ill, for surely if he were just asleep the phone would have wakened him, he took the master key and attempted to unlock Jonas' room. But when he noticed that the privacy lock was latched, he alerted the night manager. Fearing that he had taken ill, the two of them knocked and called. No answer. They walked around to the back of the hotel. Luckily, Jonas had a first floor room. Perhaps they could get his attention at the window. When they saw that the window was broken, they immediately knew something was wrong. When they looked inside the window, they saw Jonas lying face down on the blood-soaked bed. The television was on and the volume was very high. They called the police immediately.

The guest to the right of Jonas' room was a single man, Darren Schwartz, age 49, who was living in the hotel long term. He listed his profession as "inventor." He reported hearing muffled shots and possibly glass shattering around 9:30 p.m., but he assumed the sounds came from the TV. The guests to the left of Jonas' room were out for the evening. No one else heard anything or saw anything.

The Ident crew had dusted for fingerprints, filled numerous plastic bags with sweepings, from the floor, from the couch, and from the bed, glass shards from the window. The one big clue so far was a fairly clear boot print just outside the window. A plaster cast of the print was made and size and boot make were being checked. On preliminary observation it looked like a size 8 man's right boot. It was either a small man or a woman with size 10 shoes. Roger frowned. Could a woman, even a woman who wore size ten shoes (Kate wore size 10 shoes) overpower a man like Jonas who was 6'1", of muscular build and strong? He wondered.

Laird entered his office just then. "Changing the subject, I just got a call from New Brunswick."

"And?"

"The town council has come up with enough money to keep their police force on for a few more months. A committee of people who are calling themselves Keep Our Cops, complete with placards and everything made an impassioned plea to the town council and the town somehow found enough money to keep them for a couple more months."

"I so appreciate you telling me this," said Roger.

"You'll be great there."

"I'm glad you have so much confidence in me."

"Oh, yeah, and there's more."

"Let me guess," said Roger. "They're setting up snipers on the road into St. Matthews for all Mounties."

Laird laughed. "In case you want to be kept abreast of some of the other stuff going on here. One of the churches called with a B & E. Some one or ones broke in last night and stole a large quantity of holy water. Dennis took that one."

"Holy water!"

"Weird isn't it, but that's not all. A guy down on Fraley Drive called. Says his neighbor's been blowing snow from his snow blower onto his driveway on purpose. Duane talked to the old guy. Lives alone. He also talked to the neighbor. Says the old man's a chronic complainer. Duane told him to take it easy with the snow blower. Couple of reports about snowmobiles down residential streets, one on the sidewalk. Scared a kid. A few drunks. The usual."

CHAPTER 12

Even though it was only two days after the murder, reporters and media people with their notebooks, cameras and tape recorders overfilled the small gym of the Chester Elementary School. At the two entrances to the gym Chester RCMP Constables Duane Castelli and Dennis Mayweather checked for passes. The event was a closed pass-only press conference. CBC, CTV, ITV were represented as well as the American companies; ABC, CNN, CBS and NBC. The local media was also there; Chad Williamson from CKJY TV in Calgary, plus a host of radio stations from Calgary and Edmonton. The *Calgary Herald* and *Sun* were there along with The *Edmonton Journal*. Even the local Chester weekly paper was represented, their two reporters looking vaguely ill at ease and overwhelmed by the big names which shared the gym with them. Reporters sat on wooden school chairs with tubed metal legs stamped along the back with CES—Chester Elementary School. At one end of the gym a long table had been set up. Microphones were secured to it by duct tape. Cables thick as thumbs snaked across the floor, made firm by more duct tape.

At 3:55 p.m. Roger and Roy Laird walked into the noisy gym and took their places behind the long table. Questions were flung at them even before Roger and Roy sat down.

"Is it true that Sterling Jonas was going bankrupt?"

"Is it true that Sterling Jonas was meeting a prostitute?"

Roger took the mike, the crowd hushed. He read the prepared statement that the autopsy on the body of Sterling Jonas had been completed, the final forensics report wasn't in yet, but his body had been found two nights ago in room 114 of the Chester Inn. It was clearly a homicide, and police investigations were proceeding in that direction. The victim had been tied up with hotel electrical cords and then shot six times. It was not known why Sterling Jonas had come to Chester but he had apparently driven here by himself. That was about all they knew right now. They ended with a promise they would keep the press informed at all stages.

Then they were bombarded with questions to which they replied as best they could, but usually answered that they couldn't comment or they had no information at present. They had no idea why Jonas drove to Chester, couldn't comment that it was a prostitute or someone from his church, but they were following up on several leads. Also, at this point, they had no knowledge of the financial affairs of the Disciples of Grace Church, but an IRS investigation in the United States was being conducted. No, they didn't know if these were connected.

In all, the press conference lasted half an hour. When the crowd finally dispersed Laird and Roger stopped at the principal's office which was down the hall. The principal, Mary Jones, was still there, her head bent low on some papers. She looked up when they entered.

"Roger, this is Mary Jones, the kind lady who got this all set up for us. Mary, this is Corporal Roger Sheppard."

Roger extended his hand, "Yes, I remember you from when my daughter Becky was here."

She rose, smiled and shook his hand. "Yes, Becky Sheppard, I remember her. So nice to see you again."

CHAPTER 13

"God doesn't want you to be poor! He wants you to live, and that's the glorious thing, the wonderful thing—that's what grace is all about...."

Roger had arrived home to find Kate sitting cross-legged on the floor in front of the television. Her dark hair was tied back with a ribbon. She was wearing old gray sweats of Roger's, and a faded sweatshirt which read, "Super Mom."

"Hi, how was the press conference?"

"Oh, it's over. We really didn't have much to tell them." He took off his coat and grabbed a Diet Coke from the fridge and sank into the couch. Pressing the cold Coke can to his forehead, he looked over at Kate, who sat on the floor pen in hand, intent on the TV, taking notes even. Scattered around her on the carpet were clear plastic video-tape boxes and a stack of magazines and books. On the TV Sterling Jonas was sitting back in an easy chair on a lavish set, complete with the green potted plants which looked too lush to be real. To his left was a bookshelf and to his right a large window overlooked a treed park. He was talking with a blonde with high molded hair that looked like a hat. Their conversation was peppered with loud "praise the Lord's!" and "amens."

"What's all this stuff?" he finally asked.

"This guy is fascinating. Truly amazing. He basically says we should throw out the entire Old Testament, especially the Ten Commandments, that it has no relevance in our world. Interesting."

"Yeah, but where'd you get all this stuff?" he asked surveying the piles of magazines, books and videos.

"A client's mother. A real Jonas fan, poor thing. Anyway our client convinced her that maybe the police would like to see some of this. So she came and dropped it off at the house earlier. I would have told her to take it to the detachment, but I was at work. It must have been this morning. When I arrived home there was this box sitting on the porch. I couldn't help it. I decided to have a look at it. This stuff is totally incredible! This guy's theology is so off base it's not even funny, and it's not so much *what* he says. It's *how* he says it."

Roger sat down on the couch. "Yeah, that's the impression I got. A couple of times I had to look up, 'What did he say?' But I couldn't put my finger on it."

"You watched him? Where?"

"The videos of the Saddledome. CTV couriered them over."

Kate surveyed her cache of paraphernalia with something bordering on disappointment. "Oh, so this won't be new to you then?"

"We only had videos from the Saddledome. This will help Roberta. She's doing background stuff on Jonas."

Sterling kept on talking with the blonde, all smiles, all nods, and then Sterling was holding up his latest book, "Grace Can Change Your Life."

Roger asked, "Kate, do you know what happened about six years ago when all the Christian bookstores pulled his books?"

"I can't find anything here about it, but this stuff is all his publicity stuff," said Kate. "From what I remember, that was when his first wife died of pneumonia." She struggled to her feet, "but I know someone who would know."

"Who?"

"Merilee Hunt."

"Who's Merilee Hunt?" said Roger putting down his drink.

"You know. She manages Southside Christian Books in Calgary. You want me to call her?"

"Sure. Anything will help."

Kate left then, and Roger continued watching the video. Now the woman with the blonde wig-hat was singing, crooning actually on a stage set with glittery crosses, "Amazing Grace how sweet the sound...." He leaned back into the couch, his head resting against the soft back. He felt like he could sleep forever.

"I've got your story for you." Kate was standing over him, all smiles. Had he been asleep? He'd been faintly aware of sounds around him, the blonde lady singing, the photos of Sterling Jonas, Jonas lying on a bed, shot to death. Blood. And the lady kept singing. "Amazing Grace how sweet the sound that saved a wretch like me...."

"Wh-what?" said Roger sitting up.

Kate looked at him softly, then she leaned forward and kissed him on the forehead. "My poor baby, so tired..."

Roger roused himself, shaking off the somewhat unsatisfactory nap-sleep.

"Okay, here it is, listen," she sat down next to him. "According to Merilee when Jonas' first wife died of pneumonia Sterling was in Europe or someplace. She died at her sister's place, or something like that. There was this big deal about the fact that he had his secretary with him— who is now his wife, by the way—and she was hanging all over him. When he was told that his wife had died, he made this glib comment about "Well, we weren't together anyway," and then he went on to say something about his "poor wife not having enough faith for her healing." I guess he didn't even make it back for her funeral. He said something about the dead burying their dead."

"You're kidding."

"I know, the guy seems to be a class-A jerk. That didn't go over too well with the Christian booksellers, so they pulled his books, and his tapes, and his videos, and anything else he was producing at the time."

Roger leaned forward. "Do you know how old his wife is? Twenty-six. And he was sixty-two."

"How would we feel if Sara was going around with a 60 year old? I mean the guy wasn't just old enough to be her father, he was old enough to be her grandfather! Where does she come from anyway? She must have parents."

"We're only at the beginning of this investigation."

"No suspects?"

"Right now everyone is a suspect. Mick, the sergeant in Calgary, is convinced Jud did it, Jud who's the chairman of Sterling's board. Apparently they quarreled there in Calgary. Problem is his alibi is iron-clad."

"Alibis are never iron-clad. You told me yourself that normal people, innocent people don't usually have alibis for every given night, only guilty people make sure their alibis are ironclad."

"You're right, you know, except we can't break his alibi. He was in a staff meeting all evening, all evening from supper until about midnight. Mick, the sergeant from the Calgary thinks he did it. He doesn't know *how* he did it, but he's sure he did. But I'm not so sure."

"Why not?"

"I don't know. Just a hunch. I mean if he had wanted to, Jud could have killed him at so many other times. Why in Canada where he can't even have access to his fancy lawyers. I don't know, something just doesn't feel right."

The back door opened. It would be Becky.

"Hey, Becky," called Roger.

Silence.

"What's for supper?" was her first question.

"I don't know, sweetie," said Kate rising. "I haven't got that far in my day yet."

"Your mom's been watching TV all afternoon," said Roger jokingly. "How about we order out for pizza?" he offered.

"Oh, good," said Becky. "I love store-bought suppers. Can I call?"

Nothing about the move. Nothing about New Brunswick. Nothing about how they were ruining her life. Roger and Kate breathed a sigh of relief.

CHAPTER 14

She had been watching something mindless on TV when the doorbell rang—some sitcom about a family which included large bunches of relatives, aunts and uncles and cousins and their assorted friends. She had been sitting there, just sitting there on a Wednesday evening, a *work* night. But she couldn't force herself to move. Two hours ago she had arrived home from work, had sunk into her leather couch and hadn't been able to rouse herself to do anything constructive since.

She had sat through the news, feeling strangely detached from the murder story; safe in her well-kept house while reporters with their cameras descended upon southern Alberta. They had been on TV, those well dressed CNN types with their blow-dried hair and rich looking coats, standing in front of the "Welcome to Chester" sign with the horse and rodeo. They had serious expressions on their faces and were saying things like, "North of Montana, in the western part of Canada about 20 miles east of Calgary, Alberta, lies the small town of Chester. Up until two days ago, the most the residents had to worry about were what crops to plant and who would win the annual rodeo...."

If Mary Louise didn't move, never got up from this couch, maybe nobody would ever find her. Not the police. No reporters. Not even her son. Her son! She closed her eyes and leaned her head back into the leather. Shortly after she had received his letter, she had folded it in thirds and pushed it to the far back of her jewelry box. She hadn't looked at it again.

When the news ended, she sat through a sitcom about some well-dressed black family in California who slapped each other on the shoulders a lot and said "Hey." Then there was a sitcom about a single mother with dozens of kids. Were they all hers or were some of them friends? And then this one. Where do they come up with this stuff, she wondered.

At first she thought the doorbell came from the TV. So she ignored it. Then she heard it again. Two short bleeps. It's got to be Perry, she thought. Earlier Perry had called.

"Do you have supper on?"

"Not yet," she had said.

"Well, come over then. I have gobs."

"No thanks, Perry. I'm terrible company tonight."

"You're never terrible company, Mary Lou. If you don't come over I'll be over there to fetch you."

"No, the truth is, I'm sick. I'd be terrible company because I'm sicker than a dog," she had lied.

Perry called her Mary Lou, ever since she had confided in her friend that she really *preferred* Mary Louise, but Mary Lou would do.

So now Perry was here. Perry, her dearest friend in the entire world—Perry, like a sister to her; Perry, who had no idea about David or Sterling Jonas, or anything about her life before she moved to Alberta. But Perry respected her, didn't pry, she respected her privacy.

All through university and then graduate school she had lived alone. Well, except for the two months she roomed with Ada, a flighty curly-haired petite girl who seemed to have no end of friends. Mary Louise's cash flow was low, and she felt that sharing apartment expenses was perhaps one way to alleviate this struggle. Most everyone else did it. So she had advertised in the university newspaper, and Ada arrived. During those two months, Ada often invited Mary Louise to go out with her and her friends, to a movie, to a bar, to a concert. Mary Louise usually refused.

After only two months Mary Louise told Ada that it just wasn't working out and that Ada would have to find some place else to live.

"What do you mean, not working out!" Her dark eyes had flashed, "I pay my share of the rent. I always clean up. I never have guys over. I never have anyone over! Tell me what I've done wrong?"

The truth was that Mary Louise didn't know. Ada was right. She was a good roommate. No, the problem was Mary Louise. She needed solitude. After her classes, the thought that she had to go home to a person sitting in her living room, making tea in her kitchen was intolerable.

"I'm sorry. It's not you. It's me...."

She meant to go on to offer some sort of explanation for her inwardness, but Ada barged in, "You're right, it's you. I've never met anyone so messed up in my entire life. You push people away. I was told you were a cold fish, and I tried, Mary. I really tried to be your friend, but you pushed me away, too. And now you want me out? Well, that's fine!"

By evening Ada was gone. Mary Louise sat in the small kitchen window and watched her leave, throwing her belongings into her car and driving away. She felt a small tear escape from the corner of her eyes. Not for Ada. For herself.

Mary Louise had never shared a room with anyone since.

She allowed Perry in, but only so far. But Perry was different. Never demanding. Eccentric in her own right. The perfect best friend for someone like Mary Louise. And now Perry was here.

Slowly she extricated herself from the couch. She was chagrined that the suit she'd been wearing since school was now hopelessly wrinkled. She could have at least changed. Why hadn't she even though of changing?

Perry was not at the door. Or if she had been, she'd left. She was about to close the door when she saw it lying on her porch in the snow. Round, open eyed face looking up at her. Another puppet? She bent down. Was this some kind of joke? She picked it up. And then she gasped silently and dropped it. In the neck of the puppet was a small paring knife. A gaping hole had been torn in the fabric. The puppet's equivalent to a neck had been slit. A half scream formed around the edges of her mouth. It was several seconds before she could move back into the bright warmth of her living room and dial the number for the RCMP.

****

The dispatch operator in Calgary contacted the RCMP officer on duty in Chester.

"Something about a dead puppet," Roberta heard. "The lady sounded frantic."

"I'm on my way," said Roberta.

****

Fifteen minutes later a dark-haired olive skinned police constable named Roberta St. Marie was sitting with Mary Louise on her couch. The puppet and knife were already in a marked plastic evidence bag.

"This looks like a student prank," said Roberta.

"But mine's an elementary school. I can't imagine a group of ten year olds doing this to me."

"Oh, they're doing worse than that," she muttered mostly to herself. "Anyway, this will go to the lab first thing in the morning. We'll keep an eye on your house tonight." She rose and then regarded Mary Louise seriously. Mary Louise was shaking, shivering. And she couldn't stop. "Are you going to be all right? Is there anyone I could call for you?"

"Oh, Perry, maybe. But I'll call her. I'll be okay."

It wasn't until after she had left that Mary Louise realized that she had forgotten to tell her about the other puppet.

CHAPTER 15

"It's insane," said Perry pacing through Mary Louise's small living room, a hot mug of coffee in her hand and gesturing wildly. "They thought it was kids, did they?"

"That's what the officer said. But I don't know, Perry. 'I tell you I can't think of one student in my school who would do such a thing. By and large they're a good group of kids. I mean we have our problems, but they're all minor. And this looks so...so...."

"Vicious!" said Perry finishing the sentence.

Mary Louise felt tears forming at the corners of her eyes. She wiped them away with her fingers.

Perry sat down beside her. "Oh Mary Lou, I'm sure it looked more vicious than it actually was. You know kids. And Halloween wasn't that long ago."

"You're probably right." Mary Louise scrunched her legs underneath her on the couch. In the time between the RCMP leaving and Perry coming over, Mary Louise had changed into sweats, turned off her TV and put the kettle on for tea. "Probably in my state of mind, everything looks worse than it actually is. This is such poor timing."

Perry faced her. "What state of mind?"

"Oh," Mary Louise groped for words. "I haven't felt well lately. Touch of the flu," she said quickly.

Perry shrugged her shoulders and stood there looking at her friend, hands on both hips. Perry was short, slim and worked at home as a freelance commercial artist, designing

CD covers, promotional brochures and ads. She wore long flowing caftans left over from the 1960s, or oversized cotton shirts of her husband's over stirrup pants. Her hair was extremely short and spiky and in the time Mary Louise had known her it had gone from jet black to salt and pepper. Now it was getting more salt than pepper. On her face were oversized wire rimmed glasses which magnified her eyes and gave her an owl-like expression. She and her husband Edwin, married for 26 years were as different as two people could be. Edwin was an accountant who wore a tie on Saturdays. His hobbies were crossword puzzles and designing computer games. Often if Mary Louise dropped in on an evening, she would find the two of them deeply engrossed in a game of Scrabble or Chess.

"I think you should spend the night at my place," Perry said finally.

"I'll be fine."

"No. really. You look a wreck."

"Oh, thanks, you're full of compliments."

"No, seriously, I think you should come."

"What I need to do is to get into my own bed and get some sleep."

"If you're sure...."

"I'm sure."

Later that night Mary Louise wasn't so sure. Her dreams were filled with wide-eyed puppets, knives at their throats. Only in her dream blood spurted from the necks of the puppets. At one point Mary Louise woke in a haze of sweat and fear. PJ was meowing wildly. Rousing herself out of deep layers of dark sleep, Mary Louise got up and turned on light after light until her entire small house was bathed in light.

Darkness hath no fellowship with light. Words, strange religious words from a past she had rejected, were filling her mind. She padded into her living room and snuggled onto her couch pulling her afghan tightly around her. With all of the lights blazing, she slept until morning.

CHAPTER 16

At his desk the following morning Roger skimmed through the previous night's reports—the odd occurrence of a puppet and knife being left on the doorstep of an elementary school principal, more holy water being stolen from St. Anne's and couple of "drunk and disorderlies" down at the Green Lantern Pub, plus the complete forensics report on the Jonas murder had arrived via e-mail from Calgary. He called up the report on his computer screen and read through it carefully. It was a lengthy report, detailed and written in police-ese. Page after page outlined the contents of the numbered evidence bags which had been collected at the scene. Most of the fibers belonged to one of two people, Sterling Jonas and "Person Unknown." "Person Unknown" had spread his or her prints all over the room which meant "Person Unknown" had never been arrested, had never been fingerprinted. So, the crime was not premeditated. Most criminals now, even petty thieves, wear gloves, thought Roger.

The clearest bit of evidence came from that right boot print. The boot had come from a man's size eight CEBO rubber gum boot made in Czechoslovakia and at one time sold all over Canada. Roger looked at the picture of the boot on his computer, then a picture of the plaster cast. Fortunately, the murderer was not wearing new boots. Brand new boots or running shoe patterns indicate little. With wear, a forensic technician can determine whether the person was pigeon toed, whether he walked with a limp, even if he was heavy or light. In this case they had determined that the perpetrator walked with a slight limp. He was probably right handed, read the report.

Roger continued. He was stunned to learn that Jonas had been undressed and tied up *after* he was shot. He shook his head at that one. Why go to all that trouble tying someone up after you shoot him? A forensic psychologist had determined that the perpetrator was probably enraged. No kidding, thought Roger. Certain things about the crime suggested premeditation—the choice of room, the reserving of that room. Yet certain aspects were sloppy—the broken window, the abundance of fingerprints.

Partway through the report Roberta entered with a sheaf of faxed papers and placed them on the desk in front of him. "These are going to be of interest to you, Corporal."

The papers bore the official logo of the United States FBI. Before she left Roberta asked him. "Did you read the overnight dispatch? Some clown put a knife in a puppet's neck and left it on the doorstep of a teacher. Can you imagine? Kids can be so cruel sometimes. And she was really freaked. I sent the knife and puppet into Calgary this morning."

"I skimmed that report," said Roger absently glancing at the fax. "Who was the teacher?"

"Mary Jones."

Roger looked up. "Mary Jones? The principal of the elementary school?"

"That's the one, I guess." She turned to go. Roger called after her, "Oh, Roberta, before you leave, I've got something for you," and he pointed to the box from Kate's client's mother.

She glanced at it.

"It's videos, magazines, news clippings about the life and times of Sterling Jonas."

"Where'd you get them?"

"A Jonas fan."

Roger rose, picked up the box and carried it out to Roberta's desk. "Happy reading," he said.

Back at his desk, he was halfway through the FBI fax when the phone rang.

It was Mick. "You want to know a fact that could wrap up this case pronto?"

"What's that?"

"You'll never guess who wears size eight shoes."

"Yeah?" But Roger's mind was not on Mick. The slick fax pages were proving to be very interesting. Very interesting indeed!

"You want to take a guess?"

"What?"

"Have you been listening to me?"

"Oh, Mick, sorry. I'm just reading something here that's incredible."

"Yeah? Well, I've got something more incredible than that—Jud Soames wears size eight shoes. The boot print is a size eight. You've read the report by now? One of our officers just happened to go up to his room last night to talk with him and just happened to look at his shoes. I mean they were right there, lined up beside his bed. Don't need a search warrant to go looking into shoes, not when they're just lying there in full view. And just happened to notice the size. Eight."

Roger whistled. "Wait till you hear what I have here. Listen to this. It seems Jud has been embezzling big time from the Disciples of Grace. The IRS said the audit wasn't for Jonas' sake, but for Jud Soames' sake, and that this audit was actually requested by Jonas because he suspected Soames of helping himself to Disciples of Grace funds. Can you imagine someone doing that? According to this, Sterling Jonas had made complaint after complaint to the IRS. Finally he called the FBI. What kind of televangelist worth his salt does that!"

"A desperate one?"

"Yeah, but why was he desperate? What was he desperate about?"

"Whatever it was," quipped Mick, "it got him killed."

Roger sighed, said nothing. "I suppose Jud's long gone back to Oregon now."

Mick said, "You haven't heard? The planes aren't fly-ing—the storm has grounded them. So Jud is safe and sound in the Four Seasons."

"We've got motive and a boot print in an uncommon man's size. Enough, I would say, to bring him in for further questioning at least."

CHAPTER 17

Someone, it could have been Ed, it could have been Jennifer, had propped the puppet on Mary Louise's computer. Its soft cloth body had sunk into the top of the monitor, and it's ceramic face looked at her sideways, green clown eyes with the painted on tears. She picked up the puppet and scrutinized it. She was calmer this morning. She had had a good talk with herself at breakfast. She had told herself that if this puppet thing had happened even a month ago, she would have shrugged it off as a silly student prank, which was entirely what it was. She also told herself this morning over coffee that she was sure that if she checked the TV listings for the past couple of nights she would find a movie about decapitated puppets, or puppets who came to life and threatened entire villages. She wouldn't bother calling the RCMP about this puppet. It was probably stupid of her to waste their time last night as it was.

During recess, the time when she usually refilled her coffee cup and chatted with those teachers who were not on duty, she stayed at her desk with the door shut. Most of the talk in the staff room was still about the murder. Someone had flicked the TV and an anchorwoman was urging viewers to tune in a week from now to a special one-hour profile on the life of Dr. Sterling Jonas, from his humble beginnings in a small Montana church to his multi-million dollar publishing and television industry in Portland, Oregon. Inquisitive reporters were digging further and further back into his life. Mary Louise was beginning to get nervous. Inquiring minds always want to know everything. In the earlier years when she had heard he was proclaiming that he had no children and never had, that was fine with her. "I don't have a father either," she would say out loud, "and I never did." Still, she wondered how an entire congregation in Billings, Montana, could have so easily forgotten her existence. She remembered some of the faces now—Mrs. Leiber who was so enormously fat she had her own special chair in the back of the church. She wore tent dresses made of two double bed sheets. Sometimes when Mary Louise and her mother visited Mrs. Leiber they would be given heaping bowls of Neapolitan ice cream to eat. She never remembered a Mr. Leiber, but there must have been one or she would have been called Miss Leiber. People never made that mistake in those days.

Then there was the Blatz family with their dozen or more children. She lost count, along with everyone else. But she remembered Mrs. Blatz as a tired woman with stiff, frizzy gray hair which looked like a Brillo pad. She thought back to the Sunday after church when the Blatz family had piled into their station wagon. They had gotten all the way out to their farm before they realized the youngest Blatz, a boy of four, had been left behind. Mary Louise remembered him sitting on the steps of the church crying.

There were more; the Busbys and the Lowells, the Fishers and the Melencrantz sisters—two old maids, spinsters, they used to be called, who lived together. Spinster? Like she was now? No one used the word spinster anymore. In fact many of her married friends even seemed to envy her: "You just go home after work and don't have to make supper for three kids and a husband and do all the laundry until midnight!"

But what about the kids her own age, the kids in her Young People's group—friends, school chums; Arlene and Sally, Jon and Chuck? And Eleanor, her best friend from church. She wondered, did her father pay off all these people to keep quiet? She doubted that. People who are paid to keep quiet only keep quiet for so long. No, it had to be something more insidious. There were times she wanted to call up some of those people to find out just how he had gotten all of them, *all of them*, to keep quiet when he came up with his pronouncements that God had left him childless. How could they have been so deceived?

But now, these fancy-haired reporters with their cameras and endless staffs were getting too close to home. All it would take would be for one person to come up with the name Marylouise Jonas. "Please God," she found herself thinking and then shaking her head at her strange tumbled down prayers to a God who was merely a part of the past.

Rising from her desk she roared into the staff room, "Where is a good war when you need one?"

"War?" asked Jennifer looking up from her desk.

"Yeah, a war, to get our minds, not to mention the TV reporters on to some new topic for a change! Someone do me a favor and go drop a bomb on a third world country!" She said it with more vehemence in her voice than she really felt.

Monique looked up from the photocopier, adjusted her glasses and looked over at Jennifer who just shrugged. Mary Louise slammed her door behind her.

CHAPTER 18

"What is it with you people? You think you can call us up any time during the day and night and we're all going to bow down at your beck and call?"

"Take it easy, Mr. Soames." This was spoken by Roger. Mick, in his usual outspokenness, seemed to be making things worse. "We appreciate your coming down here," Roger added.

"You appreciate my coming down here," said Jud in a singsong attempt at mimicry. "It was more like I had no choice. Am I under arrest or what?" His face appeared more lined and sunken than it had appeared two days earlier. His eyes were ringed with gray and he was unshaven. To Roger's experienced eyes it looked as if he hadn't slept in days.

They were seated in an interview room at the RCMP headquarters in downtown Calgary. The room was windowless and stark. The only furniture was a wooden table, three wooden chairs, a telephone and phone book. The only wall adornment was a frayed 8 1/2 by 11 sheet of paper outlining the detained person's rights to legal counsel.

"No one's arresting you. At least not this week," said Mick.

"Great, spout off, I'm all ears. I know—where was I the night that Sterling Jonas was murdered? Is that what you want to ask me? Go ahead, ask me, I'll tell you. I was at a Disciples of Grace meeting all evening. But you already know that. I was at the hotel the entire evening."

Mick said, "We've got a positive ID on your footprint at the scene that verifies that you were there." Roger knew that wasn't entirely true. It was a ploy to get Jud scared enough to confess.

"My footprint?" Jud looked genuinely surprised.

"Your footprint," Mick repeated.

"That's insane. I was at the hotel the entire night. You know that. You've checked it out thoroughly."

"Then how did your footprint come to be outside the window at the room where Jonas was murdered?"

"I don't know, maybe someone took my shoe out there, but I certainly wasn't there."

"Wrong answer," said Mick leaning toward him.

But Roger had his doubts. A hastily put together search warrant had not come up with the rubber gum boots that made the prints. And somehow old black rubber boots bought in Canada didn't seem in Jud's style. Also, Jud Soames did not walk with a limp. If anything, he walked with his feet slightly splayed. The only thing they were going on was size. Size eight. Was that enough?

Jud said, "I refuse to answer any more questions until I have my lawyer present."

"That would be a good idea, Mr. Soames. We gave you that option at the beginning of this interview, as you will remember," said Roger motioning toward the phone. "You said since you had done nothing wrong that a lawyer was not necessary."

"Yeah, well, I want one now. And maybe I should tell you that Denise and I will be renting a car and leaving just as soon as I get out of here."

"The roads are bad," said Mick. "I wouldn't advise it."

"What are you going to do, arrest me for driving in the snow? Or for wearing the same size shoes as the killer."

"That's not all we have. If that was all we had, that wouldn't be much," said Mick.

Jud looked up.

"An audit was being carried out on the Disciples of Grace was it not?"

"The pagan American government is doing audits on all

of God's servants. You think that's news?"

"That an audit on the Disciples of Grace was being carried out at the *request* of Sterling Jonas?"

"That's insane. Why would he do something like that?" But Jud looked uncomfortable.

"Because he suspected you of skimming off the top of the Disciples of Grace."

"That's a lie!!!"

Mick's face was very close to Jud's, but Jud did not back up. "How many times did Jonas confront you before he went to the police?"

"You are horribly, horribly misled, my friend. I have absolutely no idea what you are talking about."

Roger spread out the file of faxed letters in front of Jud. For a few minutes he looked at them. Finally, he said rather quietly, "This still doesn't prove anything."

"It gives you a motive," said Mick quietly.

"So? I didn't do it."

Roger said, "Tell us about it. Tell us about the argument you had with Jonas the night before the last meeting of the crusade."

"There was no argument."

"One of your staff witnessed the two of you arguing."

"Who? Phil? It had to be Phil. Let me tell you something. Phil Kolanchuk is a big mouth and a drunk. You can't believe a word he says."

Mick said, "These papers prove that all was not sweetness and light between David and Jonathan."

"It doesn't prove anything."

"It gives you a motive."

"Motive? What motive?"

"It was clear you were skimming off the top of the Disciples of Grace," said Roger.

"I was just taking what was rightfully mine." He said it quietly, his head down.

"Dr. Sterling Jonas didn't think so. He called it, I think, stealing. Here it says, right here—stealing."

Jud Soames put his head in his hands. For several minutes no one said anything. Then Jud said, "Sterling was destroying the Disciples of Grace...."

"Would you like a lawyer?" said Roger gently.

Jud ignored him and went on. "I was the one who built up that organization. I made Sterling into what he was. It was me. I did it. I made the Disciples of Grace into a well-respected organization. He had the charisma and the looks, but I was the power behind the charisma. I was the brains. I handled all of the money, I invested it so it grew. He was nothing without me. But Jonas wanted to change things. But I told him no. In fact here in this crusade he had some crazy idea to come out and tell the people at the Saddledome about some personal spiritual journey he was on. Some poppycock about getting right with the Lord. And then he planned to resign. But he listened to my advice. He had to. The act didn't change. I threatened him...."

"Are you sure you don't want a lawyer?" This was from Roger.

At the same time Mick said, "You threatened him?"

Jud ignored this and went on, "I told him after this crusade he could come out with this spiritual confession and all that bull, but the Calgary Crusade was our biggest money maker and if he didn't stick to the act for this crusade, I would tell the world about Helene and him."

"Who is Helene?" asked Mick.

"His first wife. Everyone thought the man was so good, but the man was scum. I was sick when he got involved with Denise. That was even before Helene died. He treated people like scum, you know. Look, I may have hated him, but I didn't kill him." He was talking very fast. There was a thin film of froth around the corners of his mouth.

"What about Helene?" asked Roger.

Jud looked up, eyes wide. "It was the way she died...."

"And what way was that?"

"I ca-can't," his voice broke. "I can't talk about it. Why don't you talk to Muriel?"

"Who's Muriel?" Roger's voice was gentle, pressing.

"Helene's sister."

"What does Muriel know about Helene's death?"

"She was there when Helene died."

"Where does this Muriel live?"

"Down in Montana somewhere. I'm not sure. Sterling knew. He knew exactly."

"What is Muriel's full name?"

"Muriel Ames. Look, I can't talk. I don't have all the facts. Muriel does. I shouldn't have mentioned her." There was an edge of franticness in his voice, and somehow Roger knew he was telling the truth.

"You shouldn't have, perhaps, but you did," said Mick. Jud's eyes were wild as they flitted from Mick to Roger and back again. But he wouldn't say more.

Later, when they had released Jud, Mick said to Roger, "He did it. I don't know how he did it, but he did it."

But Roger wasn't so sure.

CHAPTER 19

Yesterday David saw Mary Louise for the first time. He had taken to driving by her house at least twice a day; once in the morning and once at night. There was a vacant lot and a large evergreen tree across the street from her place which offered a bit of seclusion. Yesterday he had pulled his Datsun under it and was reading a paperback book and listening to his praise tape when a white Honda Prelude drove into the carport. He sat up in his seat. She got out. He stared at her open mouthed. It was her! It had to be! She was tall, and there was something familiar about the way she carried her upper body when she walked—sort of the way he walked. He could see that! He stayed in his car for fifteen more minutes, shaking, exhilarated, before heading back to his motel room.

So, he'd seen her. He wasn't about to knock on her door and say, "Hi, are you my mother?" That night he prayed about it and still he did not know what to do.

It wasn't as though his real parents had mistreated him, he thought as he munched through the cheeseburger he'd ordered at the Chester Coffee Shop. They hadn't. They were wonderful parents. It wasn't that. It was sort of a feeling that somehow he didn't fit in one hundred percent. For one thing, at 6'4" he towered over all his relatives. Aunts, uncles, grandparents, cousins—he was taller than all of them. And his hair was dark and thickly wavy and he tanned easily. Every summer his skin turned a rich brown. His family were all petite, pale-skinned blondes who freckled in the sun.

As soon as he was old enough to understand, they had told him that the mother who had given birth to him was a teenage girl who had loved him very much but couldn't take care of him. When he turned 13 they gave him the note and the cross on a chain that had been left in his blanket the day his parents received him. He knew his birth mother had named him Sean. He knew the hospital where he was born. The cross was inscribed with the name Marylouise Isaacs. Was that his mother's name?

When he turned 20 he approached his parents with the idea of trying to find his birth mother. At first that had upset them. His mother had sat on the couch for a while, looking down at her hands clasped in her lap. "Oh, David," she said, "I don't want you to be disappointed...." His father hadn't said anything. But as he began to get closer to actually finding his mother, they started getting interested, even enthusiastic. "This is just like being a detective!" his mother said one evening when David had spread his papers all over the kitchen table.

He had contacted an organization called Parentfinders and was given a search consultant who showed him how to look up old records. He made many phone calls and ran many ads. He finally discovered that Marylouise Isaacs was probably his great-grandmother, probably his maternal great grandmother since there were no more Isaacs after she died. The trail eventually led to the name Jonas. Putting two and two together he wondered if Marylouise Jonas was his mother. Somewhere along the line the trail of Marylouise Jonas had led him to Mary Louise Jones. Even before he'd seen her he was fairly sure he had the right one. Two days ago he'd talked to his hotel manager.

"Ms. Jones? Yeah, both my kids had her. A good teacher," he had offered. "Is she married? Don't seem to remember her ever being married or even shacking up with anyone, so far as I know. Yeah, she's a friendly sort. Lives in a tiny little house, but everyone says the inside is something to see! I guess on a principal's salary with no dependents."

"Tell me, is she tall?"

"Tall?

"Yeah, tall, is she tall? What color hair does she have?"

"I don't know...yeah she's tall...Why all the questions?"

David had shrugged and muttered something and the motel manager had regarded him with hooded eyes as he walked out.

"More coffee?" The heavyset bleached blonde waitress was standing over him, coffee pot in hand. She smelled faintly of garlic and cooking grease.

"Uh, yes, please." Then he said, "Do you live around here?"

"You trying to pick me up?"

"No." David smiled at the ludicrousness of that suggestion. "I'm just curious about something."

"Yeah, I lived here all my life."

"You happen to know a teacher named Mary Louise Jones?"

"Mary Jones?"

"Yeah, that's the one, but I think she's the principal now. Do you know her?"

"Sort of. Not really. My kid had her, for all the good it did him."

"She a good teacher?"

"Yeah, I guess as teachers go. Me and teachers don't get along and that goes way back."

"What's she like?"

"I don't know. As I said, what're you asking about her for?"

"Just curious," he muttered.

She left, but David could see that through the window her gaze followed him as he got into his car and drove away.

CHAPTER 20

When Roberta entered Roger's office carrying an armload of yellowed newspapers, he was on the phone. She smiled, turned to leave and he lifted an index finger and motioned her to wait. A few seconds later he hung up.

"That was New Brunswick." He shook his head. "I've got to be nuts going into a situation like that. If I wasn't so sure it's where I'm supposed to be going, I'd turn tail and head to the farthest coast!"

She leaned toward him suddenly intent. "What do you mean where you're *supposed* to be going? How can you be sure of something like that?"

"You're talking about your own transfer, aren't you?"

She leaned back and nodded, her dark hair framing her face. "I'm from the north originally you know. And that's where I'm going again. I never thought I could ever get used to a place like Chester and now I feel like I'm going to miss it."

"No doubt you will."

"Can I be honest with you?"

Roger regarded her. "Sure," he said.

"So often I have felt like the *only* reason I was accepted into the RCMP Academy was because I'm a woman and part Cree Indian. I hate being on the wrong side of some government quota system—I feel like I've had to prove myself twice as hard as everybody else."

"Roberta, you're a good cop. I mean that."

She smiled. "Thanks, but a part of me is kind of afraid to go back north as a Mountie. Especially when I lived up there. When I accepted the transfer I thought it was a good idea, but now I don't know. How can you be so sure you're doing the right thing?"

"Sometimes I'm not sure at all. I've a 14 year old daughter who is not head-over-heals about leaving here and that's a concern. But I pray about all these things, Kate and I both do. We both feel God is leading us east."

"I used to pray" said Roberta. "I grew up a Catholic, you know, but then I stopped praying, kind of drifted away." She shrugged her shoulders.

"God's still there, Roberta, and He's interested in you and waiting for you to drift back."

"You think?"

"I'm sure," he said.

She was quiet for a few minutes and then said brightly, placing the papers on the table, "You want to see what I found?"

"Love to."

She spread the papers out. They were a series of *Calgary Heralds* from eight years ago.

"Newspapers," he said.

"Ahh, but not just any newspapers."

She opened to the Religion Section, the first one on the stack. "The last time Sterling Jonas graced this fair city was eight years ago. At that time his venue was not the Saddledome, but a large church in the northeast, fairly close to Chester, I may add. These papers are from that time."

He scanned the story in front of him. It was entitled "The Soft Cults" and was the story of a young woman who had escaped Jonas' clutches and was now, or at least at the time the story was written, living in Calgary. The article didn't give her real name, but she described an ordeal of many months of psychological abuse in which her finances, her career and her personality were systematically taken over by the Disciples of Grace. The article quoted a Calgary psychologist, a Dr. Viola Mosaic whose specialty is people coming out of cults, and said that the Disciples of Grace fit the description of a classic cult: Strong, charismatic leader; the loss of individual free will; the suppression of women." It was a well-written article, and Roger noted the byline—Ned Sampson. He wondered if Ned Sampson was still around, and would Ned Sampson be willing to give him the real name of this young woman and her boyfriend, who was called only "J" in the story.

The following day's edition of the *Calgary Herald*, which was the next one Roberta opened to, included more about the crusade which was featuring dramatic healings. About a week later the Letters to the Editor featured a scathing letter from a Mrs. Alma Fields, who had written: "How you can dare to call the working of God in our time a 'cult' is beyond me. Let me tell you what this 'cult' did for me. I was crippled over with multiple sclerosis, barely able to move, my vision was practically gone. I had no strength in my legs. Then I went to a Sterling Jonas crusade down in Washington state. When Jonas placed his hand on my forehead I felt a tingling, I knew God had healed me. And He had. I walked out of there that night, and for three years I no longer show any signs of the disease. I am healed, now you tell me whether this is the workings of a cult or not?"

Fortunately, letters to the editor are signed, and often include the sender's address. He went through further papers and found more names in the Letters to the Editor, people alternately praising him and condemning him. "This is great stuff," he said looking up at Roberta.

Together they made a list of people from eight years ago, who had written either in praise of Sterling Jonas or in criticism. Eight years was not a long time to hold a grudge.

CHAPTER 21

When her mother died, Mary Louise didn't cry. She had read about it in the paper, a short article no longer than an inch long. "Helene Louise Isaacs Jonas died today at her home in Billings, Montana, from complications of pneumonia. Helene was the wife of evangelist and head of the Portland based Disciples of Grace empire, Dr. Sterling Jonas. Ms. Jonas was 57." Those few words told her a lot; that her mother's home was Billings, Montana, while her father lived in Portland, Oregon.

Mary Louise had clipped the small column out of the paper and placed it on her dresser, waiting for the tears to come. They didn't. Eventually the clipping found its way into a small compartment of her wallet, behind her credit cards.

For some reason—and at the time Mary Louise wondered if Sterling had something to do with it—the media hardly mentioned her death.

Out of curiosity she had tuned into Sterling's live weekly broadcast the Sunday after her mother died. He never mentioned her. Never once. Instead, he pranced around the stage amening and hallelujahing with his pasted-on white-teeth smile and blow-dried hair. It had sickened her. She had turned it off. To think she was spawned by this man—that the same odious blood that ran through his veins ran through hers. It was unthinkable.

She was reflecting on these things as she stood in the 12-Items-or-Less line at the grocery store. In her cart were milk, coffee, a loaf of cracked wheat bread and a few cans of soup. The store was busy and noisy-bright. Directly in front of her a toddler was facing her from his grocery cart seat. His mother, young and pony-tailed was leafing through a woman's magazine from the rack. Mary Louise noticed a number of the tabloids were featuring stories about Sterling Jonas, and at least one was claiming that his faith in miracles had raised him from the dead and that he was now in South America preaching to the Amazons. "Elvis and he," thought Mary Louise.

The toddler grinned and extended a sticky hand toward Mary Louise. She smiled and touched the little hand. She wasn't sure whether it was a boy or a girl; but to her, all babies were boy babies. Little boys; four years old, five years old, eight, nine years old, 14 years old and now 19, 20. Every year that passed she observed the antics of boys who would have been Sean's age. She watched them learn to ride two-wheeled bicycles, play little league ball, take swimming lessons, score goals in minor hockey. She watched boys grow up and enter junior high school. She watch groups of them skateboarding in their bulky jeans. She would see pictures of high school students in the local paper, basketball teams on the way to the provincials, students receiving math and science awards and scholarships. And then the yearly pictures of all the graduates which always took two full pages in the Chester paper. Was Sean's picture in a paper somewhere, smiling thoughtfully in a graduation gown?

She reached into her wallet to make sure she had cash to cover her purchases, and her fingers found the yellowed obituary. And there in the 12-Items-or-Less line she brought it out and read through it again. Mary Louise had run away, out of her own free will she had left and had never gone back to her mother. Did her own mother grieve for her the way she did for Sean, noting the months, the weeks, the years? What anniversary did her own mother commemorate, the date of her birth or the date of her leaving?

Her only memories of her mother were of a frail woman, incapacitated by her many illnesses; weak emotionally, weak spiritually. But was she really? Or did her father's opinion of her mother color her own memories? Remembered snippets of childhood scenes came to her mind.

Helene, I can't trust you with the simple chore of ironing my Sunday morning shirts?....Helene, this chocolate cake tastes like rubber. You don't plan on serving this to guests do you? Marylouise, your mother is ill. You're going to have to make supper again.

Did she ever even try to understand what lay beneath the surface of her mother's weaknesses? Was she an emotionally battered woman who saw no other way to break free except by dying?

Tears began to catch at her eyes and she wiped them away with the back of her hand. But they kept coming. The toddler watched her curiously while she stood there holding the obituary and silently weeping; the tabloids of her father's death surrounding her, until the cashier had to say, "Miss?" and the grinning little toddler was being wheeled outside.

CHAPTER 22

Around 5:30 that afternoon Roberta came into Roger's office with the news that the first name on the list, Alma Fields had died three years ago. Roger had been trying without success to locate Muriel Ames in Montana. The Montana State Police had no record of her after six years ago. "It's like she dropped out of existence," the chief had told him. "But we're going to check into this and we'll get back as soon as we can, maybe later today."

Roberta said, "The house at the address was answered by an old man who told me he was Alma's husband and that she had died."

Roger frowned.

"He told me she suffered a long time with MS."

"What was this husband like?"

Roberta grinned. "I know what you're thinking but the guy couldn't have done it. He could barely get around in his walker. He didn't even seem to know Jonas was in town, or that he had died. I think he was hard of hearing, too."

"So she wasn't healed," Roger mused.

"Neither was Jonas," quipped Roberta. "Anything in yet on that murdered puppet?"

"Murdered puppet?"

"Yeah, that puppet left on that teacher's porch? Tim's been calling it 'the case of the murdered puppet.'"

"Oh, that. Yeah, something about that came in a little while ago. Strange, though. The puppet had no prints."

"So, the kids wore mittens."

"The puppet and knife had *no* prints. It's as if they were washed clean. There were water stains on them."

"So, the kids dropped them in a puddle or the snow."

"Possibly."

Roger looked back at his computer and Roberta stood there, hands fidgeting a little. He looked up. "Roberta?"

"I just wanted to thank you, Corporal, for talking to me earlier about moving and God. I used to think religion and believing in God was something you eventually outgrew. But here you are an adult, a corporal, soon to be sergeant, someone who's seen life at its worst, and yet you have a neat way with people. You can see the best in everybody, and you have a faith, a spirituality."

Roger smiled. "You're giving me a swelled head."

But Roberta didn't smile. She said, "I'm going to miss working with you, Corp." She paused. "I was thinking about, maybe, I don't know, going back to church, trying it again."

"That would be neat, Roberta."

"....Try to find a dimension of spirituality in my life, I'm told we all have this. Sometimes it just gets suppressed. At least that's what I've read."

"I've got an idea," said Roger leaning forward. "I know Kate's part of a Bible study group, a small group where people, especially people like you, can ask questions, stuff like that. It's for people who are searching. Is that the type of thing you'd be interested in? Would you like me to talk to Kate about it?"

"Sure, yeah."

When Roberta left, Roger turned once again to the list. There were a total of 11 names, Roberta had taken six and he promised to call five. He could have given this task to Tim or Dennis, but something about this murder was intriguing. And then there was Laird who had said, half joking, "You're the best with religious crimes 'cause your the religious one here." So this was a religious crime.

He scanned the list of people who were mentioned in some

way or another with the newspapers of eight years ago. Either they had written letters to the editors or their names had been mentioned in connection with the crusade:

Dr. Viola Mosaic
Rev. John Justus
Pamela Erschew
Paula Becker
Phillip Tatterly

Dr. Viola Mosaic was a practicing family psychologist in downtown Calgary. He dialed her number. Even though it was early afternoon her answering machine stated that office hours were Monday through Friday 8 a.m. until 1 p.m. He tried her home number and heard yet another answering machine. A lilting female voice with a slight British tinge to the accent said that she was not available at the moment, but if you would be so kind as to leave your name and number, she would get back to you as soon as possible. Roger did.

Rev. John Justus, a local minister, had written a guest editorial condemning Sterling Jonas as a fraud and urged Christians not to attend the meetings. Roger reached Rev. Justus on the first ring. He was still at the same address, still in the same office. Roger hoped all of his contacts would be this easy to reach.

"Rev. Justus, this is Corporal Roger Sheppard of the Chester RCMP," he said when Justus answered. "We're investigating the death of Sterling Jonas. I understand eight years ago, the last time Jonas was in Calgary, you wrote an editorial condemning his ministry as a fraud."

There was a pause. Then, "Boy, you guys are thorough! Well, I suppose I did just that. When was this you said?"

"Eight years ago."

"Eight years ago, ahh. I remember that. I was concerned with some of his teachings...."

"Did you ever meet Jonas or have any contact with him?"

"No, I did not. I have never met the man. I'm just familiar with his teachings. I've read most of his books. That's enough."

Roger said, carefully choosing his words, "I know this may be a difficult question to think about, much less answer, but I want you to, if you would, think about the people who attend your church, or who have attended your church....who may have some information into the death of Sterling Jonas. Can you think of anyone?"

There was a pause. "I'm not so sure what you're asking, but sure, if I hear anything I'll call."

The next on the list was Pamela Erschew. At the time of writing, she was a university student who had written a rebuttal to the Justus editorial. When he reached her phone number, an older woman answered who identified herself as Phyllis Erschew. She said that Pamela was married now and living in Toronto. Yes, she remembered the Letter to the Editor that Pamela wrote, and as far as she knew, Pamela had never met Sterling Jonas, had never attended any of his meetings, was not in the least religious, but just felt that free speech should be honored in every case, not just for those individuals with whom we agree.

The name Paula Becker caught Roger's eyes immediately; her address was listed only as Chester, Alberta. She had written a cheerful Letter to the Editor full of high praise for Jonas. She encouraged people not to condemn him until they had gone to a meeting and seen for themselves. She wrote: "I haven't been to a Sterling Jonas meeting either, but I certainly wouldn't judge him until I had. I'm planning to attend tomorrow night and I'm expecting my miracle from God then!"

There were no Beckers in the Chester phone book. A quick scan of the Driver's License information on the computer listed Paula Becker as "Deceased." She had died four years ago. "Well, that settles that," thought Roger.

Phillip Tatterly no longer lived at the address shown. A quick check of Phillip Tatterly revealed that he had moved to Boston, Massachusetts, a year ago. Roger called the Boston Police Department and talked to the sergeant there who promised to check into the whereabouts of Phillip Tatterly. It was a long shot, he admitted, but they were checking everything.

Dead ends. All of them. If he and his staff called every single person who had ever attended a Jonas meeting, or written a letter about, or supposedly had been healed by Jonas in all of southern Alberta it could take months or years. Plus, lately the detachment had been inundated with tips. The Calgary detachment of the RCMP had loaned a few constables to the case, and they plus Duane and Tim were taking every one of these tips down and then methodically categorizing them. Roger could only hope the murderer would make some mistake and reveal himself. But for now, they had nothing but a size eight boot print.

CHAPTER 23

Howard was very pleased with himself. Plans for the daughter were coming along nicely. The puppets were adding a nice touch, he thought, especially since no one except that nosy Mrs. Philpott knew about Paula's puppets. And nobody would believe a crazy old lady. He puzzled over one thing, however; who was David Brackett and how did he fit in? Well, he'd leave that for the time being.

Lately he was hearing the voices again, like the time right after Paula died. For a long time the voices had been quiet. Now they were back. And this time the voices weren't frightening him like they did at first. It was sort of like welcoming old friends back. Now, at least he wasn't alone anymore.

The thing was, he was feeling a lot better lately, too. His stomach wasn't bothering him nearly so much. Even nosy Mrs. Philpott said to him. "My, you're the cock of the walk these days, Howard."

And at work Father Graeme noticed. "There's spring to your step these days, Howard."

"Yup, there is," was Howard's reply. I mean why shouldn't there be a spring to his step? After all, he, Howard Becker, had gotten away with murder!

He really didn't know what possible use the holy water would have, but the voices were telling him to take it, and Howard always obeyed the voices. His trunk was full almost to the top now . At the very bottom of the trunk was his father's gun which he had rubberbanded in paper towels from the men's bathroom.

Yup, Howard Becker was very pleased with himself.

CHAPTER 24

When Mary Louise parked her car in the carport she felt an inexplicable unease. She glanced around her, wishing fervently that she had remembered to leave the outside light on before she had gone to work in the morning. The little it would cost her on her electricity bill to have it on all day might be worth it for her peace of mind. Holding the handles of her plastic grocery bags in her left hand, she unlocked the door with her right. The air in her house was cold and dry, but there was something else, a mustiness. She was reminded faintly of the paper bag which had housed the little puppet. Fear trembled in her body as she placed the bags on her kitchen counter and then walked through the small house turning on light after light. "Stop it," she told herself. "Get a grip, Mary Louise."

Using the remote control, she flicked on the TV, as much to hear another human voice as anything, and then put the kettle on for tea. PJ sidled into the kitchen meowing loudly. "What is it, boy, what's wrong?" She stooped down to pick him up but he fled from her. She followed him into her bedroom where she found him cowering under the bed. "PJ, come on, it's okay," she pleaded; but he wouldn't budge.

"It's me," she thought, "my stupid fears are now transmuting themselves onto my feline." She changed out of her work clothes and pulled on a pair of jeans and an oversized sweater. She still felt uneasy as she poured the hot water into her tea pot and added some loose tea. The quickest way to combat this foolishness, she told herself, is to get straight to her books. Her stupid response to a student prank had cost her many hours of study. She had a lot of catching up to do. She headed to her oak desk, reached for her pen and instantly froze. She managed a half cry, a sharp intake of breath. Someone had been here! It was more than the darkness. It was more than the cold. It was more than the puppets. The pen was not how she left it. That morning she had written a quick note in her daybook and then she had laid the pen down—with the writing tip facing the wall. That's how she would have left it. Not facing her, not facing into the room. She twirled around the room then, twirled and twirled like a little girl trying to get dizzy. Someone had been here. She knew it. She could *feel* it.

With a small part of her mind still functioning, she retreated to the kitchen and flung open the cupboards and pulled out the drawers. They weren't right. The cans and boxes were lined up too neatly. She had left the Cheerios on the other side of the Shredded Wheat. She knew she had. The forks and knives and spoons—too neat. She wouldn't have left them like that. Hurriedly she ran from room to room opening cupboards, pulling out drawers. Nothing was how she left it.

She kept money in a small square hinged box in her top drawer—not a lot; just grocery money. It was still there; the bills neatly stacked. She never put them like this, fives stacked on top of tens which were stacked on top of 20s. Next she checked her jewelry box. Over the years she had bought herself some expensive pieces—an emerald ring and a diamond brooch. They were still there. She felt in the back of the box for Sean's letter. Gone! Frantically she searched, dumping the contents of the box on the bed, spreading the necklaces, the earrings, the bracelets the brooches on her bed, pricking her fingers on the pins and crying out. But it was not there.

She stumbled into the living room and reached for her purse. Where was that business card? Frantically she dumped the contents of her purse onto the couch. There it was: Cons. Roberta St. Marie. "Call me if you have any questions, any problems," she had told Mary Louise. When was that, just last night? It hardly seemed possible.

With clumsy fingers she pressed the numbers. "Please be there, please be there," she said out loud into the receiver.

Roberta was there. In halting sobs Mary Louise told her that her house had been broken into.

"We'll be right over. Are you alone?"

"Yes."

"There's no one in your house right now?"

"No, I don't think so."

"Would you go over to your friend's house right away?"

"Yes."

Fifteen minutes later Mary Louise, Perry, Roberta and a constable who introduced himself as Tim Erickson were back in Mary Louise's house and seated in the living room. "Was anything taken?"

"No."

"Damages?" This was from Tim Erickson.

"None," she paused. "I know what you're thinking, but I'm not crazy. Everything looks as though someone's been in here. It's hard to explain. But all of my stuff is put away more neatly."

"More neatly," said Tim.

Perry rose and pointed her finger in his direction. "You listen to her," she said. "She's the sanest person I know."

Looking at her loose rose colored caftan, topped by Edwin's ratty old gray cardigan sweater, her loopy glasses down around the bottom of her nose, and scruffy hair, Mary Louise could see that he wondered whether that was saying much.

Mary Louise looked around her room, glanced into her living room and then gasped.

"What is it?" said Perry.

"My CD's. I had them stacked on the left of my CD player not the right."

"Are you sure?" asked Roberta.

"I'm sure. At least I think I'm sure."

"You better take her seriously," said Perry a note of threat in her voice.

"We are taking this seriously," said Roberta who shot a

look at Tim.

For the next half hour the four of them went through the house systematically opening drawers and closets, looking for anything amiss. It was clear that Tim was skeptical. Roberta, however, took a lot of time talking to Mary Louise and reassuring her that they would keep an eye on her house that night. Perry persuaded Mary Lou to spend the night with her, and Roberta nodded her approval. Roberta and Tim also evaluated Mary Louise's locks and advised her to get new ones as soon as she could. Tomorrow, if possible. The windows were especially vulnerable, Tim pointed out.

When the police officers left, Perry packed a couple of cans of cat food in a plastic bag. "We'll take PJ, too," she yelled into the bathroom where Mary Louise was gathering a few toiletries into her cosmetic bag.

"You're a doll."

"I know."

Mary Louise dragged her overnight bag from the floor of her closet and when she opened it up on her bed, she felt the blood drain to her feet. She screamed—a wet, strangled sound. Perry was instantly beside her.

"Oh my God!" said Perry loudly as she looked inside the bag. At the very bottom was another puppet, another smiling clown with big ears and a floppy yellow polka dotted hat with a couple of rusty jingle bells attached to the end. A large knife was at its throat.

The police were back almost instantaneously, and the puppet was dropped into a plastic ziplock bag and taken away. Even Tim paid more attention now, promising that they would keep a watch on the house tonight, and yes, it was very wise of her to spend the night at Perry's. Tomorrow when Mary Louise was at work, they would send in a crew to dust for prints. They told her they would have to take her prints as well, and also the prints of any friends who had been in the house. Theirs wouldn't remain on record, they were assured, it was just to differentiate with those that the intruder may have left. Mary Louise nodded numbly.

An hour later Mary Louise, Perry and Edwin were seated at Perry's kitchen table. Mary Louise's hands trembled as she brought the cup of coffee to her mouth.

"They couldn't possibly think it's still kids," said Edwin over the tops of his half glasses.

"I don't know what they're thinking," Mary Louise said. "But I think they're taking the whole thing a bit more seriously now."

"Even that young upstart of a cop," said Perry. "I couldn't believe the nerve of him!"

Edwin laughed. "Too bad I wasn't over there. I could tell them you are the most logical person I know."

"Next to you, that is," said Mary Louise with a smile.

From Perry and Edwin's basement guest room, Mary Louise called Ed Thiessen and told him that her house had been broken into and they were fingerprinting it, and she was needed down at the detachment tomorrow morning to give them her fingerprints. She also had to arrange for a locksmith and probably wouldn't be in until the afternoon. He told her to take all the time she needed, and he'd cover for her afternoon class if she didn't make it in.

"You just don't know anymore," said Ed. "This used to be a safe town, and now we're just as bad as Calgary. Was anything taken?"

"Nothing of value," she said quickly.

"Does this have anything to do with the puppet thing?"

"Yes," she said.

"Well, if you need anything, you just call. I also want you to know that Carla and I have plenty of room on the farm, especially now with the kids all gone and married. If you want to come and spend a few days."

"Thanks, no, Ed. I'm staying here with Perry and Edwin. I plan to move back into my own house tomorrow. I should have deadbolts on my doors and these special window locks by tomorrow."

"Too bad it's come to that," said Ed.

"Yes," said Mary Louise.

CHAPTER 25

It was the second night she had dreamed the dream: *It is night and she is standing on the landing of a wide wooden staircase. She has never been in this house before but she knows instinctively that there are at least two floors above her. She is consumed by fear and frantic to get down the stairs and out and away. Someone is following her, something is following her, something dark that she cannot name. On the top of the landing she looks down ready to descend. And freezes. At the bottom of the stairs is a sea of disembodied heads; puppet heads with emotionless plastic eyes in unsmiling ceramic faces. Heads with no bodies, just wisps of shredded cloth. Childish faces. Clown faces. Animal faces. Grinning faces. Weeping faces. Laughing faces. They are all looking up at her.*

She awoke with a start, and sat up straight in the unfamiliar room. It took her a minute to realize she was in Perry and Edwin's guest room. She hoped fervently she hadn't cried out. She didn't want Perry scurrying down the stairs like a mother hen. She glanced over at the bedside clock: 3:43 a.m. She felt PJ at her feet complain slightly at the disturbance.

She lay back under the covers. For several minutes she lay there, knowing that sleep would be a long time coming, if ever. She felt chilled suddenly, and pulled Perry's wool quilt close to her face. Night time was always the worst; the memories, the thoughts of a life passing by. Sean, all grown up now. A young man. David, his name. What did he look like?

About a decade ago she had awakened very early one morning, a feeling of despair shrouding her like a cloak. Somehow she knew that sometime during the previous week Sean had died. Sean had died. She could feel it, she could sense it. She knew it. After all why shouldn't he be dead? Children die all the time. Car accidents. Bicycle accidents. Maybe he was riding his bike out in the front of his house and a truck, or a drunk driver struck him killing him instantly. Maybe his school bus toppled in the snow.

After that night all of her thoughts of Sean were preceded by "if." If Sean is alive, he will be riding his skateboard. If Sean is alive, he will be going to the high school prom.

But Sean was alive and trying to meet her.

She scrunched her face into the quilt, trying to talk herself into sleep and away from the fear that was paralyzing her. She thought about the quote which was printed under her name in the yearbook when she graduated from the University of Calgary. "I am the master of my fate; I am the captain of my soul."

Mary Louise was in control. That's how other people perceived her. That's how she wanted them to perceive her. She worked hard to get people to think of her like that. She had no need for God, especially for her father's God. Her mother had been weak, and she hated her for it. But was it hate, or was it fear? Fear that she would turn out the same? Had this fear toppled her over the other way?

Her mother sang sometimes. Odd that she should remember that now. Snuggled into a wooden rocking chair, the rungs squeaking on the bare floor, back and forth, back and forth while her mother sang, "Dapples and grays, pintos and bays, all the pretty little horses." Her voice was breathy, the voice of a child.

Mary Louise rose from the guest room bed. She hated being dependent. If she were back in her own home now, she could go into the kitchen and put on the kettle for tea, and then turn on the light and read a book. But this wasn't Mary Louise's house, and she couldn't do as she pleased. She stood by the guest room window which faced the back yard. The moon was large, a looming round face in a black sky. She could see her own house a small black shadow across the yards. She could see the gazebo, shuttered and still.

Why was this happening? Who was doing this to her? "Shh," she warned PJ who was purring loudly thinking it was surely breakfast time by now. "Why? God, why?" she said, surprising her self yet again with the beseeching to a God she didn't know. "I am the master of my fate. I am the captain of my soul. There is no God, it's only me. I have done this. I have ordered the course of my life. I have worked hard for what I have. I will not thank God for my blessings; I create my own blessings, I work hard to bring them about. And if I fail, the blame is equally mine. I am the captain of my soul. The captain of my soul. My ship. My life. I need no one." She hugged herself in the darkness. Then why did she feel so alone?

She thought of her son again and the letter he had written. The one that was now gone. Again, she had failed. She did not have the address any more, hadn't even bothered to copy it down elsewhere.

She shivered suddenly and tried to stop the thought that was tumbling around in her mind. Her son. The puppets. Her father's murder. All happening at once. A little too coincidental perhaps? She put a hand to her mouth and gasped. Could it be her son, her own son who was tormenting her with puppets? Had she spawned a son like his grandfather? She moaned slightly, and sat down on the edge of the bed shivering uncontrollably. Could her son, her Sean, have somehow found out about his grandfather and then.... No, it was not possible. It was unthinkable. She grabbed the quilt and drew it around herself. She could not allow that to be possible. No, somehow she had been mistaken ten years ago. Her son was not dead. Her son was a monster, a bad seed, juvenile delinquent whose adoptive parents had despaired of him long ago. Perhaps they had even abandoned him, and now he was coming to torture her for leaving him. Somehow she knew this was true, instinctively she knew this. She made fists of her hands and then bit them to keep herself from screaming.

All these years of watching other boys grow up, boys in her class, boys in the neighborhood, boys in pictures in the newspapers, scholarship receivers; she had always pictured her Sean a good son, kind, gentle. But what guarantee did she have that he was any of this? She had deluded herself all these years. He was not dead, she had been wrong about that, she knew that now. He was a monster.

And why shouldn't it be? Her family tree was nothing to write home about. Her own mother was weak. If she wasn't physically sick, she was taken to bed with depression. Her aunt Muriel was a rebel, ran off and got married when she was 15. His grandfather? Well, it goes without saying. And Sean's own father? A hoodlum who tore around on a motorcycle. Who knew how many illegitimate kids he had running all over the country, all like him, with leather jackets and motorcycles. The only bright light in Sean's family tree was Marylouise Isaacs. She was a good woman, strong in her faith, strong where her own mother was weak. An angel. A soldier.

She groped for a bottle of aspirins from her makeup case and swallowed three of them with the glass of water she had taken to the guest room with her. She lay back down, curled herself into a fetal position under the quilt hugging her knees tightly to her chest. She wept then for all the lost things in her life. Weeping, waiting for sleep. "I am the master of my fate, I am the captain of my soul. I am the master...."

CHAPTER 26

When Roger arrived at work the following morning, there was a phone message waiting for him; a Raymond Vorhees from Portland, Oregon.

Roger dialed the number. The male voice was distant, the accent definitely American with a hint of the deep south. "Is this Sergeant Roger Sheppard of the Mounties?"

"Well, not quite," said Roger with a little laugh. "I'm still a Corporal. How may I help you?"

"Uh, my name is Vorhees, Raymond Vorhees. I'm on the board, well, was on the board as of a month ago of the Disciples of Grace. I'm calling from Portland."

"Yes," said Roger grabbing a pen and opening to a fresh page in his notebook.

The voice was tight, strained. "I thought you should know something about Sterling and Jud." He paused.

Roger made encouraging noises and Raymond Vorhees continued. "The relationship between them had deteriorated. Maybe you already know that. I remember a time when they were friends, good friends in fact."

"What happened to change that?"

"I don't want to incriminate Jud...."

Jud is already incriminated, thought Roger.

"...But there are some things you should know. Sterling wanted to change the ministry. Lately, he did. And Jud was still in the old style. And Denise. Poor Denise was in the middle."

"How was Denise in the middle?" Where Denise fit into all of this was something of a mystery to Roger.

"You don't know?" asked the voice on the phone.

"No, I'm sorry. I don't."

"Denise is Jud's daughter. That's not something that's very well-known."

It hit him then. Of course! That made perfect sense; Jud's protectiveness, the way he was always hovering around, packing her clothes, answering questions for her as if she had no mind of her own.

Vorhees was talking, "....month ago Jud fired me from the board. Strange things were happening. There was this tension all around the office, you could cut it with a knife."

"What caused this tension?"

"That's what I'm getting to." He stopped for a second and Roger heard him cough nervously. "Let me tell you something that I witnessed a month ago—the day before I was fired. Maybe that will help clarify things."

Roger waited.

"I was walking down the hall to my secretary's office when I saw Jud come storming out of Sterling's office. I don't think I'd ever seen him so angry. He walked past me. I don't know if he even saw me, but he was yelling to no one in particular, 'The guy is losing it, totally losing it.' Well, Sterling and I have always had a fairly good relationship, so I thought that I should go in and find out what the matter was. His door was ajar and I opened it and there's Sterling with his head in his hands sitting there in his big office in his leather chair and crying like a baby. I wasn't sure what to do. I told him, I said, 'Is there anything I can do?' And then he told me that he was sick of his life and this ministry. He told me he had treated his first wife so very badly. Then he also told me something that really shocked me. He told me that he had a daughter. I didn't know whether to believe him or not. I'd seen the evidence of his drinking. There on his desk were two glasses, obviously Jud and he had been drinking. I don't know how much Sterling had drunk, but it was getting fairly common knowledge that he was hitting the bottle. So I don't know at this point whether it was his talking or the bottle, but he told me he had a daughter that he hadn't seen in nearly 30 years. I asked him where this daughter was and he said he didn't know. That she'd just run off when she was a teenager and that was the last he'd seen of her. I asked him if he had ever tried to contact her and he said no, that when she left they didn't even try to find her. He had told everyone in his congregation that she was his foster daughter and never really belonged to him at all. His wife was never the same after this daughter left. Then he started going on and on about his first wife, how fragile she was, and how he should have taken better care of her—of her and his daughter. He'd lost both of them, he told me. He told me that God was never going to forgive him. I stood there wanting to tell him all the right things, but I found I couldn't say a thing. The next morning his secretary hands me a pink slip!"

Roger tapped his pen on his notebook. Daughter? Sterling Jonas had a daughter?

"My last contact with Sterling was the following morning, the pink slip in my hand asking why? And it was like the previous day had never happened. He was cold and hostile. When I mentioned this daughter, he laughed and said that he was drunk and crazy the day before and I was really stupid if I couldn't tell the difference and to forget everything I had heard. Well, as you might imagine I packed up my desk and was out of there within the hour. I don't know if anyone else knows about this daughter. Perhaps this isn't news to you, but I thought I ought to call."

"Did Sterling happen to mention the name of his daughter?"

"No."

Then Roger thought of something else. "His first wife, Helene. Did she have family, people she was close to?"

"As far as I know, her only family was her sister; she was with her when she died."

"Muriel Ames. We're told she's in Montana somewhere.

We haven't located her yet."

"I can tell you exactly where she is and it's not Montana. She's in Washington state, a suburb of Seattle. Moved there just after Helene died. Somehow she's still connected with the Disciples of Grace, but I'm sorry, I don't know how or why, I just know she is. I found that out just before I left the complex."

Raymond Vorhees gave him Muriel Ames' address and phone number. This was too easy, thought Roger. Vorhees concluded by saying, "I wouldn't call her. I'd go and see her if I were you."

"Why's that, Mr. Vorhees?"

"She'll hang up on you. She's a very bitter woman."

I'll keep that in mind."

Their phone conversation ended, Roger began making doodles on a scratch pad. So Sterling had a daughter—has a daughter, maybe. He did some quick figuring. She would probably be in her early forties now. Living where? Doing what? Had she harbored a grudge all these years?

But maybe Sterling was drunk. Maybe none of this was true.

CHAPTER 27

By the time Mary Louise was up and dressed, Edwin had left for work and Perry was in her studio working on a sketch that was going to be used on a cardboard container of laundry detergent. They wanted a rural scene, a clean scene; wild-flowers, log cabin, a couple of deer.

"Nice," said Mary Louise from the doorway. She had already helped herself to coffee.

"It's dismal," said Perry standing back, pen in hand. "They wanted a Canadian scene, that's what they said, *Canadian* scene. I told them I'd paint them a night scene of Toronto—Sky dome and space needle. They said, 'No, no. We want Canada.' So I said, 'Okay, how about the Saddledome?' They said, 'No, no, we want *Canada*—woods and wildlife and stuff.' I said 'This is Canada, friend, what do you think? We all live in log cabins with deer walking around?'"

Mary Louise laughed in spite of herself and looked at her friend. Today Perry was wearing a long white cotton shirt, with the sleeves rolled up, an old one of Edwin's no doubt. It reminded her of the smock shirts that children were once re-quired to bring to school for art.

"Anyway, I'm just about to quit. Are you ready to go?"

"Any time."

"Good, let's go get our fingers smudged," she said wag-gling her fingers in front of her.

Half an hour later they were in the detachment subjecting themselves to pads of ink and more questions. Were there any students, past or present, that Mary Jones could name that might want to do this? What was the significance of the puppets? Did Mary have any idea? Did she ever use puppets in teaching? They also asked her about her habits, any changes lately, things that might have happened that might shed some light on these puppets? Nothing but the puppets showing up out of the blue?

"That's right," said Mary Louise. "Nothing but the puppets showing up out of the blue." But her eyes didn't meet the constable's.

It took forever, but finally they left the detachment with the promise that everything that could be done was being done. Outside of the detachment chatting animatedly with each other, and deciding on where they should go for lunch, neither one of them noticed the small man in rubber boots and baseball cap who clutched his stomach and watched them from across the street. After they drove away, he limped back down the street.

CHAPTER 28

Raymond Vorhees was right about one thing, thought Roger. Muriel Ames did not like phone conversations with police. As soon as Roger identified himself and explained what he wanted, she hung up. He tried again. She hung up again. When he dialed her a third time, the phone rang and rang.

Half an hour later he dialed her number again.

"Hello," she said. Her voice was raspy and sounded like she was on the back end of a cold.

"Mrs. Ames...wait, don't hang up. This is not about Helene. This is about Helene's daughter."

"Helene's daughter! How do you know about her?"

"Sterling confided to a colleague about her and that colleague passed the information on to us."

"He wouldn't do that."

"Wouldn't do what? Confide in a colleague?"

"That's for sure. As far as Sterling was concerned, that little girl ran away and she no longer exists."

That "little girl," thought Roger would be a woman in her forties.

Roger asked, "Do you know where this girl is now then? Have you been in contact with her?"

"No, and if you're thinking what I'm thinking, that his girl went over from wherever she's living and killed him, well, she did the world a favor then."

"Mrs. Ames," he said tentatively, "You're one of very few people who knew Sterling and Helene from the old days. I'd like to talk to you about him."

"I ain't talking. This does my angina no good I can tell you. I said enough already. Shouldn't have said what I said."

"Why not, Mrs. Ames?"

"I got enough troubles now." She hung up.

Roger stared for several seconds at the dead receiver. What was the relationship between Sterling and Muriel Ames? The entire thing was so very murky. Maybe he should fly down to Seattle and talk to Muriel face to face. He took all of his concerns to Laird—that Muriel was the last person to see Helene alive and that Muriel may know something about this alleged daughter. Laird had said go for it and Roger went back to his office and booked a flight for the following afternoon. Just before he checked out for the day another call came for him. It was Dr. Viola Mosaic returning his call.

"Dr. Mosaic, thank you for returning my call so quickly."

"I don't know how I can be of help." Hers was a pleasant voice, almost musical. He couldn't quite place the accent. British? East Indian?

"You are quoted as specializing in cults."

"I do work with people in cults, among other things, yes."

"I understand you have knowledge about the Disciples of Grace."

"Let me think, yes, eight years ago I worked with a few young people who had just come out of that, and yes, I would classify that as a cult."

"Why?"

"That is a difficult one. Because you see, on the outside he preaches a message that can be received by everyone. You don't have to join his church in Oregon to be a follower of Sterling Jonas. You can do that in the privacy of your own home. Just watch his program, send him a check and you'll be on his mailing list forever. But if you do decide to go down to his headquarters and *join* his church, you will be treated very differently."

"How so?"

"It's a subtle form of mind control. On the outside Sterling wanted very much to be accepted by the mainstream churches, but deep inside he wanted power, control."

"You seem to know a lot about it." Roger was taking notes rapidly.

She laughed. "I've had experience with that group, but there are others like him. Many others."

"So what would happen if you went down to Portland and decided to join his church?"

"I'm sure it differs with each individual, but I would guess the Church, that's Church with a capital C, would slowly begin to take over your life. Sterling and his elders would begin to have control over where you send your children to school, whether they take piano lessons or not, even who they eventually marry. There's a real suppression of women in most cults, as well. Women are allowed few places of leadership if at all. This is not true of all cults, mind you, but the majority."

"You'd classify the Disciples of Grace a cult."

"Oh, most definitely."

"Any ideas about who might have killed Sterling Jonas?"

She laughed. "Ah, now you're asking me to do your work. I have none. It could be a power struggle at the top, it could be as simple as someone holding a grudge because Sterling didn't heal their mother like he promised he would."

"Thank you, Dr. Mosaic. If we need to, can we call you as an expert witness?"

She laughed again, that lilting laugh. "Oh, most definitely, Corporal. I would be happy to help."

CHAPTER 29

The day had been a long one and it was going to get even longer. When Roger pulled into his driveway he saw Kate standing in the window in her best black dress, a string of pearls at her neck, her thick, dark hair swept up on her head with a jeweled barrette. He thought, uh oh, what important date had he forgotten.

What he had forgotten was the real estate board's annual Christmas party in the Sheraton in Calgary.

Forty-five minutes later Kate and he were sitting at a round table covered with a white linen table cloth and a centerpiece of pine and candles, and munching on a mixture of spinach leaves and mandarin orange slices. In a record ten minutes he had showered and changed and climbed into his one and only suit which he wore to weddings, funerals and to the annual real estate board Christmas banquet.

Because they were late, the only available space was at a table with two couples who introduced themselves as the Williards and the Luxmauers. Rose Williard, a real estate broker from Calgary, was a pale wispy woman who looked like she had maybe spent all of five minutes choosing her dress for tonight, a flowered print with pink the predominant shade. Her husband Dobson was a small, nondescript brown-haired, brown-suited man who wore large brown glasses that dwarfed his face. Medium height, medium build, no distinguishing features, thought Roger.

Kent and Doreen Luxmauer couldn't have been any more

different. Kent was president of the Calgary real estate board and now earned so much money that he could spend all summer sailing his yacht on the west coast. This was a fact he let everyone know. He was a large, freckled, red head with a florid face and features that looked too big for his face. Doreen, his wife, was a tall angular woman with a long straight nose and dramatic high cheekbones. Her very straight, chin-length hair was a blackish purple color which hairdressers probably referred to as "Midnight Blue," but to Roger's eyes did not look like the color of real hair. She wore long green earrings and an ankle-length straight black dress.

When their salad plates were taken away, Roger leaned over and whispered to Kate, "I'm flying to Seattle tomorrow."

"You're what?"

"Seattle. I'm going there tomorrow."

"Whatever for?"

"Business. I'll tell you later."

"When will you be back?"

"Probably the day after. Shouldn't take more than that."

"I got news, too," she whispered. "Becky's math teacher phoned. She wants to see you and me and Becky. Becky has missed some assignments. It's going to affect her mid-term mark if she doesn't get them in. The teacher wanted to know if there was trouble at home."

Trouble at home! Roger shook his head. Why, when kids goofed off did the teachers automatically assume there was "trouble at home"? "Did you tell her there was no trouble at home except for Becky goofing off?"

"Shh, the teacher was very nice. I told her we were moving and that Becky was having difficulty accepting it."

All of this was done with whispers. The waitress was passing out bowls of soup to the other tables, bypassing theirs.

"What are we, chopped liver?" called out Kent.

"Shh," commanded Doreen.

Roger leaned over to Kate again, "You still go to that Bible study for new Christians, or whatever you call it?"

"I haven't been for a while," Kate whispered back. "I hate

to go when I'm not bringing anyone. That's the whole point of it you know."

"I know. I may have someone for you to bring from the detachment—Roberta."

"Roberta! Really, she's interested?"

"I'll tell you all about it later, but yeah, I told her you'd call her."

"Great! I will."

Rose turned to Kate then, and in a few minutes the two of them were involved in conversation. Becky, Seattle, the move east and the Jonas murder would have to wait. He decided to engage Dobson in conversation. The poor man was just sitting there staring forlornly into his empty salad plate.

"So, Dobson, tell me, what do you do?"

"Well, right now, what I'm doing is sitting here waiting for the soup."

Roger looked at him and then realized that the man was trying to make a joke. So he grinned.

Then Dobson said in a mimicking tone, "So, tell me, Roger, what do you do"

Two could play this game. "I'm a civil servant."

"Federal or provincial?"

"Federal."

Kent chimed in now. "So you're with the feds. And it's my tax dollars that pay your salary, right?"

"Right." Roger grinned.

Kent chuckled. "So you better be giving us bang for our buck."

"Oh, I do that all right." This was fun.

Doreen said, "I used to be with the provincial government. I was a secretary. Now they call them, I think, Administrative Assistants, some fancy name like that." She held out a piece of bun with her left hand. "What branch of the government are you with?"

"Justice." Roger winked at Kate who was listening, clearly amused.

It was about this point that Kent took over the conversation sparked by a question from Dobson about sailing on the west coast. He went into a long monologue about his boat, and how it was really the best boat out there and how he got it for the best price going and on and on until Roger looked around wondering when that next course was coming. It really did look as if the waitress was deliberately ignoring their table. It was him, he was sure of it; he had the knack of always sitting at the wrong table. Don't sit next to Roger at a church potluck, you'll be sure to be the last to get your food. Looking around he figured that he was probably the only RCMP member in the place, maybe even the only cop. He guessed there were more than 200 people in the room; and if this banquet was anything like previous banquets, the eating of the food would be followed by hours of speeches, clapping until his hands were sore and he was left wondering what he was clapping for. This would be followed by the opening of the bar and dancing. It was about at this point he usually persuaded Kate they had enough. Still, Kate liked to go to these things, so he went. After all, she did go to the RCMP Regimental Ball for him; the one event during the entire year when he wore his RCMP red serge. But, come to think of it, Kate enjoyed that, too, mingling with the other members' wives and admiring each others gowns.

When he turned back, the conversation had drifted away from sailing on the west coast to the latest tabloid offerings about Sterling Jonas.

Rose was saying, "....just don't see how sane people can buy those magazines! They are just pure garbage."

"I agree," said Doreen. "I saw one yesterday that said Sterling Jonas had risen from the dead!"

"You bought that one, you mean," said Kent.

"I did not! That one in the family room came from my sister."

"Yeah, but you read it cover to cover, I'm sure," he said.

"Yeah, well, so did you for that matter. I saw it in your bathroom."

"The funny thing," said Kent. "was that we had real estate

meetings in the Four Seasons the entire week Jonas was staying there, just last week."

"Oh yeah?" said Roger.

"Yeah. We had that room booked about a year ago. I mean it was strange that we're there the same time. I saw him a couple times too, him and that little weeny wifey of his...."

"Seeing him is different than meeting him," said Rose.

"Wait a minute little lady, who said I never got to meet him?"

"Did you meet him?" asked Kate.

"Well, I didn't exactly meet him, but I did see him—he and that wife of his. I thought at first it was his daughter. Then someone, I think it was a valet, told me it was his wife."

"What does she look like?" asked Doreen.

"Petite, not nearly as dramatic as you, my dear," he gave a laugh. "But pretty in her own way. I can see why Sterling went for her."

"Oh sure," said Doreen. "Now you tell me you met Sterling Jonas' wife. He never tells me these things at home. I have to find out about the life and times of my husband by going to a real estate dinner!"

"So, what's she like?" asked Rose.

"Hey, maybe I should sell this stuff to the highest bidder?" He leaned back and held out both hands palms up. "Any takers?"

"Oh, shush," said Doreen. "If you're going to tell us, fine. If not, then let's move on to another subject."

But Kent, clearly the center of attention, was not about to move onto another subject.

"Okay, you wanted to know—they were fighting."

"Fighting?" said Roger.

"Yeah, it happens. Couples fight.

"Tell me about it," said Doreen.

"Did you hear what they were fighting about?" asked Kate. "Children."

Dobson said, "Children!"

"Yeah," Kent was grinning now. "She said to him that she

wanted a baby, and I heard him say, 'not at my age I don't. This wasn't one of the things I promised you. No. No way!'" Kent said all of this with wild gesticulations and did a passable imitation of Jonas' voice and accent.

Kate looked at Roger as if to say, "Sorry I had to drag you here."

And Roger winked at Kate as if to say, "No problem. This is better than television by a long shot."

"Yeah," Kent was continuing. "He said, 'this was never a part of the wedding vows my dear,' and that little wife of his was pouting."

"You're kidding!" said Rose.

Kent leaned forward, both hands on the table palms down and looked around. Clearly he loved the rapt attention of everyone at the table. Then he began laughing so uproariously that he had to wipe his brow with his cloth napkin.

He said, "See how you people eat up the gossip. No wonder the tabloids make money, no they weren't fighting. And I didn't even see them together. I never even saw the late Dr. Sterling Jonas!" He was laughing. The others at the table were looking at each other. Rose and Dobson were smiling politely. Kent's florid face was still rippling with laughter.

Doreen said petulantly, "So you never saw them at all! You big liar!" And she punched him gently in the shoulders. He took her hand and kissed it dramatically.

"What I did see," he said finally allowing his laughter to subside, "was his child bride fighting with someone else. See how quick you all are to believe the worst, that she was fighting with her husband! What I really saw was her fighting with was a short man who was wearing John Lennon glasses."

"John Lennon glasses?" asked Rose.

"Wire rims, you remember John Lennon glasses. Don't tell me I'm the only one remembers John Lennon glasses."

Dobson leaned forward, "So she was fighting with some stranger about having a baby?"

Roger was beginning to believe that Dobson had what people call a "dry" sense of humor. Maybe a bit too dry.

"No, I made that up, too. Right on the spur of the moment I may add."

"Do tell," said Doreen.

Roger asked, "Did you hear what they were fighting about?"

Kent raised his right hand palm forward. "The truth is, people that I did not hear what they were fighting about. He had her hand on his arm and she was trying to squirm away. And folks, she did not look happy. She had a scowl, a mile long and talking a mile a minute about who knows what."

"Really," thought Roger.

Later that night when Kate and Roger were in bed she turned to him, "I know, don't say it. Why didn't I choose a profession which attracts normal people, like say plumbers or airline flight attendants?"

CHAPTER 30

The early morning sky was dark and starless, blanketed with fat gray clouds. By 7:45 Roger was sitting in a booth at Jani's Coffee Shop, just around the corner from the detachment; a favorite early morning haunt for those in uniform. Across from him in the booth was Roy Laird who was working his way through a creamcheese pastry bit by bit. Next to him was Fish and Wildlife Officer Sam Freestone, a balding jovial fellow who never tired of recounting his exploits of disarming drunken hunters, or finding illegal venison in someone's freezer. Next to Roger sat Roberta who rested her head in her hands. Several times she smiled wanly at Sam's latest story. They'd had another puppet incident last night. This time the puppeteer had gotten inside the teacher's home.

Roger sipped at his coffee. On the table in front of Sam was a platter of fried eggs dripping grease, sausages, hash browns, white bread with butter and jam. Cholesterol City. Roger, with his high fiber bran muffin, no butter, was feeling very righteous.

"....So what do you think about that?" Sam was pointing his grease covered fork directly at Roger.

"Pardon?"

"This guy's weird religion. It make any sense to you?"

"If you're talking about Sterling Jonas, I think he's way off base."

"How so?" Sam looked genuinely interested.

Roger paused for a moment and broke of another bit of his

bran muffin. He had this great knack of coming up with all the right things to say about an hour after the opportunity had passed. Quietly he prayed. Then he said, "The guy says that if you just believe in God all your problems will be solved...."

"....They weren't solved for him," piped up Roberta.

"That's exactly what I'm saying. He says that if you believe, then you should have no more health problems, no more money problems, and everything you do is all forgiven even before you do it."

Sam chuckled, "So we could have all these ax murderers walking around."

"Exactly. If you believe what Jonas preached, then you're not accountable to your family, your co-workers, or to the law—you're not accountable to anyone."

Roberta said, "When he was going on and on in those videos about not being under the law, was he talking about the legal system, the *Canadian* law?"

"I think he meant the laws as they were set up in the Old Testament for the Jews, you've heard of the Ten Commandments, I'm sure...."

"Saw the movie," said Sam.

Roger continued, "....but it could refer to this Canadian law, too, I think. Because he says that whatever you do, God can't see your sin. That's not how it really is. We have to be accountable for what we do. You do something wrong, you pay the penalty."

"You do the crime, you do the time," said Sam loudly spearing a fat laden piece of sausage. Grease squirted onto the table.

"God's penalties, however, are much more severe than the law of this land. It's capital punishment big time. The wages of sin is death, that's what the Bible says. The Bible also says Jesus Christ paid the penalty for sin, took the punishment, did the time for mankind's sin, and that's where Jonas and his people have it all wrong, in my opinion. It would be like when we find this killer of Jonas' and someone else takes the blame, and then the real killer gets almost glib about it, and goes out and kills more people knowing that this other person is always going to take the blame no matter what he does."

Laird spoke for the first time, "So that's what that creep believed? I didn't get it."

"It's all Greek to me, too," said Sam mopping up the grease in his plate with a hunk of white crust.

But Roberta turned to Roger and said, "I think I understand what you mean."

Back at the detachment, Laird told Roger that he had been in touch with New Brunswick, and that it looked as though the town had definitely decided that one more month was all the money they could come up with. The RCMP was scheduled to move in two months at the outside. Already, renovations were taking place at the old police building in St. Matthews to bring it up to RCMP standards.

"What about this citizens committee to preserve the local cops?" asked Roger

"I guess they've been told there just isn't any more money. They've been assured by Ottawa that the RCMP will give them service just as good as they've been used to."

"I'm sure that's of great comfort to them."

For the next half hour they lined up the duties for the day, preparing for the time when Roger would be away. Laird said, "I've assigned Roberta and Tim to the break-in at the teacher's place. God knows we're stretched to the limit what with the Jonas thing. Why couldn't that puppet killer have done his thing a couple of months ago, or next summer?" said Laird shaking his head. "The latest puppet and knife are being sent to Calgary this morning. I think they'll be clean again. But personally, I think you should concentrate on the Jonas case."

Roger picked up his mug of coffee. "The reporter from the *Calgary Herald* is supposed to get back to me today about that woman who left the Disciples of Grace. I don't leave until later this afternoon, if I'm already gone Clayton and Dennis can visit her. I don't know what she'll have to say if anything."

"Did you read the latest report on the shoe print?" asked Laird.

"If it came in this morning, I haven't read it yet."

"I'll save you the trouble. The shoe pattern doesn't match the walking pattern of Jud Soames. But I think we already guessed that. We are looking for someone else with a size eight shoe."

"Back to square one. That won't make Mick very happy. He was so sure it was Soames."

"Mick is sure of a lot of things, or thinks he is anyway."

"Are they still in town, Jud and friends?"

"No, they hightailed it outta here the same day you had him in for questioning. Rented a car.

Later that morning when Roberta stuck her head in Roger's office door, he was in the middle of paper work; writing, signing, reading everything in triplicate. Everything had to be just so for the courts. If not, a case they'd been literally working on for years could be thrown out in an instant. He was grateful for the break.

"You drink too much caffeine," she said eyeing the cup on his desk. She entered and sat down across from him.

"Coffee's good for you," said Roger. "Cleans out the plumbing."

She chuckled. "I'm going to miss you around here. The place just won't be the same. When are you going anyway?"

"One minute you're telling me you're going to miss me around here and in the next breath you're asking when I'm leaving. Actually, the word is two months now."

"Corp, I been thinking about this puppet thing. Can we get it on Crime Stoppers? I know Tim doesn't agree with me. But my instincts tell me there's more to the story. The teacher seemed so freaked. And I'm afraid there's more on the mind of this puppet-master than just fright."

"Why do you think that?" asked Roger.

"Well, first he, or she, puts a puppet with a knife on the teacher's doorstep. The next time, only like a day later, the guy breaks into her house and puts the puppet and knife into her suitcase. Why her suitcase? Because he figured she'd be so freaked she'd be packing to go somewhere."

Roger mulled that thought over in his mind. He, too, had wondered why her overnight bag.

"You know how you're always telling us to trust our instincts," she continued. "Well, these are my instincts. I mean I don't know much about puppets, but these puppets don't look like ordinary puppets that you can buy in any department store. They had painted faces, like those old dolls you see."

"Porcelain?"

"Yeah, I think porcelain. I don't know if the report will come back soon. It's probably a low priority at this point, but I thought that maybe if we got this on Crime Stoppers someone might recognize these puppets. I don't know. I got a feeling that teacher lady is in for more threats. The whole thing has this creepy feel about it."

"Let me talk to Laird. If there is anything strange about the puppets, we'll check with this Mary Jones and see if she would agree."

"We don't even have to mention her name in the Crime Stoppers thing."

Roger nodded. "You're good Roberta."

"I know. The best. But this puppet thing is really weird. I mean who does that sort of thing?"

CHAPTER 31

When *Calgary Herald* columnist Ned Sampson called Roger with the information that Fiona Stone and her husband Jesse would meet with him late that afternoon, Roger asked, "Fiona Stone?" "Yes, one of your officers called this yesterday requesting her name, the one in the story."

"Ah, yes, the cult thing."

"Right."

"I told your officer." Roger could hear paper fluttering in the background, "I have it right here. I talked with a Constable Clayton Lavoir. He called yesterday asking for the name of my contact. I told him I couldn't give it to him until I had checked with her. I was able to call her earlier, and she said you can come over this afternoon if you'd like."

"Let's see," Roger did a quick calculation. Right after lunch he could meet with Fiona, then get Clayton to drive him to the airport where he would catch the 5 p.m. flight to Vancouver, and then transfer to Seattle. "Can we make it earlier, like right after lunch?"

"Don't know, I guess I could check."

"I'd appreciate that."

The rest of the morning Roger tried to get caught up on his paperwork, not his favorite task, and then shaking his head that when he moved to New Brunswick and took over the duties as sergeant in a brand new detachment there would even be more paperwork. "Oh goodie," he thought.

Around 1:30 Roger and Clayton took off in a police cruiser

and headed toward Calgary's southeast side.

Fiona and Jesse Stone lived in a small white bungalow in a neighborhood filled with small white bungalows all in a row. Toy houses in a toy village. Complete with real snow. It wasn't a wealthy neighborhood, yet the residents seemed to take pride in their surroundings—freshly shoveled walks, cheerful Christmas decorations made of construction paper by children were pasted in picture windows, and on the front lawns were snowmen with carrot noses and knitted scarves around their necks.

The Stone's bungalow featured bright red shutters painted with a white filigree pattern. Roger and Clayton walked down the recently shoveled cement block walkway. Near the front door a yellow plastic dump truck was parked atop a hill of snow. There was no doorbell, instead Roger rapped a few times on a pale blue tole painted door knocker.

It was answered by a slender woman with strawberry blonde hair which was very straight and hung nearly to her waist. A toddler with the same strawberry blonde hair and wearing a bright blue embroidered playsuit peered out at them from behind her mother's legs.

"Are you Fiona Stone?" asked Roger.

"Yes." The young woman extended her hand. "You must be the policemen here about the newspaper story. Come in. I've made some coffee," she said. "My husband's at work. He wanted to be here, but he doesn't get off till later and I know you said you needed to come early."

She led them through a small, square living room which was cluttered with a variety of toys, a playpen and an entire fleet of brightly colored plastic trucks. In one corner a preschooler was sitting cross legged in front of a television.

"I hope the kids don't make it too difficult for us to talk. This one is Angelica. She's 18 months. Curtis is three. He's the one watching television. Curtis, say hello."

The little boy turned. "Hello," he said. Before Roger and Clayton had a chance to respond he had turned his attention back to the show which featured a large purple dinosaur who was galumping across the screen.

Fiona hoisted Angelica onto her hip and said, "She's due for a nap soon. I was hoping to get her down before you came, but no luck. Are you ready for coffee?"

"That would be nice," said Roger thinking that this was probably his fifth cup of coffee for the day but who's counting. Clayton nodded.

Fiona settled Angelica in a highchair and put a vanilla baby cookie on the tray. Then she placed three coffees and a flowered china creamer and sugar on the table. Roger glanced around the room. The kitchen windows were curtained with a printed fabric which was bustled and full. On the walls were framed needlepoint pictures of flowers and English cottages; a small calico wreath hung on the back door and various dolls and teddy bears perched on corners and counters. Quaint. Cottagy. Kate would approve.

"I made some apple bread this morning," she said placing a china plate of sliced loaf in front of them. Angelica immediately grabbed for a fistful but Fiona rescued the plate and moved her high chair back a bit.

"There now, you eat this and let Mommy talk." Then Fiona sat down and came right to the point. "I assume you want to know about Sterling Jonas and my involvement in the Disciples of Grace."

Clayton nodded and for the first time Fiona seemed flustered. She nervously ran a hand through her long hair. "It's so hard to know where to begin," she said.

Roger said softly, "Just start from when you first met him."

"That was nine years ago." She seemed intent on getting each word right. "He came here to Calgary to meet with churches about coming back for special meetings. He spoke at our church." She looked toward Curtis and then took a long sip of her coffee. She chose a piece of apple cake and carefully broke it into small even pieces on the napkin in front of her. She stared at them for several seconds.

Her voice shook slightly as she continued. "We were all taken with him, with Sterling Jonas then. All of us were. Even my parents. He has...had this, I don't know, this magnetism about him. I remember sitting in church and listening to him talk about grace and healing and I remember saying to myself, 'I want to be like that. I want to have what he has. I want my faith to be that strong.' I was struggling then with my faith, and Sterling made it all seem so easy. So right. Nothing to it.

"He came to our house for lunch that Sunday. I felt like I was the luckiest person on the earth to have him at our house."

"He was alone?" This was asked by Clayton.

"Yes. His wife wasn't with him. I only met her a few times. She was sick a lot. They had this strange kind of relationship. At least I used to think it was strange. Now I know it was no relationship at all." She paused and picked up one of the bits of apple bread and placed it in her mouth. She chewed slowly, thoughtfully. "After dinner Sterling Jonas turned and looked at me and then he said, 'What are you doing with your life, Fiona?' Just like that. I was shocked that he even knew my name. I was all of 18 at the time and didn't have a job. I guess I was really at loose ends. I remembered hemming and hawing and saying that I couldn't find a job in Calgary. And then he said that if I came down to Portland, he'd find me a job there. It all happened so fast. One week later I was down in Portland. Some of the staff at the church had been in touch with me. They found me a job working as a receptionist at a car dealership. The manager of the place I worked was from the church, too."

"What about immigration? Living in the States?" asked Clayton.

"That was the funny thing. There was no problem at all. The people in the church took care of everything, got me a green card, found me a job, got me settled into an apartment with two other girls from the church. They took me all around Portland. I felt so loved and taken care of; for the first time in my life I didn't feel like an outsider. I felt like I was on the *inside* of something really great. I felt so lucky. My two roommates were so nice. So much of our life was taken up with the church. We had meetings three nights a week, plus Sundays of course, but that was fine with me. We were only allowed to watch Sterling Jonas programs on TV, but that didn't bother me. I was so, I don't know, *caught up* in the joy of the Lord— or so I thought."

She looked into her lap and Roger asked gently, "When did things start going sour?"

"For a long time I didn't think anything was wrong; everything seemed so *right*, but they were taking over my life little by little, and I didn't even notice. Maybe if he'd stood up wearing an orange robe with his head shaved telling us to give him all our money, it might have gotten through my thick skull! Sometimes it's so difficult to understand how I got involved with them. I grew up in a good home, what you would call a good *Christian* home. And then I go down there and everything goes out the window.

"It's not just me, though," she said her voice taking on an intensity. She leaned forward. "There are still so many people down there, and not just single people, but married people, families living right under his thumb—that's the sad part. They do everything he says. He says, 'Put your kids in Little League,' they put their kids in Little League. He says, 'Take your kids out of Little League,' they take their kids out of Little League." She reached over and stroked Angelica's hair out of her eyes. "I hate to think of kids growing up under that. Jesse—that's my husband—and I have a ministry to people coming out of cults. You probably haven't heard of us; we try to keep a low profile. People know us, so I'd appreciate it if you would keep what I say confidential. I have no desire to write a book about my experiences, nor be featured in the tabloids."

"I understand that," said Roger.

Fiona continued, "In the end I could barely eat a meal or pick out my own clothes for the next day without consulting one of the elders. I guess where it started was in the classes. We had lots of practical classes on such things as Christian conduct and dress and how to manage your money, things like that. I thought, 'Hey this is neat.' Managing money has never been my strong point. I can tell you," and she paused and laughed slightly. "Jesse despairs of me at times. Well, in the 'Managing Your Money' class, we were told that 20 percent had to go to the Church. In fact, we had to show them our pay slips to prove we weren't keeping any back. The story of Annanias and Saphira was drilled into us. There was *no way* I was going to keep any money back. But, still I was having trouble making ends meet, having enough to pay my rent, buy my groceries and clothes. Financial counselors were assigned to those of us who had problems with our budgeting. Sounds innocent enough. And at first we worked together, but my counselor kept telling me that I had no head for money. He made jokes about it; I think that was a part of the strategy. And I'd be laughing right along with him. Eventually he just took my paycheck; he paid my rent, paid all my bills and bought my groceries and even my clothes. Eventually I didn't even have fifty cents in my pocket to buy a Coke if I wanted. But oddly, this didn't really bother me. I felt like this is how you get close to God. I remember my dad called once and just about blew his stack when I told him what was happening to my pay. I found out later that he tried to get a hold of Sterling, but none of his calls were returned. About a month later he flew down to Portland and visited me but got nowhere. I was totally unresponsive to his concerns."

"But when did you realize that the Disciples of Grace Church was not all it was cracked up to be?" asked Clayton.

"I don't think I ever did, to tell you the truth. Not completely. It was drilled into us over and over that we were 'disciples,' and just as Paul had his disciples and Apollos had his disciples, so we, too, were the disciples of Sterling Jonas and Sterling Jonas had a direct line to God. And it wasn't like some cult groups you read about where the people aren't allowed to leave the complex. We all lived in Portland and had regular jobs just like ordinary people. I kept saying to myself that if I was in a cult I couldn't come and go as I pleased. That's what I kept telling my dad. "Do I look like I'm a prisoner?" I asked him. And then he said to me, 'No, you're not a prisoner physically, but you are one emotionally. I can see that.' And then he went on to tell me that the shapeless cotton dresses I was exclusively wearing were things I wouldn't be caught dead in back in Calgary. But I argued that I'd learned that life was more than meat and drink and fancy clothes. The Bible even says that. He left then, but I know that he and my mother prayed for me continually after that."

She shook her head. "When I think of it now, none of it makes sense. He had us girls wearing practically rags, yet part of his philosophy is that we should all dress rich and be rich, that Jesus Christ, himself was a wealthy man with twelve servants. Unbelievable!"

And then she said, "Denise was in my class then. You know, his wife. I knew her. We weren't roommates, but we were in the same evening classes. She was so quiet that I felt sorry for her. When I got out and heard that Sterling and she had gotten married, I couldn't believe it! I'd like to talk to her...."

"What made you finally leave?" Roger asked.

"I met Jesse. He was also a Disciple, a new recruit. He was drawn to Sterling because of a physical problem, a congenital heart problem that Sterling supposedly 'healed.' But when his problem cropped up a few months later, I guess that soured him on Sterling." She shook her head. "We began to get together for coffee. He was working in construction just down the street from where I worked at the car dealership. By this time the Church had picked someone out for me to marry. I think his name was Kevin. I remember having no thoughts one way or another about marriage to this guy, and to tell you the truth now, I can't even remember what he looks like. I wasn't in love, so I had none of those emotions, and I didn't feel revulsion either. I think by this time my emotions were so seared that I couldn't feel anything. But Jesse continued to be my friend. I didn't know he had dropped out of Jonas' church because of his healing that wasn't a healing. He didn't tell me, of course. And I guess it was a combination of his friendship and my parents prayers that I gradually began to see things in a new light." She was tearing her apple bread into smaller pieces, not eating any of it. "Jesse showed me passages in the Bible that didn't jive with what Jonas was saying, or what we were learning in our classes. I tried to tell my roommates about this, and it was like I was suddenly ostracized. Sterling took me into his office and said, 'How could I question the wisdom of a Man of God?' It was sort of like, how could I, a mere mortal, question the high and mighty Sterling Jonas? He also told me that the reason that Jesse wasn't healed was because he didn't have enough faith. He also said that I should repent of my sins in front of the whole church." She paused, "You know, that's another thing I've never understood either. He says that grace covers all, that we are clothed in Christ's righteousness. That's his message every single Sunday morning, that it doesn't matter where you came from or what you do—grace covers everything. Sterling Jonas seems...seemed to have two separate messages, one for the outside world, that God heals and makes you rich and nothing you can do can take you out of His favor; and another message for those of us who are members of his congregation, especially his young recruits. It was that we are wicked and have to constantly repent, and that it's our lack of faith that's keeping us from being healed, from being rich, and from realizing that grace covers everything. In our classes it was constantly drummed into us that we didn't have enough faith. We had to drum up more and more and more.

"By this time my roommates were monitoring every phone call I made and were on constant lookout for me to do anything strange, like pack. One of them even walked me to work every morning. My boss was keeping an eye on me, too. I felt like I was under house arrest; they wouldn't even let me call my parents. Well, one lunch hour I walked out of the back of the car dealership and never returned. I didn't even take my coat, that would have caused them to become suspicious. I left with nothing. Jesse was waiting in a car and we drove to Canada. I was absolutely shaking the whole time. Absolutely shaking. About an hour out of Portland I begged him to drive me back to church. I really thought I was going to die, that

God would strike me dead. All the way to Canada I begged him to turn around and drive me back to Portland where I could get forgiveness from the church. But he didn't. He was a rock. He just kept his eyes focused on the road ahead and kept driving. He told me later he was praying the whole time.

"Through lots of counseling and prayer I've managed to come through."

"And Jesse?" asked Roger.

"Jesse continues to be a rock." Fiona was smiling now, a broad smile that lit up her face. "And you know, after all that we went through God healed him. At his last checkup everything was clear. Everything!"

CHAPTER 32

By the time Clayton and Roger left the Stone residence, a heavy wet snow was falling, the flakes coming down already knit together in great, wet clumps.

"Some weather we're having," mumbled Clayton as he unlocked the cruiser. It was only 3:30 p.m. Roger's Air Canada flight didn't leave until 5. He had no desire to sit around the airport for an hour, nor did the drive back to Chester and then back again to the airport make any sense.

"What do you say we get a coffee somewhere?" asked Roger.

Laird looked over at him. "Corporal, did anyone ever tell you you drink too much coffee?"

"All the time. Okay, a Coke then."

"How 'bout a burger and a Coke? You have lunch yet?"

Roger thought. "No," he said. "Just that apple cake."

"Yeah, good stuff," said Laird wheeling the cruiser up the side street. Up ahead on their right a snowplow was lumbering down the road, lights flashing.

"How 'bout Micky D's?" asked Laird.

"Fine with me," said Roger.

The McDonalds they stopped at was practically empty. The only other customers were a grizzled man who hugged his coffee with both hands, and two young mothers with a bevy of little kids who ate their french fries one at a time and whined.

Roger ordered a large Diet Coke, fries and a burger. Laird ordered two burger specials and a milk. "Whole," he told the girl behind the counter, "not that two percent stuff."

"So what do you make of that story?" asked Laird when they were seated.

Roger shook his head. The more he found out about Sterling Jonas the less he liked the man. People with a motive to kill him were becoming as plentiful as worms on a rainy sidewalk. He told Laird as much.

"Yeah," Laird grunted.

Roger arrived at the airport in plenty of time for the flight to Vancouver. He grabbed his duffel bag from the back seat of the cruiser and promised Laird he'd keep in touch.

On the Calgary to Vancouver flight he had an aisle seat, which he preferred. Next to him two elderly ladies spoke animatedly to each other. Roger introduced himself, and the two ladies told him they were on their way to Vancouver to do a little sightseeing. A flight attendant offered him a *Globe and Mail* which he took, and soon the ladies were happily chatting to each other nonstop. No sooner had the plane taken off than they extracted from their immense carry-ons glass jars containing sandwiches and carrot sticks. Glass jars! Roger put down his paper and looked at them. The little woman in the middle seat turned to him, "Can you imagine, two old biddies like us, never been on a plane before. Look Evelyn, we're in the air now! You can see the houses. Look how small they are!"

Roger smiled. Evelyn from the window seat leaned toward him, "I hope you don't mind we took the window. Half way through, Ethel and I are going to change seats."

The flight from Vancouver to Seattle was full as well, but Roger was again fortunate to get the aisle seat. The window was taken by a teenage boy, slack-bodied, baseball cap on backwards who slouched into the window and plugged into a Walkman. When Roger asked, he told him that he got a week off school to visit his dad in Seattle for American Thanksgiving.

Seated across the aisle was a businessman complete with suit and briefcase. He smiled politely when Roger introduced himself, but spent the remainder of the trip immersed in a glossy covered report about trends in the oil industry.

CHAPTER 33

There was no snow in Seattle, just a dense, drippy fog that pushed the city down onto its face, suffocating it. Roger rented a GM Corsica at the airport and drove to the Howard Johnsons'. It was a quarter after nine. Saturday night in the big city. Too late to drop in on Muriel Ames? Probably. Show up on her doorstep tomorrow morning when she's fresh, he thought. Was she the type to go to church? Somehow he doubted it.

He checked in, unloaded his duffel bag and called Kate. But it was still early and he felt restless. He shoved his hands in his pockets and headed outside for a walk. Hunger prevailed and two blocks later he stopped in at a dingy cafe and ate chowder and rolls at the counter. Someone had left yesterday's local paper dog-eared and in the wrong order on the counter. He picked it up and read it through while he ate. It wasn't until page eight that he came to the latest in the Sterling Jonas murder mystery. He skimmed it looking for new information. It looked as if the reporter was on the same trail that Roger was. The reporter had talked to "anonymous" sources in Montana who said that the Helene and Sterling's foster daughter had been named Marylouise. *Foster* daughter? This was a twist. Roger folded up the paper, put it under his arm and went back to the hotel. Despite all the coffee he'd had today, and the late hour of the supper, he fell asleep easily.

Muriel Ames lived in a large ranch style home which, although imposing, looked somehow bleak and uninviting in the morning rain. He parked the rental in the carport behind a forest green K-car. He ran through the rain to the front door. The squawking buzzer was answered by a skinny tall woman wearing an oversized faded red sweatshirt. Poking out from the bottom of the shirt were two sticks of legs encased in black leggings which bagged. On her feet were scuffy pink ballet slippers. The skin of her face looked like twenty-year-old newsprint which had been crumpled up and then flatted out. Her hair was red, fuzzy and matted. She squinted at him.

"Are you Mrs. Ames?"

"Yeah?" She didn't smile.

"I'm Corporal Roger Sheppard from...."

She interrupted him with an impatient wave of her hand. "What are you doing here?"

"I'd like to talk to you about Sterling."

"I said I ain't talking. I ain't. I can't."

A large droplet of water hit Roger square on the nose. He wiped it away and regarded her. There was more than anger in her voice. Fear? He decided to play his instincts. "Mrs. Ames, Sterling Jonas can't hurt you any more."

Her face snapped around. Startled, eyes wide she said, "What do you know about that?"

So his hunch had been right. "Let's play this carefully," he cautioned himself.

"Whatever Sterling was holding over your head, he can't do it anymore."

She opened her mouth as if to say something, then closed it again.

"Mrs. Ames, we want to help you."

"You can't. I don't know what I'm going to do now. I don't know if any arrangements were made."

"Arrangements?" Play this carefully, he said to himself.

"I can't talk. You don't understand."

"Mrs. Ames, can I come in for a minute?" It was exceedingly wet on the porch.

She looked around, opened the door wider and said, "I can't believe you came all this way."

Grateful to get out of the wet he followed her into a large

living room, beige carpets, decent furniture, a large gilt framed mirror over the couch. In one corner was an easy chair with an afghan across its back. Next to it was an end table with a half empty mug of coffee, a box of tissues and an ashtray, half-filled with ashes and butts. Across from the chair the television was on, the volume muted. Some talk show he didn't recognize.

She stood at the entrance to the kitchen looking flustered, eyes darting, her bony wrists rubbing against her sweatshirt.

"So what do you want?" she asked nervously.

"I want you to tell me about Sterling and Helene's daughter. About Marylouise."

"She didn't do it."

"Do you know where she is? Have you had contact with her?"

"No, never."

"What can you tell me about her?"

Looking a bit more relaxed she said, "She ran away 30 years ago. She never wrote to no one. Not once. Not even to her dear, sweet mother, may she rest in peace." She paused and looked around her. "Would you like some coffee? I'm just having some."

"Sure. Coffee's fine."

She motioned for him to sit at the kitchen table. Then she poured him a mug out of an old fashioned electric percolator. Kate and he had received one of those as a wedding gift way back when. He hadn't seen this kind of coffee maker in years and didn't know they even made them anymore. He spooned in powdered cream and sugar. The coffee was surprisingly good.

"Coffee's all I drink," she said pulling out a chair and sitting across from him. "Can't stomach water. Can't stomach juice...."

"Yeah," said Roger smiling. "People tell me I drink too much coffee, too."

She didn't smile. "No one tells me that."

There was a silence. Roger looked out the back patio door.

"You have a nice garden out there."

"I have a garden, yes. But I could care less about gardening, about plants."

So far he was batting zero.

"Mrs. Ames," he said as gently as he could, "can we talk about Helene?"

"I could write a book...."

"You knew Sterling back in Montana, right?"

She was frowning. There were permanent frown marks around her lips. From her pocket she took out a cigarette and placed it in her mouth. She felt in her pockets for matches, turned to Roger and said, "You got a light?"

"I don't, I'm sorry," he said.

The cigarette still dangling from her lower lip she got up and rummaged through several kitchen drawers. "You don't smoke?"

"No."

"Used to be in my day a gentleman always had a light for a lady. Manners gone out the window like everything else."

Roger didn't say anything, just waited. Finally she found a book of matches and returned to the table. Her cigarette finally lit she shook out the match and placed it in a large ceramic ash tray. "So," she said, "you want to know about Sterling good-for-nothing Jonas."

Roger pulled out his small notebook from his pocket. "You didn't like him?"

"Notes? No, no." She put her hand up. Her fingers were long and looked arthritically red. She said, "No taping, no notes. You can just walk out that door."

Remembering the number of telephone hang-ups Roger said, "Fine, no taping and no notes," and he closed his notebook and put it back into his pocket. He'd have to wing it. After the interview he'd head to the nearest coffee shop where he'd sit and try to reconstruct the entire interview. He'd done this kind of thing before. "Let's just talk," he said.

"Fine," she said. "So you want to know what kind of a scum bucket he was? Tell me something," she put down her cigarette and leaned toward him, beady eyes fixed on him. "Would you like someone who destroyed your family—who killed your sister, killed your mother and caused your sister's kid to run away?"

She rose and walked to the window, looking out through the uncurtained glass into the cheerless day. Her back was to him, her shoulders heaved slightly and her hands curled into fists at her sides.

She finally spoke, "He destroyed me, too. After Helene died my husband, he was my third husband, walked out on me. After 16 years he walks out on me, just like that. He says to me, 'Muriel, you have a problem with rage.' I said, 'No kidding, tell me something I don't know.' And then he says, 'As soon as you deal with that problem you call me.' But he died on me, dropped dead five years ago, so I move to this cheerless city."

"Why Seattle?"

She leaned back and laughed. "I picked it out of a hat. That's how I done it, put all the places I wanted to live in a hat. Seattle it was.

Wanting to get back on topic Roger asked, "What do you mean when you said Jonas killed your sister?"

"Okay, I'll tell you. I been thinking about this lately, ever since that scum bag died, that I should tell someone. I don't know what they'll do to me, probably make me move into some dump for old hags; but I kept this too long on the inside as it is."

Roger was confused but simply said, "Go on."

She paused for a few minutes and then began. "My sister Helene did not die of pneumonia. Complications of pneumonia." She laughed. "I know the death certificate says pneumonia. What she really died of was syphilis."

"Syphilis!"

"Don't sound so shocked. Syphilis. And that's God's honest truth."

"Syphilis is not a deadly disease...." protested Roger.

"It is if you're too embarrassed to go to the doctors; it is if you're too *mortified* to go to the doctors, which is what my sister Helene was. Sterling, the creep, the one she got it from, got over it just fine. A couple of doses of antibiotics later and he's out with the hookers again. Meanwhile Helene, the innocent victim, she's the one who dies."

Roger was incredulous. "Why didn't Helene get help?"

"She didn't want it. Was too scared. Never went to the doctors, nothing. By the time she came to me it was too late."

"But why?" Roger's mind reeled.

"Because Sterling—that creep—was telling his doctor, who by the way is a Disciple of Grace, lives right down there at the complex and is in his pocket big time, that he caught it from his wife who was fooling around. If you ever met Helene, you would know how stupid that statement was. So Sterling's doctor calls Helene with this information that she better get herself to a doctor and quick. She told me later he insinuated it was her lifestyle that was causing all these problems for Sterling and how that would reflect bad on his ministry. Well, you had to know Helene to know just how terrified this made her. All of this I find out later. She just gets sicker and sicker. When she finally comes to me, she's on death's door. She told me all of this before her mind went. She was blind at the end, too." Muriel was pacing as she talked in-between taking deep puffs of her cigarette. "I never seen nothing like it."

"When she died, I was all for telling the world how she died. But then Jonas' doctor got to me and somehow the death certificate read complications of pneumonia. And then Sterling calls and says that for the future of the Disciples of Grace it would be better if the world didn't know that Helene had had many affairs, and to keep quiet he'd set me up with a pension. Told me I could buy a house, anywhere I wanted long as it wasn't Portland. That's how come I chose Seattle, and he sent me two thousand dollars every single month. Now, with him dead, I don't know. At the time I thought to myself, I would never win here. No one would believe a bitter old woman."

"What about your husband? Did he know what was going

on?"

"He didn't care. He didn't know. He was off in his own little world half the time, lived at his office five days out of the week. He's what you'd call a classic workaholic. He left me money, too, but not enough to keep this house."

"All this is true?" he said quietly.

"Do you think I could make this up?"

Roger looked into the coffee. He knew instinctively that she was telling the truth. And he began to wonder how many more people Sterling had paid off. The more he waded into the dealings of the Disciples of Grace the murkier and fouler it got.

"Tell me about your mother. You said he killed your mother."

"Our mother was a saint," she said. "She's what you would call a perfect Christian mother. There were just the two of us, Helene and me. Our father died when I was little. I was the rebellious one, left home when I was 15, got married. But Helene was the gentle, pure one who married a man who walked all over her. I wasn't around a lot, but I do remember when Helene got married our mother was deadset against it. She said Sterling would not amount to much and there was a darkness, I think that's what she called it, a darkness in Sterling that she feared. Mother was the only one who saw him for what he was. Helene was dazzled by him—this personality-plus, good-looking-guy, going-to-be-a-minister—who wanted to marry her. But mother saw past that. When Sterling began having his affairs, the truth of Helene's situation destroyed mother."

"Were you close to your sister at this time?"

"Not really. I saw them at Christmas. But you gotta remember, I was like the black sheep of the family—never went to church. Still don't."

"Did you know Helene's child, Marylouise?"

"She ran away when she was a teenager. Girl after my own heart." She chuckled, but there was no mirth.

"Do you know where she went?"

"Nah, when I heard she left I said to myself, 'Way to go, girl!' But it broke Helene's heart. By this time she knew all about Sterling's affairs. But Helene and I weren't close. We never were close until she was dying. Then we talked. Sterling destroyed our entire family and I will dance on his grave!"

Roger studied her, then he said, "Sterling Jonas has been murdered. Apparently there were many people who felt like you do about Sterling...."

"If you're asking me if I killed him the answer is no. Why would I kill him? He was sending me two thou every month."

She didn't do it, Roger knew. But this daughter. Where was she? And the doctor? And Jud Soames? Any number of board members all with motives?

When he left Muriel Ame's blood-money home, he stopped at a Dunkin' Donuts, ordered a coffee, decaf this time, and a corn muffin, sat down and wrote word for word as much as he could remember about his interview with Muriel Ames. When he got back to his motel, there was an urgent message for him.

CHAPTER 34

David sat on the edge of his bed with the phone cradled in his lap. He had gone to church that morning, Chester Community Church, but during the music, during the message, during the prayer his mind was elsewhere. It was with Mary Louise. He looked at his watch. He knew his parents would be home from church now and he felt like calling them. Usually he called in the evening when the rates were cheaper. He always tried to make everything sound cheerful during those calls, like he was having such a ball sightseeing, having as wonderful time as a tourist in Alberta. Notes on postcards: "Scenery is here. Wish you were beautiful. Ha ha." So far, he hadn't told them about Mary Louise. He knew they were interested, but knew they were kind enough not to bring up the subject until he did. And he didn't. He didn't know why, but he just couldn't. He couldn't tell them that he'd seen his mother. But he was afraid to meet her. His search consultant had been right; until his birth mother called him, he would just have to sit it out.

Yesterday when he had driven by Mary Louise's house he had seen a police van parked there. He had parked in his spot across the street and watched for a few minutes. Police officers dressed in heavy blue overcoats carried little black tool boxes into her house. Mary Louise wasn't there, but he saw that her neighbor was directing traffic. He'd seen this woman before, she was hard to miss with her short hair, huge goggle glasses and long dresses over work boots. The officers went inside and shut the door. So much for that. David had gone back to his motel.

He picked up the phone and called home.

His mother answered.

"Mom, hi!"

"David! Where are you?"

"Still in Alberta."

"How are you, David?"

"I'm having a really nice time here. The weather's kind of bad, though. But I'm spending time in Calgary, seeing all the sights, doing some Christmas shopping....Have I gotten any calls or letters?"

"Just one, David."

"What? Who called?"

His father came on the extension. "I took the call, son. It was a woman who called, asking for you. She wouldn't leave her name."

"A woman? Who was it?"

"She wouldn't leave her name. She wanted to talk to you."

"What did she sound like?"

"She had a deep voice," said his father. "It was probably nothing, son. Could've been someone about your Israel trip."

"Yeah," said David rubbing a hand through his hair, "but the Israel people would have left their name. What did she say?"

"She wanted to speak to you, and when I told her you weren't home, she asked where you were."

"What did you tell her?"

"That you were on vacation."

"Did you say where?"

"I said Canada. She asked where in Canada and I said Calgary. I hope I have done the right thing, son. Maybe I shouldn't have told her where you were."

David sat down heavily into the bed. His mind reeled.

"I'm sure it was nothing, David. I'm sure it was those Israel people." It was his mother on the extension now. "We've been praying so much for you, your father and I. Are you sure you're all right?"

David hoped his voice didn't shake on the phone. His birth mother had called, he was sure of it, and yet he couldn't show too much excitement over the phone. He said, "If that person, that woman calls again, could you give her my motel phone number here in Chester?"

"Will do, son," said his dad.

"When are you coming home?" asked his mother.

"I don't know, it may be soon. I'm just going to get a few more Christmas presents. You know, the three of us should come up here some time, maybe for the Stampede." He was conscious that he was talking too fast, but his mind was racing. "I've toured the Stampede grounds and the museum. It's really neat. You would like it. Well, I'll let you know when I'm coming home. If she calls back..." He paused.

"We'll tell her your number," said his father.

He heard a knocking on his door. The motel manager? He didn't know anyone else here.

"Gotta, go Mom, Dad. There's someone at my door."

A few seconds later he opened the door to two uniformed members of the Royal Canadian Mounted Police.

CHAPTER 35

He got through right away to Laird. "Head down to Portland," Laird said.

"Portland?"

"Down to the Disciples of Grace headquarters."

"Really?" Roger was incredulous.

"Yeah, Denise Jonas called. She wants to talk to you."

"To me? That girl hardly said a word the last time I spoke with her."

"Yeah, well, she's talking now. Wants to talk to you. No one else will do, she said especially not that short guy who was with you."

"Mick."

"Yeah, Mick, I guess. I don't know what her problem is with him. I mean he can get a little bullish at times, but he's an okay investigator."

"So, you want me to go down there?"

"For the last time, yes. We thought since you're halfway there already, you could just drive the rest of the way. Get a good look at the inside of the Disciples of Grace. Wouldn't hurt."

"I'll check out, change my flight and head down right now. Does she know I'm coming?"

"Yeah, we told her. She said today was good. Jud is away, so are half the board of directors, something to do with putting the funeral on satellite. Oh, yeah, before I forget, we're bringing in a suspect on that puppet thing. A neighbor of Mary

Jones' called. She's spotted a blue Datsun, Washington plates, hanging around Mary's house. We're taking care of it here."

"Great, fill me in when I get back."

"Yeah, and you can fill me in about Muriel and Denise."

After getting Denise's number, they said good-bye. Before getting on the road to Portland, Roger made two phone calls. The first one was to Kate to tell her he'd be delayed a day.

The second call was to Denise. The afternoon was fine, she said. Her voice sounded tentative, unsure and Roger wondered how much effort it was costing her to meet with him. She told him she'd wait for him around the back of the complex and she told him how to get there.

By noon he was behind the wheel of his rental heading south on I-5. He had a rough idea of where the Disciples of Grace was located. The Portland police had said stay on I-5, it's the easiest thing in the world. Drive right through the city until you're practically out of town. It's on the right. Signs all over. You can't miss it.

Portland was experiencing similar weather to Seattle's. Drippy and dull. Fog bearing down like a weight. Welcome to winter in the Pacific Northwest.

He saw the spire from the large Grace Cathedral before he saw any signs. He took the closest exit. Up the exit ramp, turn right at the stop sign, down about a quarter of a mile and you should see the driveway.

Roger drove up the wide asphalt driveway. By this time the Sunday morning crowd had dispersed. The church, itself was an impressive, long, low-slung affair of concrete and glass rising at the front end into a massive spire complete with a large lighted cross. He'd love to get a look at the inside. He glanced at his watch. Half an hour until he was to meet with Denise. He decided to chance it. He pulled up next to a large Lincoln Continental and got out.

The foyer of the church was circular and rimmed the auditorium. It was spacious with a high ceiling and lushly carpeted in a pale rose color. In some ways it resembled the foyer of any upscale church with its coat racks, book tables and posters advertising Sunday School. The one difference was that in the large wall space over the main auditorium door, where you'd expect to find a portrait of Christ or a cross, there was a large oil-painting of Sterling Jonas. He was seated in the portrait, his hands resting on a Bible. For several seconds Roger stood there gazing up at the imposing figure.

"May I help you?"

Roger turned. Seated behind a counter marked "Information" was a woman. He hadn't noticed her before.

"So that's Dr. Jonas," he said.

"Yes, is, or was. You heard that he has passed away?"

You'd have to have just gotten back from Mars not to know that fact. He said, "Yeah, I heard something about that. Tell me, do you give tours of this place?"

"We do, or did in the summer."

"Boy, I'd love to see this place," he said looking around. She glanced down at a calendar on her table. "Well, I don't know, this being Sunday and all." She looked up. "Maybe. I guess I could. Probably just the sanctuary, though. No one's over at the office complex."

The sanctuary would have to do.

From a bottom desk drawer she pulled out a ring of keys. "Follow me," she said.

Roger followed her down to the end of the foyer where she introduced herself as Sonya Terrence and began talking in a memorized tour guide voice about architecture and the vision of Dr. Sterling Jonas.

Roger interrupted her, "How long have you been with Jonas?"

This seemed to make her stumble in her speech and she faltered. "Just six months."

"You enjoy it?"

"Oh, yes., Dr. Jonas is a wonderful, was a wonderful boss." She looked down. "I was so fortunate to get this job, I mean...." She seemed flustered, and then she turned and unlocked the sanctuary door. He followed her in.

It was dim, windowless and opulent, with the predominate color being roses and blues. Roger looked around. It was by far, the biggest auditorium he had ever been in, and that included the trips he and Kate had taken to see the Calgary Philharmonic Orchestra.

"Wow," was all he could say.

She was walking down to the front and Roger followed. It seemed to take forever. Down at the front she pointed out the platform, the choir loft, and the instruments which included a grand piano, pipe organ and a full set of drums. The sound system was completely hidden, the mikes were cordless and the podium was glass. The platform was surrounded by a brass rail.

"Could we go up there?" asked Roger pointing to the carpeted stairs which led to the platform.

She faltered. "I don't think so. That's one of Dr. Jonas' rules—only ministers of God are allowed past the altar rail."

"The holy of holies," thought Roger.

Back through the sanctuary and to the doors again, Sonya used a different key. He was then given the grand tour of the Sunday School classrooms, a couple of fireside lounges, music rooms and a smaller auditorium which would be the envy of many a small church. Sonya explained that this was often used for weddings and funerals.

Twenty-five minutes later they were back where they started.

"Thank you," said Roger.

He left. The tour hadn't given him any information on who his murderer was, but what it did do was to give him just a little more insight to the man, Sterling Jonas. And he didn't like what he saw.

He pulled out of the lot, and following Denise's instructions he drove around to the back. He passed the office buildings. Next to the complex was a humungous square foundation hole. Construction vehicles lay idle. A large white sign proclaimed that this was the future site of the Disciples of Grace College and Seminary. He exited out the back and found himself on a gravel service road which wound around behind the complex. In the distance a tall wrought iron fence was partially hidden by a hedge of trees and foliage. Running parallel to the gravel road was a paved road which led to a gate, the kind where punching the correct sequence of numbers allowed you access. Denise had said to stick to the gravel road. He did. Every so often through the trees he could glimpse the private residence of Dr. Sterling Jonas; massive, white, wide porches, with landscaping only a full-time gardener could care for. Finally, he reached an open gate at the back. Denise was standing there, diminutive figure in a navy raincoat that looked too large for her. Her head was down, her hands were stuffed in the pockets. He pulled up to her and rolled down the window. She said nothing, but pointed to a marked parking spot beside a back door which led into a large windowed porch or solarium. He parked and followed her in.

The back door led into the solarium. It was quite warm in the windowed room, although dim. Along one wall were a row of hooks. Since she made no move to offer to take his coat, he hung it on one of the empty hooks. She left hers on, despite the warmth.

She turned on a bank of lights and sat down on a straight back wooden chair, her coat still tied tightly around her. "Thank you for coming," she said. Today she wore no jewelry or make up. Her brown hair was pulled back into a pony tail.

Roger sat across from her on an overstuffed wicker couch gaily printed in green and white. The windows looked out on the vast Jonas grounds, dismal in the rain. With the lights on the solarium was surprisingly cheerful, filled with green healthy plants. They hung from the ceiling on hooks, sat in rows on wooden racks and sprawled all over the floor. Across from Roger was the largest Boston fern he had ever seen. Rooted in what Roger thought was an exceedingly small pot, it spread at least six feet in all directions.

"That's a beautiful plant," he said pointing.

He readied himself for a noncommittal answer, instead she brightened and said, "I know it is." Then she looked around.

"This is my room," she said.

She rose. "I have something to show you. It might help with the investigation." She walked over to a small oak secretary desk with the plants draping around its sides, Roger hadn't noticed this piece of furniture before. She unlocked a drawer with a small key and withdrew an envelope. She handed it to Roger. It bore the return address of the Four Seasons Hotel, which made Roger wonder initially if it was from an employee of the hotel where they had stayed. Across the front one word was scrawled one word: "Denisy."

She explained, "Sterling used to call me Denisy. He gave me this just before he went to Chester. I never showed this to my father. I never showed it to anyone."

Roger pulled out one sheet of hotel stationary and read:

Dearest Denisy,

It's difficult to write this, to admit that everything you have strived for, you have worked for is a total sham, but it is. It's taken me more than 60 years to realize that my whole life has been a sham. I have wronged so many people that I cannot begin to name them. And you, my dearest child love, I have perhaps wronged you the most. You are but a child, yet I decided that I had to have you, like David in the Bible. Even though your father protested, my wishes won out. So I married you. Since we have been married I have to say that I have come to love you, to appreciate you for who you are and not for what you can give to me.

Roger looked up at her from his reading. Her small face blushed, "It's okay," she said, "Please read it."

If I have seemed distant in the past few months it's because I have done some soul searching, which I haven't been able to share with anyone. I have begun reading the Bible. Does that surprise you? In the past I would come up with an idea, turn it into a theology, and then look around the Bible for a few verses which would prove what I said. I wrote many books based on one or two verses.

But three months ago I started reading the Bible straight through and I have learned so much, particularly from Paul's writings. I have come to see God in a clear way, as if 'something like scales have fallen from my eyes.' I have come to see that so much of what I taught and clung to was utterly false.

After this crusade I plan to resign from the ministry. And, Dear Denisy, I want to let you go, too. I weep as I write this because I don't want you to leave me. I am hoping, I am praying that you will stay with me. I need you, but if you wish to leave, I will not stop you. You are too young to be saddled with an old man like me.

We will talk about this when I get back from Chester. There is a person there that I must see—that I must make things right with before I can move on. When I get back we will talk. There are so many things I want to say.

I love you,
S.

Roger folded the letter and placed it back in the envelope. When he looked up, Denise was looking at him, her green eyes almost transparent. She looked small and childlike to him with her wide freckled nose. Her beseeching look. He handed the envelope back to her.

"Denise," he said. "I'm so sorry."

She looked away. "I thought maybe," she blinked away the tears. "I thought maybe knowing the last part about Chester would help you."

"When did he give this to you?"

"At breakfast, the morning before he went to Chester. I think he wrote it the night before."

"And no one else knows about this letter?"

"No."

"Not your father?"

She looked up. "Especially not my father. He hated Sterling."

Roger said, "Do you have any idea who he wanted to meet

in Chester?"

"No, I would tell you if I could. But," she looked down and smoothed her raincoat in her lap with motions of her hand, "it wasn't my father who killed him. I know you were thinking it was, but I know it wasn't."

"How do you know?"

"Because well, my father hates all of this publicity. That's what he objects to, and if he wanted to destroy Sterling, he could have used other ways. He was already using other ways."

"What other ways?"

"Blackmail? I'm not sure." Her hands were moving faster now up and down on the lap of her coat, as if she were trying to clean them on her lap. "There was something. I really don't know."

Muriel Ames, thought Roger. He said, "Did you know about Sterling's daughter? About Marylouise?"

Her eyes widened. "No, I heard something once, but Sterling told me she was his foster daughter. They only had her a few years. That's what I thought."

"It appears it was his real daughter."

"Where is she?"

"That's what we'd like to know." Then he said, "Do you have any personal papers of Sterling's that we could have a look at?"

She stood up. "Jud wanted me to get the stuff ready for him. But maybe I'll give it to you if that would help." She walked out of the room.

When she was gone, Roger watched the rain against the windows. The afternoon was getting darker; the rain and the darkness racing to see which would envelope the city the quicker. Roger felt an inexplicable sadness. The strange father-daughter relationship between Jud and Denise. Helene dying alone of syphilis, Muriel the renegade, Marylouise, the runaway daughter, and now Sterling's apparent deathbed reversal and moral confession, or was that, too, the act of a consummate con artist? The snake-oil man—sell your healing and forgiveness in one package deal. You never have to worry about sin anymore. Be well. Be healed. Be forgiven. In ten easy installments. Instant breakfast. Fast food. Buy now pay later. No one wants to grow in Christ the long way. Even Jesus spent a month in the wilderness growing, praying, meditating, but no one wants to do that now.

These thoughts were shambling through his head when Denise returned with a small square cardboard box.

"If you want these things you can have them," she said. "Take them away and take them home. I don't want them anymore."

"What will your father say?"

She shrugged. "I don't know. I'll tell him I lost them."

Roger took the box and looked inside. He saw what looked like a few bank statements, a pack of rubberbanded letters, a black leather daytimer with the name Dr. Sterling Jonas in gold script along the bottom. Roger also saw a Bible, a stack of church bulletins, and some paperclipped sheets which looked like minutes of meetings.

She took a deep breath and sighed, "I'm giving these things to you now because I know you'll probably just come for them at some time with a search warrant and I want to give them to you of my own free will."

It was the longest speech he'd heard her make and she wasn't finished. "I trust you. I know you're trying to find Sterling's killer, and I believe what Sterling wrote was true. I'd seen changes in him, too. Although we really didn't talk that much anyway...." Her voice faded away. "I'm packing now, too," she said more quietly. "I can't stay here anymore."

When he finally left he headed north again, sadness descended on him like the dark clouds building on the horizon, and a sky which drizzled rain and fog in the same breath.

CHAPTER 36

They had made a mistake. They had asked him a lot of questions, like his full name, where he was from, and what was his business in Alberta. At first David thought it had something to do with the border. Maybe he was supposed to fill out some forms or something there. But if that was the case, it would be the fault of the border crossing guy to make sure he had them, and he hadn't. So what was it? And then it struck him. His car! He could slap his forehead with the palm of his hand. He had a lot of good qualities, said his mother, but organization wasn't one of them. He'd paid his car registration at the end of October, and had forgotten to affix the little sticker to his car license plate. It was still in his glove compartment! Of all the stupid idiotic things to forget! Boy, he thought, they sure made a big deal about those kinds of things up here.

"If this is about my car," he said, "the registration's in the glove compartment...."

But they just looked at him and said, "Mr. Brackett, does the name Mary Jones mean anything to you?"

"The principal of Chester Elementary School?"

The young male perked up. "So you know her?"

"No, I don't."

"Then how did you know about her?"

"I mean I know who she is, but I've never met her. Is she in some kind of trouble?" A line out of some detective show.

"If you don't know her, would you mind telling us what you have been doing parked in front of her house for the past few days?"

David put his head in his hands. So, she'd spotted him. And reported him. And of all the answers he could say, none would be good. "It's personal," he said, which was not the right thing to say because he was now being urged to "accompany them to the detachment."

They said nothing on the short trip; he sat in the back of the police car, like some criminal, a divider separating him from the two officers in the front. He'd watched as they left the hotel and the hotel manager standing in his picture window looking at them leave.

At the detachment he was ushered through a back door to a small square room which looked like one of those interrogation rooms in movies. On the wall there was a poster informing him of his right to legal counsel. But no one had arrested him, or maybe they had and he didn't know it. Maybe in Canada they don't have to "read you your rights," like they do in the movies.

"Am I being arrested?" he asked the woman cop. She was cute, he noted. Dark, wavy hair, small, but she looked muscular. Probably jogs five miles a day and has a black belt in something, he thought.

She looked up at him. Her name tag read, Cons. R. St. Marie. She looked tired; there were circles under her eyes.

They said no, that they just wanted to ask him a few questions. They told him he could have a lawyer, and that they'd provide one for him. As soon as he was allowed back he'd get his car registration for them.

And then they asked him again about Mary Jones. He just groaned and put his head in his hands, realizing that he was not making a very good first impression. *It's called harassment, David and it's against the law.*

After a long pause, "I know it was stupid. I promise I won't do it anymore." A nice reply if you are ten years old and your mother has just caught you with your hand in the cookie jar—not a good answer to two police officers.

One of the officers placed a color photo of what looked

like a doll on the table in front of him. Next to the doll was a paring knife. "Recognize this?" said the officer whose name tag read: Cons. T. Erickson.

He looked at them blankly. "No." he said.

"Well, then how about this one?" And he plunked another color photo on the table. This one had a smirk smile, like a court jester, and with the fringed hat with bells. David studied them without speaking. They were puppets, he saw.

"No, I've never seen these puppets,"

"You know they're puppets."

"Well, anyone can tell they're puppets...."

"Some people called them dolls..."

"Well, they're puppets, you can see the hand places."

"And how do you know so much about puppets?" asked the young man again.

"I don't know a lot about puppets. I only know that these are puppets, anyone can see they are puppets."

"Anyone familiar with puppets, you mean."

David was getting exasperated. Just what were they accusing him of. He decided to take the direct approach. "Just what are you accusing me of?" he asked.

"Nothing yet, Mr. Brackett. We just wanted to see if you recognized these."

"Well, I don't. Other than to say they are puppets."

The young woman spoke now. "Mary Jones has been threatened," she said. "And these puppets were left at the scene."

"Someone's threatening her?" asked David incredulously. "Why?"

"We were hoping you could tell us about that," said the young officer.

"Is she in danger?" He began racking his brains. He had spent a lot of time under the tree across from her house. Yet he had never seen anyone enter or anyone else there.

"You never did tell us why you have been parked in front of her house."

"And asking questions about Mary Jones to people around

town," said the woman police officer.

He sighed. He could write a book on how not to find your birth mother.

"I won't park there again, and as for the puppets, they aren't mine. I think I'll just go home now."

"Mr. Brackett, you don't seem to understand," said the woman. "Mary Jones has been threatened. Someone has been in her house. Someone who left no prints, but who left this. First one was left on her front porch, and now one was left in her closet. You are the only person who has been lurking around her house."

"I haven't been lurking around her house."

"But your car was seen parked across the street from her house on more than one occasion," said T. Erickson.

"I would just sit there and read. It was a nice place to park my car." David was groping.

"Across from Mary Jones' house?"

"I guess, yes."

"And you seem to have a keen interest in Mary Jones despite the fact that you say you never met her," said R. St. Marie.

"I guess, yes, she's someone I'd like to meet."

"Why?"

He almost said "it's personal" again. "It's personal" would just be an open invitation for them to dig and dig. No, he'd have to come up with something else. But he couldn't lie. That much he knew. These people have all sorts of ways of figuring out if you're telling the truth or not. They even have machines for that sort of thing.

"Mr. Brackett, we're waiting for an answer."

He blurted out. "We, my family and I think she may be a long, lost relative."

"A long, lost relative," said T. Erickson dryly.

"Yes." That would do just fine. "A long lost relative."

"So," he continued, "why don't you just go up and knock on her door and ask her if she's this long, lost relative."

"It's just not that simple."

"Why not?"

"Well, if you knew our family history, it has more ins and outs than a soap opera. It's not that simple." David smiled.

T. Erickson sighed and shook his head. Then he said, "Okay, so Mary Jones is a long lost relative who probably stands to inherit a million dollars and you have come to spy her out to see if she's worthy."

"Not exactly in this case."

R. St. Marie turned to him, "Are you a private investigator, Mr. Brackett, because if you are you should have told us."

"No," the idea was appealing. "I'm just a member of the family."

For the next hour they grilled him, but he stuck to his story, wouldn't budge from the long lost relative bit, and flatly denied the fact that he knew anything about the puppets.

In the end they let him go.

CHAPTER 37

Supper had been one of Perry's vegetarian bean dishes, good certainly, but Mary Louise had hardly tasted hers. Johanna was home for the weekend and her young presence provided a needed diversion from conversation about puppets, threats and finger prints. Mary Louise had kept up a cheerful banter. Johanna had inherited her mother's eccentricity and her father's analytical mind. She wore her hair long, straight and had her mother's clothes sense, or lack thereof. This evening she wore an oversized nubby brown sweater over tattered bell-bottom jeans. It would seem that both mother and daughter shopped at the same 1970's inspired boutique. But Johanna also had inherited her father's mind, hence her choice of computer science rather than something in the arts, ala Perry. Over a pre-dinner glass of wine Mary Louise heard all about Johanna's first semester in Computer Science at the university.

"...And then he said, I couldn't believe it, but he said he'd *moved* the date of the assignment until next Thursday, and I just about rose up and kissed the man. I had forgotten all about it. I hadn't even *started* it...."

Johanna was a special child to Mary Louise, and while she sat and listened to her animated anecdotes from first semester she thought of the time when the precocious little nine-year-old Johanna had run across the backyard to her house, knocking very primly and saying in her serious way, "I made you something in school today," and then she handed Mary Louise a large heart-shaped valentine fringed with doily. "I made one for my mother also, but I told my teacher I needed two, one for my mother and one for my auntie. She said it was perfectly all right."

For one year, grade five, Mary Louise had been her teacher. Johanna was an exceptional child, smart and very serious, a perfectionist. When she moved on to grade six, Mary Louise missed her.

Three years ago at just about this time of year Mary Louise had taken Johanna into Calgary to go Christmas shopping. It was the second week in December and there should have been snow on the ground. Instead, the two of them wore only light jackets. It had been an extraordinarily long and warm fall. Good for the farmers, everyone said. Good for those who didn't like winter. Johanna had said, "I know this is good weather for the farmers, and every one is cheering about it, but, Aunt Mary Lou, I wish there was snow."

"There'll be snow soon enough," said Mary Louise. "And in three months time it'll be slushy all over the ground and we'll all be sick of it."

"I know, but it's Christmas. All the Christmas cards are pictured with snow."

And then Mary Louise had told her about people who lived in Australia where Christmas was in the summer. And how when she was there she spent Christmas with a family on the beach.

"You've been there?"

"I've been there."

"You've been all over."

"I know. I have no children to eat up all my money. Who better to spend it on than me."

"But you buy me things. Mother says your too generous."

"I know," and then Mary Louise had reached over and hugged the girl as they walked through the glittery mall. "You're the one eats up all my money."

"You should have been a mother, auntie. You would have been a good mother, buying things for your kids all the time."

When Perry cleared the supper dishes away and brought

out coffee and dessert, Johanna got up, kissed her mother and
her father and Mary Louise and said good-bye and that she
had to get back to Calgary this evening for a study group and
then to her apartment. As she was lacing up her high brown
boots she turned to Mary Louise, "When are you coming to
Calgary again?"

"I don't know. The next time I need to do major shopping
again, I guess."

"Next time, call me. We have to go on our annual Christmas shopping expedition, remember?"

"A yearly tradition. I won't forget, Johanna."

Johanna left then in a flurry of coats, plastic containers
full of leftover casserole and pillowcases full of clean laundry.

"She misses you," said Edwin when the three of them were
again seated around the kitchen table.

"I miss her, too. I really do. I miss her running through
the backyards to my house, playing with PJ. She's a great
kid."

Perry spoke now. "You've been a real role model for her,
you know. She told me she wants to be just like you. Doesn't
ever want to get married, wants a career, her own life."

"It's not all it's cracked up to be," said Mary Louise looking down into her coffee.

With the three friends sitting around the table in the quietness of a winter evening, Perry leaned toward her and said,
"Mary Lou, now you can tell us what's wrong."

Mary Louise looked up. This would be a perfect time to
tell them all about Sean and her father. Maybe they could help
her, advise her, bear the pain with her. Instead, she said,
"Wrong? Nothing's wrong?"

"Nonsense. Edwin, now you tell me, does Mary Lou look
perfectly okay to you?"

Edwin shrugged, "Well, I should think Mary has a good
reason for not being perfectly okay."

"The break-ins?" said Perry. "There's more to it than that.
I know Mary Lou. I've never seen her more distracted."

Mary Louise looked at the two of them, talking about her

as if she wasn't there.

"Wait a minute, you two. I have good reason to be...."

"No you don't," Perry said. She rose then to fetch the coffee pot. "Edwin, you've always been able to talk sense to her..."

Edwin looked helplessly at Mary Louise, a half smile on his face.

"Perry, Edwin, there is nothing wrong," she protested. "My house was broken into, I've had to get all new locks, miss a day of work, and get, among other things, finger printed. Other than that my life's peachy!"

"Perry," asked Edwin running a hand over the top of his almost bald head. "What are you getting at? Why doesn't Mary's explanation satisfy you?"

"Oh, Edwin," said Perry sitting down. "Mary Lou is always so...so in control...."

"Dear, if we'd been broken into, threatened by some bizarre person or persons, students, perhaps, who kept leaving puppets with knives, I daresay we would be out of control, too."

"Oh," said Perry with a wave of her hand, "You're probably right."

And Mary Louise breathed a sigh of relief.

CHAPTER 38

Because most of the detachment's efforts were going into the Jonas murder, Crime Stoppers wasn't used for the puppet caper, despite Roberta's protests "that someone out there knows something." Instead, on the six o'clock news, in a one-time segment only, Roberta was filmed holding up the puppets asking that if anyone recognized or knew anything about them, would they please contact the RCMP immediately. The news item came right after the update of the Jonas murder case so everyone naturally connected the two.

On his first morning back from Portland, Laird filled Roger in on the news item and Roger filled Laird in on the Disciples of Grace Church and his conversations with Muriel and Denise. Back in his office he received a call from an IRS official in Montana.

"I'm not sure you're the one I should be talking to.... Can you hear me?" said the female voice on the other end. The connection was poor. The lines cracked.

"Yes, I can hear you, talk loud," said Roger.

"Okay, eight months ago I received a strange call from Canada. The person said he was a private investigator hired by some bank in Portland, Oregon, representing the estate of Helene Jonas. Well, right off I thought that was strange, since I think she's been dead for a while, and I didn't know banks hired private investigators. Well, maybe they do, I just had no experience with that. The fellow wanted to know all about Sterling Jonas. What we had found out about the audit. Who stands to inherit his money should he die and did I know of any dependents who would stand to inherit. All sorts of things. At first I answered as best I could, but then I began to get suspicious."

"Why?" Roger twiddled his pen between his fingers.

"I don't know, it's kind of difficult to explain, this person just went on and on asking questions like some robot or something; it sounded like he was reading from a script or something."

"Male or female?"

"I know this sounds odd, but I couldn't tell if the person was a male or a female. I mean it could have been a female with a low voice, or a male with a high one."

"Did you get this person's name?"

"No, I kept asking for it, but he or she kept evading my questions by asking more questions of his or her own."

"You said the call came from Canada. How did you know that?"

"At the very beginning he said he was calling from Canada. I was sure that he did. But when I tried to press him or her at the end he tried to evade my questions. We have a call display phone that logs in the phone calls made to us. But it was blocked, which means it either came from a cellular, a phone booth or out of the country. That's why I'm sure it was from Canada. I filed it away thinking it was a crank until this whole thing came up. There was a thing on the TV here that said that if you had any information we were to contact the RCMP in Canada. They gave an 800 number. That's when I thought about that call. I hope this helps."

It was a long shot but Roger called the Chester Inn and asked to speak to Penny Perkins.

"You said it was a male voice that made the reservation for room 114. Could it have been a female?"

"No, definitely not. It was a man with a deep voice."

"There was no mistaking that?"

"None. I remember thinking what a deep voice the guy had."

"Thank you, Miss Perkins."

"Interesting," thought Roger when he hung up.

CHAPTER 39

"Right foot, left foot, raise your arms, right, left. That's it!"

Aerobics. It was something Mary Louise did on occasion. Whenever she felt like she was getting out of shape, out of control, she would sign up for another five weeks of after-work torture. This was session number one of five. There were 16 others in the class. Some she recognized—mothers of students, a teller from the bank she used, the lady down the street who worked in a florist shop—all hiphopping and sweating to the music, and following the antics of the instructor at the front with her neon pink exercise tights and shoes as white as photocopy paper.

"Right knee, bend it, that's it, that's it."

Although her body complained, she bent it. When she was upright, again she felt a surge of dizziness. But it was more than being out of shape. It was a feeling, that inexplicable feeling that she was always being followed, always being watched. She looked around her. Nothing but red faces grunting with the rhythm. It had to be her imagination. Either that or she was going crazy.

Because Mary Louise was jumping around in the aerobics class she missed the puppet announcement on the six o'clock news. The police had told her it would be on, that was enough for her. The less she thought about it, the better. If she could get it out of her mind, then Perry would quit asking her what was wrong, or stare at her with sad cow eyes.

The class was "cooling down" now, stretching comfortably on their floor mats. Finally. Mary Louise closed her eyes.

Later, after she had showered and changed, and was making her way through the parking lot to her car, she felt it again. She glanced over her shoulder. Nothing.

She had read somewhere that you should always have your car keys out and ready when you approached your car in a parking lot. No fumbling around in your purse. A key ring with a flashlight was even better. How about a key ring with a gun? She held her keys pointed out in front of her like a weapon. She thought of car-jackings, things that happen in cities, not in small towns. The community recreation center parking lot, although well-lit, was foreboding with numerous dark places to hide if you were so inclined.

As she approached her Honda she did see someone. She jumped. A little man in an army jacket leaning against a light post seemed engrossed in his newspaper. Once she was inside with all her doors locked and her engine purring, she expelled her breath in one long stream.

Forty-five minutes later she took a cup of hot Earl Gray tea into her living room and turned on the television. She flipped from channel to channel before settling on an old movie from the movie channel. That was one of her vices. She subscribed to cable—the full package—all the movies, everything; but seldom watched it. She was telling herself that she paid for the privilege of having it there for the few times when she wanted it. Now was one of those times. She curled up in her leather couch with PJ and covered them both with an afghan. She was asleep when a face peered in at her through the partially drawn curtains; she didn't see the scowl; didn't hear the scrape of the rubber boots as they tramped underneath her window. It wasn't until the following morning that Mary Louise discovered what he had left.

CHAPTER 40

Howard hadn't seen the Mounties with his puppets on the news; he had been out walking. So when Mrs. Philpott from upstairs came down and said she was going to call the Mounties the following morning and tell them about the puppets, he just stared at her.

"I knew these were devil toys and now it's confirmed. You killed that TV preacher with those puppets. I saw it on the news. I'm going to the Mounties and you can't stop me," she told him. Her long beak-like nose wobbled when she talked.

A roar, a sound like all of the voices at once, screaming and shouting filled his head. He covered his ears and rushed at her.

But she was gone, her gray skirt bustling up the steps to her apartment. He went back to his bed where he succumbed to a stomach cramp so violent that he doubled over, hardly able to breathe. When the spasm passed, and he had no way of knowing how much time had passed, he made his way up to her apartment and unlocked the door. He had a key. He "borrowed" hers once and had a duplicate made. One never knew when these things would come in handy.

It was dark when he stole into her room and placed a pillow over her sleeping face. It was surprisingly easy. It was only a matter of minutes before she finished squirming. Then he carefully put the pillow under her head, straightened out her flailing arms, pulled the blanket to her chin and left her grimacing in death.

****

It was Mrs. Swanson's habit to visit Mrs. Philpott at least once a week. At least once a week in the morning they would sit and drink tea and eat strawberry squares and gossip. If the life and times of Chester, Alberta, weren't exciting enough, they would talk about who was having an affair with whom on the soap operas. This morning Mrs. Swanson was carrying a Tupperware container of rhubarb squares.

She knocked. No answer. She called "Yoo hoo." Still no answer.

She tried Mrs. Philpott's door. Unlocked, which surprised Mrs. Swanson considering how careful Mrs. Philpott was about everything. "You can't be too careful," was what she always said.

Mrs. Swanson wandered through the living room calling, "Yoo hoo, yoo hoo." The living room was neat as a pin, thought Mrs. Swanson, and the kitchen, too, but then Mrs. Philpott's motto was "A place for everything and everything in its place."

She kept calling as she wandered from room to room. She pushed the door of the bedroom open, and stood there for several seconds, her voice dying on her lips, bile rising in her throat. For at once, she knew that Mrs. Philpott was not sleeping.

She raced into the front room and called Dr. Mack Blake.

****

Dr. Blake was Mrs. Philpott's doctor, a young man in his thirties who'd taken over the practice from Dr. Ernest Filger, who'd been Mrs. Philpott's doctor for 30 years. With the practice Dr. Blake had inherited a lot of elderly patients, Mrs. Philpott and Mrs. Swanson among them. A few minutes later he arrived at the house and examined the dead woman.

"She died in her sleep, did she doctor?" asked Mrs. Swanson.

Dr. Blake frowned. People don't die in their sleep unless

they're already sick. A stroke? A heart attack? Except Mrs. Philpott was healthy as a horse. That's what she always told him, "I'm healthy as a horse doctor, I don't know why I'm wasting your time."

And in truth she was healthy. So why would she die in her sleep? And something looked strange in the way she was lying there. He'd seen people who had died in their sleep. She did not look like that. Suspicious deaths were to be reported to the RCMP. In fact the way to guarantee an autopsy was to report the death as suspicious. He dialed the number for the RCMP.

CHAPTER 41

That morning when Mary Louise fetched the *Calgary Herald* from her front step as was her custom, she almost didn't see the small brown paper bag which during the night had blown against the hedge beside the porch. She knew what it was. "Don't even look at it," she told herself. "Leave it there and go in right now and phone the police." But she didn't. Some latent motherly instinct that she couldn't define demanded that she protect him. She took the paper bag in with her paper. The top of the bag was folded over and stapled. She undid the top and dumped the contents out on her kitchen counter. Another puppet. She sighed, almost resignedly. And then she saw what looked like a folded piece of paper clipped to the puppet. She opened it up. It was a sheet of lined notebook paper. Words and letters from magazines had been cut out and pasted to form a message: "God's judgment. Your mother is dead, your father is dead. You are next, Marylouise!"

She dropped it to the floor and sat down on the cold kitchen floor.

"My God, my God," were the only words she could utter. Over and over again, she said them. As a prayer she said them. She couldn't go to the police. Not now. There would be too many questions, all those years of keeping everything hidden. And then there was the little matter of changing her name illegally, which probably amounted to a charge of forgery and a prison sentence for her. "Oh, Sean, Sean," she called. But it was not Sean, it was David, the monster she had birthed. She imagined him growing up in an orphanage where abuse was commonplace, or shunted from foster home to foster home, all the time nurturing a hatred for the mother who had abandoned him. "But I didn't want to leave you, they made me. They made me! I wasn't even supposed to see you!" She pleaded to an empty room.

A few moments later she rose from the floor. She couldn't stay here. That much was for sure. She walked around her living room making sure that all the doors and windows were bolted, walking, walking. She made plans. First, there was PJ. She'd pack him up and take him to the animal hostel in Calgary. She often left him there when she traveled. He would be treated well. Maybe she should phone first. No, it was only 6:30 in the morning and probably if she just showed up, cat in hand they would surely take him. Wouldn't they? She'd make up some story about forgetting to phone. She was a good customer. Surely they wouldn't refuse her.

Second, she'd have to get a note over to Perry, without actually talking to her. In the note she'd include a set of keys for her new locks. Perry always had a set of keys to her house. She'd tell Perry she'd had an emergency and could Perry watch her house and water her plants. And she would add a line about thanking her for being a good friend. If she mailed it this morning Perry would probably get it tomorrow.

Then there was the little matter of work. If she called now she could leave a message on Ed's voice mail at work, that way she wouldn't have to talk to him in person. She made the call. "Ed, this is Mary Jones. I know this is extremely short notice, but I've had a personal emergency and will be gone for at least a week. Sorry, but it's something that can't be helped. My fifth graders have an essay due, just collect them and put them on my desk and I'll get to them when I get back."

Fear and coffee kept her going the next hour. She found PJ's carrying cage and folded a blanket inside. As expected, PJ was no where to be found. She'd pack for herself and then worry about him later.

She pulled out her suitcase and opened it rather tentatively.

Empty. She filled it with clothes, sweaters and jeans, underwear and sweat pants, throwing things in willy-nilly. By 7:30 she was ready. The animal hostel didn't open until 9 a.m. She tidied up her home, putting things away, walking, walking. And then she sat down. In the quietness and darkness she sat, unmoving until 8:30. The phone rang once. She ignored it. After four rings her answering machine picked it up. Ed. But she couldn't hear what he was saying.

The only voices she heard were the voices in her memory: Her grandmother saying, *"Mary Louise, you are such a special child, don't ever lose your love for the Lord;"* her father standing over her, *"You have plunged my entire ministry into contempt;"* her mother, *" I'm not well, Mary Louise, please try to have some patience;"* Aunt Muriel laughing at her, *"You don't want to be living here forever do you?"*

At 8:35 she put PJ in the carrier despite his protests and pulled out of the driveway. She dropped the letter for Perry in the mailbox at the post office and headed out on the highway. The urgency to get away was overwhelming. She drove west into Calgary, the sun rising behind her, chasing her, moving her forward.

She knew exactly where she would go. Four years ago Mary Louise and the teachers in the Chester school division had rented the grounds of the Rocky Mountain Retreat Centre for two days of "educational visioning." Nestled in the foothills of the Rocky Mountains, the center featured lots of rugged, well-kept cabins each with a fireplace and kitchenette. A cozy restaurant and gift shop featured the work of local crafts people and artists and also home cooked meals. The hotel proprietors were Carolyn and Van Randolph, a couple in their mid-sixties, pleasant, homey, out doorsy people; just the type to run a mountain bed and breakfast. The last time she was there she remembered snuggling down into the quilt in one of the cabins and feeling safe. She had told herself that if she ever needed a place to run away to, this would be it.

At 9:15 she dropped PJ off at the Animal Hostel. She kept her voice even as she told the woman there that she would be gone for a week and forgot to call for an appointment, but hoped that it would be no trouble. The woman who wore a t-shirt which read, "I love animals;" the word "love" being replaced with a heart, smiled and said that it was no problem, PJ was a wonderful kitty and everyone here loved him.

She made good time on the highway. She kept the radio off, listening instead to classical CDs. It had snowed, a skiff of snow they called it, but the road was well plowed and she reached the Rocky Mountain Retreat Centre an hour later.

There had been a lot of changes in four years, a paved driveway and parking lot, more cabins, an expanded restaurant. She parked and got out. The air was fresh and crisp. A woman, wearing a patterned ski sweater and looking to be in her mid-twenties was behind the counter.

"Can I help you?" she asked.

"I would like to rent a cabin for about a week. I know I don't have a reservation, I just came on a chance that you would have something."

"Well, you're in luck. The skiing season hasn't started, and it's not summer. In fact, we have plenty of cabins. You'll have your choice."

"Something out of the way, picturesque."

"Are you a writer?"

"No, why?"

"We get a lot of writers in the off season."

"No, I'm a school principal as a matter of fact, here on a mini-vacation. The last time I was here was for a staff retreat. When I was here a few years ago there was a couple by the name of Carolyn and Van Randolph who were the owners. Are they still here?"

"My grandparents, yes. They're here. Both of them are hunting guides. My grandpa is out now with a group from California. Grandma's around somewhere."

Mary Louise chose Mountainberry, the furthest cabin into the woods. It was only after she had closed and locked the cabin door behind her did she feel safe. She had told Ed a week. A week should be enough time to decide what to do.

Hire a private investigator? A body guard? After she had lunch in the restaurant, a gigantic buffalo burger, she rented cross country skis and skied by herself along the trails behind her cabin. It was the first time in a long time that she didn't have that feeling that someone was following her, watching her.

CHAPTER 42

On his way home, Roger drove down Main Street. He had spent the day at his desk. Besides the nuisance crimes such as the theft of holy water and the underage snowmobilers, there was another disturbing crime, that is if it turned out to be a crime at all. An elderly woman had been found dead in her bed that morning. The doctor seemed a little less than certain that she had died of natural causes. Her body was in Calgary right now awaiting an autopsy. Then, there was the puppet caper, plus the Jonas thing which they weren't really making a lot of headway on. Even though they had received hundreds of tips, they really had no idea who Jonas planned to meet in Chester.

He was late. Tonight was the night they were meeting Sara's famous Mark for the first time. Pulling into the driveway, Roger saw a small Ford, gray and rusty with a University of Calgary sticker on the center of the back window. So Mark and Sara were here. He walked through the garage and whistled as he came into the kitchen. The smell of Italian food was in the air, lasagna probably. Which also meant loaves of hot garlic bread and a green salad. Sara must have chosen the menu. Still whistling he walked through the kitchen and into the living room. Kate sat facing him from an easy chair. To his back were Sara and a girl with very long brown hair which was tied back in a pony tail. He wondered where Mark was and who was this new girl that Sara had brought, when the two of them turned around and Roger saw that the "girl" was a young man.

"Dad, this is Mark," said Sara.

The boy with the long hair said, "Hi, Mr. Sheppard. Sara's told me so much about you."

"Hello," said Roger. "So, ah...." he couldn't get his eyes off that hair. "So, Sara tells me you play in an orchestra?"

"Band."

Sara piped up. "Mark's in a Christian alternative rock band."

"Whoa, run that by me again."

Sara pronounced each word very slowly. "Christian alternative rock band."

"We call ourselves the Dog Ear," said Mark. Roger noticed he was also wearing an earring.

"Nice name."

"They're really good. They're gonna be in Calgary Fest next summer," said Sara brightly.

"So tell me, what's Calgary Fest?"

"Only the biggest Christian music festival in the province, and practically the whole west. Dad, you must've heard about it."

"Sorry," he said raising his hands.

From a chair in the dining room Becky chimed in, "If it was a Christian festival and there were no drugs or illegal stuff going on, chances are he didn't."

"Well, anyway they're on the Showcase Stage, not the Main Stage, but you have to audition to even get a place on the Showcase Stage! Which means next year they could be on the Main Stage.

"That's great," said Roger somewhat doubtfully. There was a pause in the conversation and Mark filled it.

"So you're a cop. Excellent."

"Yeah," said Roger.

Kate rose, went into the kitchen and a few minutes later called that dinner was ready. The family moved into the dining room. The lasagna that Kate placed on the table looked and smelled absolutely scrumptious. It was only then he realized how hungry he was. Had he even had lunch? He couldn't remember. Across from him sat Mark and Sara. Mark was wearing a black t-shirt which read "Hell is for Wimps." At least it was clean.

After the prayer, Mark said "Cool," and Roger asked him what "Alternative" meant in connection with music.

"We're an alternative music choice."

"Alternative to what?" asked Roger.

"Alternative to top 40."

Roger waved his hand in front of his face. "I'm lost here."

Sara turned to Mark. "My dad doesn't understand these terms, his idea of cool Christian music is Johnny Cash. Okay, Dad, here's the rundown. First there's mainstream, they're the top 40 and get played on Christian top 40 stations. Then there's alternative. It sounds a little different, not so smooth, not so...."

"Polished, machine-produced," offered Mark.

"Yeah, and alternative music is only played on certain stations, or on alternative shows on a top 40 station."

Roger said, "So, all in all they're not played as much as top 40."

"Right," said Sara, serving Mark a large wedge of lasagna.

"And if they're not played as much, then it stands to reason that the alternative musicians don't make as much money as top 40 musicians."

"Well...." said Sara looking up.

Roger continued, "And that the top 40 is more polished and the reason that they make more money is their sound is more polished."

"That's right," said Mark again.

"Well, knowing the top 40 is played way more often and the recording artists make more money, sign bigger contracts, wouldn't any alternative band *aspire* to be in the top 40?"

Mark shrugged and looked over at Sara. "Dad, you don't understand, alternative people like to be alternative," she protested. Behind her he could see Kate frowning in a "please-don't-say-anymore-Roger" gesture.

Roger did his best not to goad Mark any further. Instead, they talked of aspirations, goals, music and courses of study. During the supper Roger discovered Mark was pinning all of his hopes for a future in music on Dog Ear. At one point Roger asked the significance of name Dog Ear to discover it had none. But that's how the alternative music scene was, Mark explained. The fact that all Top 40 groups have significance to their names, and alternative groups do not.

"Oh," said Roger.

Kate was doing her best to keep things cheerful and Becky kept interjecting with comments like, "Cool earring, Mark."

Sara was as bright as ever, talking about music and Christian vs. secular and Christian rock concerts, and how Dog Ear once played in the basement of the SUB and a whole lot of people came, and it was cool. And this was at *lunch time*, she said. "And you should have seen them, everybody said they were awesome!"

Roger had to ask it, "So, tell me Mark, how do your parents feel about your musical aspirations?"

"My parents?" He shrugged. "They're cool with it."

Partway through the meal the phone rang. It was Roberta at the detachment office.

"Sorry to bother you at home, but Mary Jones' neighbor Perry called a little while ago. Mary's left town. She left a message with someone at the school that she was taking a week of personal leave, but Perry's not buying it. She was screaming that Mary's been kidnapped and we'd better do something about it."

"Maybe the lady really did just take off for a personal emergency."

"Perry's not convinced. She'll never be convinced, and Perry's the sort of person who will bug us until we do something."

"What did you tell her?"

"The usual, that we'd look into it, but Mary Jones was a grown woman and allowed to go away for a while if she wanted. But Corp?"

"Yeah?"

"What if she really was kidnapped?"

"Did anyone check if she took her car?"

"Her car's gone. Should we put out an APB for her car?"

Roger thought. "Let's wait," he said. "See if anything turns up tomorrow."

"Perry's gonna have our heads."

"Well, that's Perry's problem."

When he returned to the table the three of them were devouring a cheesecake confection Kate had whipped up; no doubt it was out of her new Low-Fat Cookbook. The conversation was still Christian music and the state of Christian radio in Canada. This was another of Mark's dreams—to set up a Christian rock station that played nothing but alternative. Twenty-four hours of Dog Ear.

While Sara eyed him dreamily, and Becky continued to ask him questions like, how long did it take you to grow your hair, and what kind of conditioner do you use, Kate just kept smiling, and Roger began to sincerely hope that Mark wouldn't become a member of this family. The father of his grandchildren. The carrier-on of Sheppard blood. He choked on his coffee.

CHAPTER 43

"What should I wear to work today?" Kate was standing in front of her closet considering.

"You work today?" Roger was stumbling bleary eyed into the bathroom.

"I'm not scheduled to," she called, "but I told you I'm having lunch with Derek from the agency. He's going to give me some pointers on getting my real estate license."

"That's good," he called in.

"I'm thinking about maybe waiting until we get to New Brunswick though. But I don't know if the requirements are the same. That's one of the things I want to know. He said he'd look into it for me."

Roger walked back into the bedroom, rubbing his head with his hand. "That's good."

"Are you even listening to me?"

Roger stopped and looked at her. "Of course I am, honey. I'm really proud of you. Really."

She smiled. "Thanks," then she looked back to her closet. "But now back to the main question—what to wear?"

"You look good in anything."

"Oh, thanks, Roger! And, don't forget. We have an appointment with Becky's teacher at four."

"I wrote it down, I won't forget."

"I better phone Adele to remind you anyway."

By the time they were downstairs for breakfast Sara had already left for university and Becky was sitting in her robe in front of the television. Another special report on the life and death of Sterling Jonas. She looked up when they came down. "So what did you think of Mark?"

"He seemed like a very nice boy," said Kate filling up the coffee pot and turning it on.

"So, what do you think?" She had turned to her father now.

"I'm sure he has some good qualities."

"What about Dog Ear?"

"Well, Becky, I really haven't heard his band yet, so I really can't judge it."

"Trust me, Dad," said Becky. "You're not going to like it." Then she paused and gazed into her cereal bowl. "I just never thought Sara would end up with a guy like that."

"Who said anything about ending up with him? She'll probably have a dozen more boyfriends before you get to be a bridesmaid."

"Not Sara," said Becky hopping off her stool and grabbing her back pack for school.

Later in his office Roger was pacing in front of his desk thinking, not about Jonas and the latest clues, but about his daughter and Dog Ear when Roberta stood in the door way with two cups of coffee in her hand.

"I brought you coffee, cream and double sugar."

"Thanks, you didn't have to."

She entered and put his coffee on his desk. "You're pacing. The Jonas murder really eating you, eh?"

Roger turned to her. "What would you do if your very sane and very smart teenage daughter was dating a guy with a pony tail, an earring and plays in a rock band?"

"Becky got a new boyfriend?"

"Sara."

"Sara! Smart, serious Sara. The one with all the scholarships?"

"The very one."

Roberta chuckled. "Well, I say good for Sara."

Roger grinned. "You're not helping here."

Then she said, "I've got a brother living up in the Peace

River country, Corp. He's got long hair in a pony tail, two kids, a wife and does family counseling."

"Maybe the long hair's not so bad, but why an earring?"

Roberta smiled and shook her head, "That's what we're all going to miss about you, you're so...so...."

"Straight?"

"You took the words out of my mouth!"

Then there was a pause. Roger said, "I know you didn't come in here to talk about my daughter's choice or lack of it concerning a boyfriend."

"No," she paused. "Perhaps I'm wasting your time."

"You're not wasting anybody's time, Roberta."

"I mean, I went in and talked with Sergeant Laird about Mary Jones disappearance. And all he said was that they couldn't do anything about it, she was a grown woman, blah, blah, blah."

"He's got a lot on his mind," said Roger.

"Yeah, the Jonas murder, who's gonna take your place, who's gonna take my place. But this puppet thing is a bit weird. I've just got this deep gut feeling that something is really wrong here, I don't know. Can't put my finger on it, but all sorts of things are happening now. It's like the full moon is out or something, and now we've got an old lady who might have been killed."

"I don't think that case has anything to do with the puppets or with Jonas."

"Maybe not, but don't you think there's an awful lot of strange things happening all at once."

He thought about it. There were a lot of strange occurrences in this small town; the puppets, the disappearance of Mary Jones, the possible murder of an elderly woman, the theft of holy water from St. Annes, snowmobiling down main street at night, not to mention the murder of Dr. Sterling Jonas. But if they were related, what was the common thread? He shook that off as too fanciful. He was tired and letting his imagination run wild. The autopsy report on the woman will probably reveal that she died in her sleep of natural causes, a stroke, perhaps. The puppet incident was kids, as was the theft of holy water. The Jonas murder was the only serious crime here.

Later that afternoon, the autopsy report was e-mailed to him from Calgary. Mrs. Florence Philpott had indeed been murdered. The constriction of her lungs showed acute suffocation, and finding a few pillow fibers in her nose and mouth clinched it. She'd been suffocated with a pillow. Good work, Dr. Blake.

So now they had another murder. Now, when they were stretched to the limit with the Jonas thing. Even though a number of constables had been brought in from other detachments to help the over worked Chester detachment, Roger, himself was operating on about five hours of sleep at night and fueling his days with coffee. He liked to keep in shape, but he had missed his early morning jog for about a week, and he couldn't remember the last time he had read his Bible. He had even missed church last Sunday because he was on the job in Seattle.

CHAPTER 44

It was really very simple finding out where David Brackett was staying. Those people at the other end of the phone number in Washington had said their son, they called him their son, was in Calgary. So from his phone booth he started with the A's in the motel and hotel listings. It only took him one phone call to realize that hotels don't give out the names of their guests. He had tried that with the Ace Hotel in Calgary.

"Do you have a David Brackett as a guest in your hotel?"

"I'm sorry, sir, we can't give out that information."

Angrily he had banged down the receiver. He stomped his feet in the phone booth. It was cold. If his stupid landlady hadn't been so cheap, he would have had a phone of his own in his own room! But now she was gone. Like Paula. Yesterday morning the doctor had come and then an ambulance and the Mounties had taken her body out, covered up in a white sheet out to an ambulance. He had watched all of this from his basement window. He always thought that was odd. An ambulance was supposed to be there for sick people—not dead people. Watching them take Mrs. Philpott away, with that idiotic Mrs. Swanson wailing along beside, made him think of another night when they had come for Paula. He had yelled at the ambulance people, but nobody listened to him. "You're not supposed to put her in that ambulance van!" As soon as she left is when the voices started.

On the ledge in the booth was someone's half drunk cardboard cup of coffee. He hadn't noticed it before. Looking at it

made him sick; why do people leave their food remains behind? He hated other people's garbage. The dregs of human
beings, castoff, muddy grimy slime they left behind as they
walked, like slugs along a cement wall. With a piece of Kleenex
from his pocket, gingerly he took the paper cup, opened the
door of the phone booth and flung it far into the asphalt of the
parking lot. A gas station attendant who was filling someone's
auto tank looked up in surprise.

He was smarter on call number two. He called Anderson's
Bed & Breakfast and asked to speak to David Brackett who
was a guest at their place.

The man said, "Just a minute." And then he returned with,
"I'm sorry, we have no one here by that name."

"Oh, maybe he hasn't checked in yet."

"Perhaps not, sir."

He hung up and laughed out loud again. He had a pocket
full of change, but then he had another idea. Maybe David
Brackett was really in Chester. After all, he had found the
letter in Mary Louise's house in Chester. It was too bad, but if
this David Brackett was any relation to Mary Louise, then he
had to be destroyed, too. God's judgment on the whole Jonas
clan, and he was God's avenging angel. No one from that
family shall live! Just like in the Bible where they had to kill
all the people of a certain tribe, women and children and all
their animals, livestock and maid-servants and man-servants.
He remembered Paula telling him about that once. She went
to a lot of Bible studies. He never did.

He remembered that Mary Louise had a cat which had to
be killed, too. The first time he had tried, the cat had screeched
and hissed and clawed at him. He still had the scratch marks
to prove it. No, he'd get the cat another time.

He punched in the numbers for the Chester Inn.

"I'm sorry," the lady said, "We have no one here by that
name."

"Oh, then I guess he hasn't checked in yet," said Howard.

He got lucky on his ninth call.

"I'll connect you to his room," a man said when he punched

in the numbers for the Whispering Pines Motel.
Howard hung up the phone, and then called for a cab.

CHAPTER 45

David was sick of the four walls of his hotel room. Plus, he was running out of money. It seemed like every other day he was taking more money out of the bank machine. He was leaving soon for Israel. He had a lot saved, plus his church at home had given him some financial support, but right now he wasn't working. For one entire year he would be relying on the gifts of others before he came back and finished Bible school and then got a job as a youth pastor or maybe a missionary. His dad had told him not to discount that. "Maybe God will use this Israel trip to lead you into some new avenue of service for Him." And here he was, wasting people's money on a wild goose chase.

Mid-afternoon and Chester was seeing the first sun in about a week; but instead of warming the town, all it did was to cast long buttery colored rays upon the ground, a mere taunt of what sun was supposed to do. David buttoned his coat to his chin, stuffed his hands in his pockets and left his room. He stopped at the office to ask where the path behind the motel ended up.

"Down to the ravine, it's about a two mile walk."

"Ravine. Is there a creek there or something?"

"Ravine, yeah, everyone around here just calls it the ravine. But there's a creek down there. It dries up in the summer sometimes and freezes in the winter. A good time to go down is on a Saturday or a Sunday morning. You can make a fortune in beer bottles; it's a favorite party place."

"Even at this time of year?"

"You'd be surprised. Oh, did you get that call? Someone called for you a little while ago."

"No," said David. "Was it...was it a woman's voice?"

The man winked at him. "Sorry, no, a guy. Probably he hung up, though."

He left. He was hungry, and his stomach was growling, but to save money he was only eating two meals a day. He only had about a month before he left for Israel. How he had wanted to meet his mother before he left! He was sure it was God who helped him find his birth mother so quickly. And then she hadn't written back. As time passed he became impatient. But he had to admit ever since he had gotten in his car and driven to Alberta to look for her, he had felt that God was a million miles away. But he was just not able to accept the fact that God wouldn't want him to find his mother. As he headed down the path, small tears wet his cheeks. He began to realize this one area he had kept to himself. He was hardly willing to let God have it, hardly willing to even pray about it in case God didn't want him to find his mother. So he had kept this to himself.

It was quiet in the ravine. He saw only one other person, a woman jogging up the hill, her breath expelling in small white puffs of air. David said hello when they passed and she nodded. There were a few leafless trees which skirted the gravel ravine road, in contrast to the straight flat fields, now white, up above. He could see the creek in the distance, it's edges beginning to be covered over with snow. The sky above was blue, a blue so viscous it seemed solid. He stood still for a moment and watched it. And it was as God himself suddenly spoke to him, "Don't you know me, David, even after I have been with you for such a long time?"—Jesus' words to Phillip in the Bible. Jesus, saying to him, "Have I been with you for so long and still you do not trust me, do you not know that I love you?"

David stopped. All was quiet. The jogger was far up the hill. He could barely hear her running shoes crunching rhythmically on the snow. He looked up into the blue sky, and for the first time realized he had run ahead of God. He as much had told God, "This is what I'm doing. Make my mother call me." And up here in Chester his prayers had been, "I demand You, God, to make my mother call me. It's only fair that You do, after all You took her away from me at birth. It's only fair You get her to call me now." That's what he'd been telling the Lord, and all along God had been calling, "David, David, don't you understand I love you and have your best interests in mind? You want to do great things in Israel for me and yet you cannot trust in this one thing?"

David sank to the ground. In the distance he could hear the gurgling of the creek as it clung to the last vestige of summer before the ice came. David, in his desperate search for his birth mother, had almost become like the ice, threatening to freeze away his Living Water. The crisp snow was cold on his knees as he knelt in the path way, but he hardly noticed. On the creek, the sun splashed, and David almost laughed out loud for the joy that welled up in him. It was as if the Lord Himself called from the creek, "Come, I am the Living Water of life, don't let your worries about your mother freeze out your love to Me. I love you. I love you more than you can know."

For a long time David knelt on the path laughing and crying, just him and his God, feeling the presence of God wash over him like a warm breeze on a cold November day. He didn't know how long he stayed there, he only knew when he rose, it was with the confidence that God was sovereign. God was in control. As he stood, reluctantly turning his back on the creek to ascend the path—for suddenly he realized how cold he really was—he made a decision. He would leave for home tomorrow. He ascended the path.

A little way up he saw walking straight toward him a short man in a khaki army jacket and black rubber boots. The man grimaced from time to time, and walked with a slight limp. When he was a few feet from the man, David stepped aside to let him pass. The man stopped, regarded David intently and said, "Are you David Brackett?"

David was taken aback. Before he could answer, the man bent double and clutched his stomach.

"Are you all right?" asked David moving toward him.

He straightened. "Of course I'm fine." To David's ears the sound almost came as a sharp rebuke.

"I said, are you David Brackett?"

"Who wants to know?" David was feeling uneasy. After his little sojourn into the police station, he hesitated on the question.

"I want to know, or I wouldn't have asked the question, stupid."

David was flustered. A part of him wanted to run. He suddenly thought of his birth mother and the threats that had been made against her. Yet another part of him wanted to reach out to this man who was so obviously in pain. When the man groaned and bent double again, David put his hands on his shoulders.

The man immediately straightened up and jerked his shoulder away. "No one ever touches me! Do you hear? No one ever touches me!" Then he looked deep into David's eyes and shuddered with horror. "You are him! I can see him in your eyes! You are part of him. I knew you were related. I knew it by the letter!"

The man was clearly delirious, thought David. "Let me drive you to the hospital or to a clinic."

"No one is to touch me, no doctors, no one. No one ever but Paula! No!"

"Okay," said David backing up, his hands up in mock surrender. "I won't touch you, I promise."

"Good, now I want to know. Are you David Brackett?"

"I'll answer that question for you if you promise to tell me why you want to know."

"Fair."

"Yes, I'm David Brackett. Now how do you know me?"

But the man backed away, a mocking laugh at his face. "I knew you were! I just knew you were! You are a little sniveling rat who deserves to die just like your whole family and all

your animals and cattle and maid-servants and man-servants.
No one shall live!"

David backed away, open-mouthed, as the man danced in
front of him pointing his finger and shouting.

David turned and ran then all the way up the hill, locked
himself in his car and drove the rest of the way into Chester,
right to the front door of the RCMP detachment.

****

Howard had to get the gun. Trouble was, it was over at the
church where he worked and it was a long walk from the ravine into town. And his keys were in his apartment. So, he'd
have to go there first anyway. He felt around in his pockets.
No money. Why hadn't he thought of that when he came out
here? He shrugged. There was no getting around it, he'd have
to walk all the way into town. It was cold and bright when he
reached the top of the ravine and started down the highway.
Too bright. He hated the sun. He shielded his eyes.

Another problem was his stomach was hurting more and
more. Sometimes it bent him double and he'd have to stop,
crouch down on the snowy pavement until the spasm passed
and then move on. He was sure it was because there were still
people on this earth who were related to Sterling Jonas. As
soon as they were destroyed, his stomach would stop hurting.
This he knew for a fact. He got up and began the five mile
walk back into town. He had to get the gun.

CHAPTER 46

Roger was out when David arrived and told Dennis that a crazy man had threatened him in the ravine. Roger was over at the fourplex where Mrs. Philpott had been murdered, interviewing the three other tenants. Clayton and Duane were up to their eyeballs with Jonas murder tips; Roberta was following up a puppet lead she had made at the Actor's Guild in Calgary and Tim was out talking to Father Graeme at St. Annes about yet another theft of holy water. So when the report had come that Mrs. Philpott was murdered, Roger was the only one available. The tenant right below Mrs. Philpott, a Howard Becker, was out when he arrived, so he talked with the other three. The other basement apartment was rented to Neil James, a 25 year old farm hand who commuted to Frobisher's Dairy Farm every day. He was usually out the door by five a.m. and not home until nine at night or later. A quick call to his boss confirmed that the evening Mrs. Philpott was murdered, Neil had been working, so he never heard anything or saw anything. In the apartment directly above Neil James was a newly married couple, Lori and Ben Sweeney. Lori Sweeney was a short, round blonde woman in her early twenties who answered his questions with wide eyed wonderment and a lot of "oooooohs" and "nooooos." She said over and over again that she hadn't heard a thing! She and Ben had rented a video— they hadn't heard a thing. Honest! If they'd known something like this was going on, well, they would have called the cops right away. They really would have. She kept shaking her head and saying things like, I can't believe something like this happened here! Right here in this building! Wait till I tell Ben!

By the time Roger had left the Sweeney apartment, the man in apartment #1 was returning.

He introduced himself when Roger inquired, as Howard Becker. He'd just been out walking, he said, and that accounted for his breathlessness. No, he hadn't even heard that anything had happened to Mrs. Philpott. She was the landlady, owned the building, and no, he never had any trouble with her. She was a fine woman. A fine woman. He paused and grimaced, bent over holding his stomach.

Roger moved toward him and said, "Are you all right?"

In obvious pain, he stood and said he was okay and it was just a touch of indigestion. Then he told Roger that he worked as a janitor at St. Annes and Roger duly noted it in his notebook.

"St. Annes," said Roger. "The church with the recent thefts."

"Ah yes," said Howard, "there are some insane people in the world. I and Father Graeme are keeping our eyes open."

On the way back to the detachment, the first sun he'd seen in many days reflecting on his windshield, Roger wondered what was familiar about the name Becker.

Back at the detachment the waiting room was full. There were a couple of CNN reporters he recognized, still kicking around the Jonas murder and wondering why there hadn't been a press conference lately. He waved them off saying that as soon as they had new information there would be one. In the middle of the melee with her head leaning against the wall was Mary Jones' neighbor Perry, a folded letter in her lap. A young man was talking animatedly to one of the constables on loan from Calgary. Roger heard snatches of the conversation as he walked toward his office. "Wild man!...cattle would die...and woman folk...Polly, he said the name Polly, or Paula."

As Roger passed her desk, Adele whispered that Mary's friend Perry had demanded to see him and that no one else would do. "Oh, it's so nice to be so popular. Changes will be made when I move east, I tell you," Roger thought.

There was also a brief message for him, hand written by Adele and placed on his desk. The Police Chief from Boston, Massachusetts, had called with the message that Philip Tatterly, retired teacher was out on his sailboat, had been all summer, and now he was sailing somewhere off the coast of Bermuda. If it was important, the note read, they would check with the coast guard and get back to him. They would wait for Roger's directive.

No, thought Roger, crushing the note in his hand. It was a long shot anyway. There was a weariness about him, a pain around his eyes, the beginnings of a headache, but it wasn't a physical problem, not a physical pain, but a deep mental one born of many days of exhaustion. He looked at his watch, 2:48 p.m. Just a little over an hour before he'd have to leave to make it to Becky's school on time.

He called St. Annes and asked Father Graeme about Howard Becker.

"Howard Becker? Yes, he works here, a quiet little fellow." Father Graeme's voice was gentle and friendly.

"How long has Howard worked for you?"

"About five years, just after his wife died. He had some sort of a breakdown after she died, and then shortly after that he came to us here. But Howard is like a fixture here. He is a very private person, a loner, you might call him. We knew he had problems and we tried to create a home for him here."

"Does he have friends in the congregation?'

"I'm afraid not. Poor Howard. I hope he's not in any trouble..."

"So, he was a loner."

"Very much so. Often when he was working I would go down and chat with him. But he seldom talked. Still I tried, and several in the parish had him in for meals, but I'm afraid Howard really preferred to be by himself."

Roger thanked him and hung up.

There was a timid knock on his open office door. He looked

up. Roberta.

"You look exhausted," she said.

He smiled wanly.

"You shouldn't be taking all this on yourself, you know. You could've waited until one of us got back. We could've gone over to the Philpott apartment. There are dozens of constables from Calgary here. They could've gone, too."

"They're here to work on the Jonas case. I can't ask them to do anything else."

"Yeah, well you're going to kill yourself. Kate even says so."

"Kate?"

"We talked this morning. She wanted to know if I'd go to that Bible study with her. I told her yes. I'm really looking forward to it."

"Great!" he said.

"Soooo, do you want to hear what's been going on in your absence?"

"You mean we have more going on in Chester than two murders? Lovely little Chester where nothing ever happens?"

Roger rubbed his head. Too long on the job, he thought. He said, "The only thing I need is about a month of sleep. Sure, fill me in."

"That guy you saw on your way in? He kept going on about meeting a wild man down by the ravine. Funny thing is, he was the guy we brought in for questioning on the Mary Jones thing."

"Yeah? The one with the long-lost relative story."

"The one."

"Interesting. I'll look over the report."

"Laird's got a few constables from Calgary working on this, who, by the way, are fit to be tied because they don't think this is a major crime."

"But you think it could become a major crime."

"I do, yes."

"So, now we have one criminal almost caught. We still have two murderers out there and no suspect."

"I know. People are starting to become nervous. Everyone's locking their doors and talking about safety and the crime rate. The mayor's even talking about curfews, like this is Chicago or something. We're getting about a zillion calls."

Roger rubbed his eyes. The Jonas murder? They had potentially hundreds, thousands of suspects if you counted everyone, who according to Dr. Mosaic, was supposed to get healed and then didn't. The Philpott murder? He couldn't come up with one suspect.

While he was talking to Roberta, Perry marched in, a small envelope in her hand which she held high.

CHAPTER 47

"My son is a juvenile delinquent." Mary Louise uttered these words quite out of the blue. Carolyn Randolph and she had spent the early afternoon cross country skiing on one of the trails behind the Rocky Mountain retreat.

Earlier Van Randolph had scouted and pronounced the trail skiable. "A little early in the year," he had said to the two of them who sat eating breakfast in the coffee shop, "but it looks good. I wouldn't go off the main trail yet though," he added.

The morning had been crisp and bright. Snow glinted along the snowdrifts like it was varnished with diamonds. It had been a while since Mary Louise was on cross country skis, and she slid back a few times until she got the hang of it, but soon the two women were forging through a foot of snow, blazing the trail.

"This is better than aerobics," said Mary Louise at one point.

Five miles up the trail was a small log cabin. The two women leaned their long skis against an outside wall and Mary Louise followed Carolyn inside. It was one room wooden structure, log walls and a wood floor approximately ten feet by ten feet. Shelves lined the walls which held a variety of jars and books. A heavy cast iron wood stove stood like a rampart right in the center of the room. Above it were numerous hooks for warming mitts, jackets, hats and anything else that needed drying. Against one wall was a log table and a couple of stumps that served as chairs. Despite its ruggedness, the cabin looked new and well kept. The logs hadn't matured to a deep brown, but were pale, clean and practically dustless. Forgetting David for a moment, Mary Louise commented and Carolyn explained that Van along with their son had constructed the cabin only last summer. "The skiers always complained about not having a place to warm up half way home. So we built this. As far as I know, you and I are the first people to use this as a ski stop off."

Carolyn pulled off her striped woolen hat and shook out her hair. It was thick and gray and short. Although no one would mistake her for a younger woman, there was a glint about her eyes which spoke of physical and emotional health.

Carolyn shrugged off her down jacket. "It's so hard raising children now a days," she said.

"That's why I'm here. I'm trying to decide what to do."

"How old is your son?"

"Twenty-two."

"Ah, so you've been through the teenage years with him, and he still hasn't grown up?"

"I guess not," was all Mary Louise said.

"Where is he now?" Carolyn grabbed sticks of kindling and was laying them expertly in the wood stove on top of some crumpled newspaper. She rose and groped along one of the shelves. "Ah, here's where they are. I knew they were here," she said pulling down a canning jar full of matches.

Mary Louise responded thoughtfully while Carolyn bent low to start the fire. It lit immediately filling the room with a sudden crackling warmth. Mary Louise spread out her fingers in front of the fire.

"He's in Chester, at least for the time being. At least I think he's there."

Carolyn stood up and faced her. "I'm sure, Mary, that you did the best you could with him. So many kids just make up their own minds to go off in their own directions and there's really nothing the parents can do."

Mary Louise turned away from Carolyn and gazed out the window. Carolyn bent down and worked on the fire, poking here, prodding there and adding split cordwood from the bin beside the stove.

There was an easiness around Carolyn that Mary Louise appreciated. Gaps needn't always be filled with any old sort of conversation.

The fire satisfactorily lit, Carolyn groped in her pack for the thermos of tea and package of sandwiches that her granddaughter had put together out of last evening's roast turkey.

She set the sandwiches on the table along with the thermos, then she said, "Would you like to talk about it? I've been told I'm a good listener."

"Perhaps," said Mary Louise doubtfully. But then she was quiet. How could she share this hidden story with a stranger when her very best friend, her "sister" didn't know any of it? She kept quiet, listened to the crackling of the stove sounding like hundreds of dry sticks being broken underfoot. Carolyn opened up the sandwich wrappings, and then she said something that made Mary Louise jerk her head up suddenly.

"Before we eat," she said, "I would like to thank the Lord for our food and for this beautiful day."

Mary Louise sat as still as granite while Carolyn intoned about God and his goodness and the beautiful day, and the snow and the trail and most of all for this new friend.

When she was finished Mary Louise said, "You're a Christian."

"Yes, I am. Been a Christian for a long time. Never regretted it."

"My grandmother was a Christian," said Mary Louise. "She's the only Christian I ever knew."

"Tell me about your grandmother," said Carolyn pouring the hot tea into the two mugs she had brought along.

Mary Louise leaned back and laughed. The thought of her grandmother brought both tears and laughter. "Let's see, where do I begin? She's gone now, long ago. Died when I was a little girl. Oh, but she used to read to me from the Bible. That I remember. She made me memorize long paragraphs from the Bible. Gave me these tiny apple turnovers that she baked when I'd get them right."

Carolyn chuckled. "I've got grandkids of my own. There's a special relationship there you don't even have with your own children...."

Mary Louise turned away. "My mother might have been a Christian. I don't know. She never told me."

"And you're father?"

"My father was definitely not a Christian. Definitely not." She paused and added, "My father was a minister."

And then Mary Louise began pouring her story. She began at the beginning with her midnight flight to Canada, her father's murder, the puppets and her suspicions about David.

It took a good half hour to tell, but Carolyn never moved. The fire had died, but Carolyn made no move to stoke it. When Mary Louise finished, Carolyn reached across the table and took her hand. "Do you mind if I pray?"

"I don't know. Go ahead, if you think it will help."

Mary Louise bowed her head and in her mind she could hear the long, sonorous, thunderous prayers of her father. Instead, Carolyn's prayer was simple. "Surround our sister with your love. Hold tight to her and be her comfort."

"Carolyn," said Mary Louise when they had cleaned up the lunch things, made sure the remnants of the fire were cold, and re-stacked the inside wood box with split birch, "I have never told this story to anyone. I would appreciate it if...."

"You have my confidence." Then she paused and looked at Mary Louise. "I do think you should tell this to the police."

But Mary Louise shook her head. When they had strapped on their skis she said. "Maybe someday I will, but not now." What do you do when you suspect your own son of murdering his grandfather and threatening to kill his mother?

CHAPTER 48

"But Mary would never leave of her own accord," protested Perry. "As I've already told you, I received this in the mail. And I know Mary. She never would have done that. She would have come over and talked to me. I have her key, and fiddlesticks, I'm afraid to go into her house."

"But isn't her car gone?" protested Roger. "That indicates to me that she left of her own accord."

Still, Perry would not be placated.

In the end, Roger agreed and at 3:15 in the afternoon with Perry at his side, he inserted the new key into the lock of Mary Jones' house.

The house was empty, cleaned and looked as if Mary Jones had indeed packed for a few days away. Her large gray suitcase was gone.

"But why would she leave?" asked Perry slumping down on her bed. "Why?"

"Maybe it's like the note said, 'family emergency.'"

"But she doesn't have a family. She was an only child and her parents are dead. I was her only family. Myself and Edwin and Johanna. We were her family. Her parents died when she was young." She was speaking quietly now, more to herself than to Roger. He kept up his cursory search through the rooms, looking for something, anything that would satisfy Perry that her friend had gone away by herself.

"I checked with the animal hostel in Calgary," she was continuing. "They have PJ. And they got the same story—a family emergency. But they told me she seemed distracted, too. I knew she was acting strange. I told Edwin but he didn't see it. Neither did Johanna, although how can you expect an 18 year old to think of anyone besides themselves..."

That got a smile out of Roger.

"But I knew there was something strange about her. I've known her for 20 years—almost 20 years. You get to know a person in that time. She was there when Johanna was born, practically raised her along with Edwin and me. And in all that time," she looked up at Roger, "in all that time she never mentioned a family. No aunts. No brothers, sisters, uncles. No one. Family emergency?"

While Perry stood beside the bed talking quietly, Roger went into the bathroom and looked around. Everything looked in order, looked as if someone had packed for a week, tooth-brush gone, toothpaste gone. But when he heard Perry cry, "Oh, Mary Lou, I knew you were in trouble," he hurried back into the room.

A stricken Perry stood shaking, she thrust the note into his face.

He read the message: "God's judgment. Your mother is dead, your father is dead. You are next, Marylouise!"

He stared at the note for several seconds before the impli-cations of it reached his thinking. The first thing he said was, "Her name is Marylouise?"

"That was her real name. She went by Mary, I called her Mary Lou sometimes."

"How long have you known her?" Roger had a rush of questions.

"I told you, ever since she moved here, almost 20 years."

"Where did she come from?"

"Calgary. She was a student there. In education. She taught up north for a couple of years before coming here. Then she got her Masters. Look, why all the questions?"

"Perry," said Roger. "I need you to listen to me. This may be very important. And she could be in danger."

"Yeah, well I can tell that by the note...."

He interrupted her. "Did she ever mention to you who her parents were?"

"No," said Perry looking at him sideways. Just that they died when she was 17."

"She never mentioned that her father was Sterling Jonas, the evangelist?" Even as he said it he was unsure of what he was insinuating. Could this really be Marylouise, daughter of Helene and Sterling, the one who ran away? It could be. She was the right age. Could she have been the one Jonas went in to Chester to see? Did she murder her own father? But the note, and the puppet threats, they were all connected, somehow. And Roger didn't think she would make up these threats to throw the police off the track. That would make no sense at all.

Perry stared at him open mouthed. "What on God's green earth are you talking about?"

And then he told her, told her about the trip he had taken to Seattle, told her about the runaway daughter, about the daughter's mother dying of syphilis, of the daughter's Aunt Muriel being paid to keep quiet, of Denise. In the end Perry ran her hand through her short hair and said, "I find this so hard to believe. So unbelievable."

"Obviously it was a secret she wanted kept."

"Are you sure about this? Absolutely sure?"

"No, I'm not sure, not sure at all. But too much fits."

"Somehow I believe it. She has been acting strangely lately, quiet; I knew something was wrong. I kept insisting, but Edwin didn't see it. Mary Lou is a very intelligent, self-sufficient woman. But lately she has kept more to herself. She kept telling me she wasn't feeling well, but somehow I knew something was wrong."

"When did this strange behavior start?"

Perry sat down on the edge of the bed and thought. "You know—ever since Sterling Jonas was murdered. In fact, that very day. That's when it started." She looked at Roger wide-eyed. "I'm so scared for her," she said suddenly. "If what you are saying is true, then she has carried around this awful burden for so long."

"And she could be in danger now," said Roger suddenly.

"Does this have anything to do with the puppet threats?"

"I'm willing to bet it does."

"It's just too much of a coincidence to have all happened at the same time," said Perry.

"That's what I'm thinking, too."

"Did you check out the guy in the Blue Datsun who was hanging around her house?"

"The person from Washington on the search for the long-lost relative? How did he fit in? We did, he wasn't the puppeteer. We're sure of that, but I think we'll talk to him again."

Back in the living room Roger dialed the detachment and got immediately through to Laird. When he had relayed the story he said, "Perry's on her way down, too. I've got to get over to my daughter's school or Kate will have my head, but I'll be right over afterwards—half hour at tops. Get all that puppet info too—prints, make of the puppets. This isn't just a 'student prank' anymore. I think we're looking at the murderer of Sterling Jonas. I've a feeling this whole thing can be wound up fairly quickly."

CHAPTER 49

"I know both of you are busy and I wouldn't have called you in if I didn't think this was important." The teacher who sat across from Kate and him was in her early forties—glasses, short, straight blonde hair flecked with gray, a pale suit.

Get on with it, thought Roger, whose mind was definitely elsewhere. It was with Mary Louise Jones, or Jonas, and of a young woman who had run away and then made a new life for herself, only to have that life come back to haunt her. If, indeed, his thinking was correct. He thought about the pleasant, efficient principal who had set up the press conference for him in the gym. But then again maybe he had it all wrong. Maybe she had written the note to Jonas, to which Jonas responded? Could this intelligent, self-sufficient woman, as her friend described her, be a murderer? But then who was the puppet man? Kate was looking at Becky's grade card and nodding, listening intently. They were sitting on wooden and metal school desks in Arlene Nash's math room. The walls were decorated with posters of math equations, student essays and had that unmistakable smell of school hallways and learning.

"Do you think we should get a math tutor for Becky?" Kate was saying and Roger was taken back to reality and thought, "With my salary, a tutor? Get real."

"No, I don't really think that's necessary. She's has missed a number of assignments, but it's not because she doesn't understand the concepts. She seems rather distracted lately."

Roger said, "Is she in danger of failing?"

"She will be if she doesn't get the assignments in."

Kate frowned. "We've been told all her school years she doesn't work up to her potential. I don't know how you make a kid work to their potential."

Arlene Nash smiled. "You know, honestly, there really isn't anything you can do about that. You can give incentives, like no phone until you get your assignments done, no TV, that kind of thing, but for a kid to work to potential, it has to come from somewhere inside that kid. I hate to say it, but it just isn't there with Becky, at least not right now." She paused then went on. "I'm also concerned with the friends she seems to be keeping."

Kate said, "We've known Jody's family for years."

Mrs. Nash smiled. "That's part of the problem. The two of them seem to be trying their wings, so to speak and hanging around with the wrong crowd."

Roger said again, "Well, you can count on the fact that Becky will get those assignments in. I'll personally see that she does. And you can be assured we'll be having a talk with her about her new so-called friends." Kate looked at him and frowned and Arlene said, "I understand you are moving?"

"Yes, we are," said Kate. "And I know Becky's having difficulty dealing with that. But we can't stay here just because out 14 year old daughter doesn't want to go."

Arlene smiled and said, "Moving can be hard on kids."

"Adults too," said Kate and Roger looked at her. Maybe he was the selfish one, he thought. Taking a promotion across the country. He said, "Hundreds of kids move. They have to learn to adjust."

"And I'm sure Becky will adjust," said Arlene. "It just may take her a while."

Roger found himself saying, "We never had any problems with Sara. None whatsoever. Model student. Straight A's, then along comes Becky."

Kate shot him a look and Arlene said gently, "We're not talking about Sara."

Later as they made their way out to their separate cars,

Kate to go home and Roger to go back to the office for who knew how long, Kate said, "Roger, I'm worried about you."

"Don't be. When this case is over we'll take a nice holiday, just the two of us.."

"But that's what you always say. 'When this case is over, when this case is over.' Roger, you have to learn to be there, be all there even when you're in the middle of other things. You can't put your family on hold, put *me* on hold just because you're in the middle of an important case. Sure, we have great times when we get together just the two of us *after* an important case, but we need to be a family all the time!"

"So, what do you want me to do? Quit my job? I could do that you know, get a job here in Chester as a security guard somewhere. That apparently would be better for all! Becky included. You, too, apparently. If I just quit. Stayed here in Chester instead of moving clear across the country as you said, then Becky would do better in school!" He was becoming angry. He didn't know where the words were coming from but they tumbled out of him in a frustrated rage.

"Roger, no, it's not that. I want to move. I want to be closer to my family, I do. And Becky will get used to it. It will be nice there. It's just you—you can't operate on five hours of sleep a night. I don't care how important this case is. If you move to New Brunswick as the sergeant, and you take each case so personally, I really fear for you. I do."

"Yeah, well I gotta go." And he started to move off, his mind already on Mary Louise. Suddenly he longed to get to the detachment where things were comfortable and people didn't complain when he was tired. They just fed him more coffee and expected him to continue. He was indispensable. He was the only one who had visited the Jonas complex down in Portland. He knew how it operated. No one else did. Didn't Kate understand that?

When he got into his car he looked over to see Kate, her head bent over the steering wheel of her car. He felt a pang, but it would be as he promised. After this case wound down— and dear God, make that soon—they would get away, just the two of them. Maybe even up to Edmonton, over to Banff. It would be okay then. Kate would see. It would be okay then. Once this case was over.

CHAPTER 50

It was late afternoon on a Wednesday when Aggie Percell was rooting around the basement of St. Annes looking for the Christmas costumes. She was in charge of getting the Sunday School children ready for the annual Christmas pageant and Florence Rewzins, who led the junior choir, had told her that all of the costumes—the Mary costume, the Joseph costume, costumes for all the shepherds and the angels were in a big box in the basement cupboard. Well, so help her, she had looked in every basement cupboard in every single room, but still couldn't find them. And there was no one down here to help her either, what with Father Graeme upstairs somewhere and that janitor they had who was nowhere around. She dearly wanted those costumes tonight. She'd set aside this evening to wash and iron them and do minor repairs. Most likely the garland on the angels would have to be replaced, and the Mary costume would have to be rehemmed for the much shorter girl who was playing Mary this year.

But where was that box? She'd looked in the Sunday School cupboard, the kitchen supplies cupboard, the choir room, but still no box. She decided she'd give herself 20 more minutes. If in 20 minutes she couldn't find the box, she'd go and call someone.

Between the Men's room and the Ladies' room there was a narrow door, a door she must have seen a hundred times, but noticed it now for the first time. She tried it. It was unlocked. She poked her head into the narrow opening. It was a boiler room of some sort, dark and musty smelling. Surely Flo wouldn't have put the box in here, would she? But she'd looked everywhere else, hadn't she? It was certainly worth a try. As her eyes adjusted to the dim light she began to look around.

The room was small, about six feet by six feet with an uneven cement floor. The room, although dusty smelling, seemed empty enough. She was just about to close the door when she saw the edge of a dark box leaning against the far wall. She hunched through the narrow door sideways, begrudging herself that she hadn't stuck to her diet. The little room made her feel claustrophobic. "Just grab the box and pull it out into the basement," she told herself.

When she got closer, she noticed that it wasn't a box at all but a very old steamer trunk. Could Flo have put the costumes in here? The trunk was wedged inside a space in the wall, a small open shelf barely visible from the door way.

Aggie tried to pull the trunk out. It was heavy, but costumes were heavy, weren't they? Besides, this trunk looked big enough to house the wooden manger, the wisemen's gifts and the baby Jesus. She pulled and lugged and heaved, almost gave up, but then she thought, "I've got to get at these costumes tonight." With a final shove, the trunk budged out of its space. She dragged it by its handles across the cement floor, through the doorway and into the main part of the basement.

When she lifted the lid, she was immediately disappointed. It wasn't the costumes at all, but what looked like stacks of papers, some rubberbanded together, some loose and some stuffed in envelopes. As well, there were cassette tapes, and stacks of incredibly dirty spiral bound notebooks.

"I don't need papers, I need angel costumes," said Aggie Percell in disgust.

****

At the top of the stairs Howard Becker froze. There it was, his trunk, his special, private place sitting open in the middle of the room with a lady crouched over the top of it!

His gun was in there, wrapped in paper towels and shoved into the bottom. His puppets were in there too, also at the very bottom. He'd taken them out of his apartment and stuffed them in there after Mrs. Philpott went to the hospital. And now there was a stranger down there going through his stuff! What was she doing with his things? But there she was, picking up his notebooks, exclaiming over them, frowning. How dare she touch his things!

He clutched the railing and flexed his fingers, then gripped tightly on the rail; tighter, tighter. The voices were starting again. He could hear them in his head like hundreds of orchestra instruments tuning up before a concert. Louder, louder. If that lady, that stranger saw the gun, if she reached down the sides and pulled up one of the puppets he would have to kill her. There was no other way. He waited.

****

Well, that was a big waste of time, thought Aggie to herself as she shut the lid and shoved it over against the wall. "I'll get Father Graeme or the janitor to move it back in the closet," she thought to herself. She wiped her smudgy fingers on her slacks in time to see the janitor striding toward her, flexing his fingers, an odd, almost detached expression on his face.

"Oh, Mr. Becker," she said approaching him. "You wouldn't know where the Christmas costumes are? I've looked just about everywhere, and I can't imagine where Flo has put them...."

But her voice faded as the janitor strode past her without looking and entered the Men's Room.

Aggie shook her head and headed up the stairs. It was getting late, she had supper to make and things to do. She'd have to phone Flo this evening.

CHAPTER 51

Mary Louise thought about Carolyn's words as she got out of her wet ski things and into a pair of jeans and a sweater. Perhaps she should go to the police. After all, why was she protecting David anyway? David had already killed one person and was now threatening her. It was ridiculous to keep running. She had told Carolyn, a complete stranger, everything and the sky hadn't fallen in. Maybe if she called and made an appointment with Constable St. Marie they could sit down and she'd tell her everything. Except she didn't have David's phone number or address anymore. Odd, that David would steal the very letter he had written.

It was late afternoon in her cabin when Mary Louise made the decision to go home. She had a job, after all. She couldn't keep running forever. She was a teacher with not a great deal of sympathy for students who were truant. And here she was a truant teacher! She smiled in spite of her self.

After supper she would drive home, drop off her suitcase and then head over to the RCMP detachment. She turned on the TV to catch the early news in time to see her face on the screen and the announcer's voice saying, "Have you seen this woman?"

Mary Louise stood still, a chill gripping the back of her neck and making its tracings down her spine. She forced herself to listen to the rest of the broadcast. "Her help is wanted in connection with an important police investigation." Her mind reeled. Maybe they had found David already and had arrested him.

She put her payment, room key and a quick thank you note on the dresser and left.

CHAPTER 52

By 7:30 p.m. Mary Louise was pulling in to her carport. Anxiousness gripped her as she retrieved her bag from the back seat and locked the car. There were notes taped to her door from the RCMP asking her to contact them immediately. No doubt her answering machine would be filled with messages as well. She was surprised that there wasn't a police car sitting waiting for her to arrive.

From her porch she picked up two *Calgary Heralds*; she'd forgotten to cancel the paper. She was just about to unlock her door when she heard a voice.

"Marylouise Jonas. You can't hide anymore."

She jumped. The voice was timid, like a child's, a falsetto. She saw no one. "Who's there?" she called. In her panic she had dropped her keys, and she frantically scrabbled for them on the snowy porch.

"I said you can't hide anymore."

She looked up. From the top of her hedge a large furry rabbit puppet was waving it's floppy ears and talking. Mary Louise gasped and backed against the wall. Her keys were still somewhere in the snow on her unshoveled porch. She couldn't see them. She turned to run.

"I wouldn't run if I were you," said the puppet. "I have a gun."

Mary Louise clambered down the porch. In her rush she slipped on the snowy walk and fell, twisting her ankle. Momentarily she was stunned, which gave the "puppet" enough time to show its true self. A small unshaven man in a khaki jacket limped forward, gun in his right hand, puppet still in his left hand, the puppet did all the talking.

"What do you want?" she gasped.

"You have to come with me."

"Who are you? What do you want?"

"You ask too many questions," said the falsetto puppet voice.

Slowly she got up, but her ankle hurt severely and she began to wonder if it was broken. The rabbit puppet continued to wag its ears.

"Where's your cat?" asked the rabbit.

"My *cat*?"

"You heard me, your cat?"

"In Calgary."

"Oh no!" screamed the man using his normal voice now. "No cat—that ruins everything! You have to get the cat!"

Frantically she looked up and down the street, but everything was quiet and dark. Where were the police when you needed them?

"You want me to drive to Calgary?"

He paused, seemed to consider and then said, "All three of you should have died at one time. Avenge the death of Paula. And now I'll have to wait. Wait until tomorrow. Yes, that's right. We'll get the cat tomorrow. Now move it!" He pointed with the gun hand around to the back of her house.

"Where?" said Mary Louise.

"To that shed. Now!" He was pointing toward her gazebo. "Over there!"

She limped painfully across the snow. He followed along behind. "You can't get in there," said Mary Louise. "It's locked."

He laughed. "I have the key. On your back porch."

"Drat," she said to herself. Despite her best advice, she always hung the key to the gazebo on a hook outside her patio door.

He unlocked the gazebo and shoved her roughly inside.

She fell against one wall and landed painfully on the wooden floor.

She was not alone. Against the far wall a young man lay on the floor, hands tied behind his back, ankles tied, a gag in his mouth. He looked up when she arrived and his eyes widened.

"Everything is ruined because of the cat," said the man, still waving the gun with one hand, the puppet on the other. "Now you have to stay here overnight and I will kill you tomorrow when we get the cat." He was talking in his puppet voice again. Mary Louise just stared at him. He went on, "It's God's judgment. It's ordained. All of his line must be wiped out!"

The note, thought Mary Louise. The threats, the puppets. But who was this man? Surely not David! He was too old, too short. No. But who was he? "Get me out of here, God," she prayed, "and I promise I'll go to church." She rubbed her ankle. It hurt and was beginning to swell.

"And now I have to tie you up, too. The way I did your father. So you'll never get away. Until tomorrow when we get the cat." His voice was coming out in spurts of confused speech. Every so often he'd stop mid-sentence and clutch at his stomach.

He pulled a ball of twine from the pocket of his khaki jacket and with the gun carefully held at her head with one hand, he wound around the twine around her wrists with the other. He tied them in front of her not very tightly, Mary Louise noted. Then he tied the twine around her ankles which brought tears of pain to her eyes. He placed a piece of black duct tape over her mouth despite her squirming.

Then he locked them in the room and left. Outside of the gazebo she could hear the man retching in the bushes. Then she heard the muffled sound of feet tromping slowly through the snow.

Mary Louise leaned against the wall and tried without success to rid her wrists of their bonds.

She moved her mouth, pushing her tongue against the tape.

It tasted horribly, tasted like those puppets smelled. But she figured if she could loosen the tape then she could call for help. Meanwhile, the young man was thumping his legs against the wall.

After about five minutes, Mary Louise succeeded in loosening the tape, it hung off the end of her chin like a misplaced costume beard. Then she began screaming and calling for help, until she realized that two voices were probably better than one.

She said to the young man, "I don't know who you are or why we're in here, and I have no idea why he was so bent on getting my cat, but if you move over here, I think I can at least untie the gag in your mouth. Then we'll work on getting everything else free."

He shoved his lanky body across the floor to where she lay. A few minutes later his gag was loosened, too.

"Who are you?" she said. "What's going on?"

"I was hoping you would know." His voice was resonant and deep. "I saw him only once before. Yesterday he came racing at me while I was taking a walk and starts going on about how my whole family has to die. I have absolutely no idea what his problem is."

"Well," said Mary Louise blowing a stray hair off her nose with her mouth, "my name is Mary Louise Jones. Nice to meet you." She held out her tied arms in a mock hand shake.

"Yeah," the man said and looked down.

"So, who are you then? I have no inclination of just sitting here waiting to die. If we work together maybe we can come up with a plan."

"Yeah." But his voice was quiet.

"Who are you?"

The young man looked up. And Mary Louise gazed into eyes that were inexplicably familiar. She stared at him. It was like looking in a mirror. Thick dark hair. Slightly wide-ish nose. A wide mouth. Gentle smile.

"My name is David Brackett." He said the words slowly and distinctly. The words were like a punch that took the air out of her. For several minutes she said nothing. Just stared at him, at his hair, at his face, at his long legs.

"Baby Sean," she said finally, and her voice was a whisper.

He smiled. For a while no one said anything. The only sounds was the night wind swirling around the shuttered gazebo. Neither moved.

Then she said, "How tall are you?"

"How *tall* am I?"

She laughed. "That was a stupid question."

"I'm six foot three."

After a while she said. "Tallness runs in the family."

He said nothing, just gazed at the wooden floor. It was getting colder and Mary Louise could feel the damp cold on her toes. She could barely feel her ankle anymore. She wiggled her toes to try to keep them warm. She said, "What are you doing here?"

"I don't know. A few hours ago that man was in my motel room and made me drive him here. At which point he tied me up at gun point."

Silence. Mary Louise was rubbing her wrists against her the buckle on her loafer. If she could untie her wrists, then she could untie David and the two of them could get out of here.

David said, "It's funny we would meet here. In your shed."

"It's a gazebo." Mary Louise understood that their conversation was strained, that they were talking about all the wrong things. Tallness and gazebos. They should be getting caught up on 25 years. They should be smiling and hugging, like they do on talk shows. "Come and meet your mother whom you haven't seen in a quarter of a century!" And then they would parade out on stage to bright band music and the applause of half the country. Not this.

"What's a gazebo?"

"In the summer I take the shutters off, pile them underneath and sit out here and read. Sometimes Johanna comes over. I used to read to her out here sitting in lawn chairs. It was sort of our special place, and then I decided to build a gazebo. Now she's too old for me to read to, so we just come out and talk. It's our special place for talking."

"Who's Johanna?" His voice was strained.

"A neighbor girl. I never had children of my own....I mean...." She looked down.

"It's a good place for talking," he said quietly.

A long pause. Mary Louise felt she ought to say something, that something was somehow required of her. She was the Mother, after all. She said nothing, just stared at the white wooden boards of the floor of the gazebo. They would need painting in the spring. Funny, she would think of it now.

She said, "We should be screaming. Someone might hear."

"Yeah," but he was looking down. His voice was strained. Only a mother for a couple of minutes but already she was failing. She felt a couple of tears form at the corner of her eyes. "Stop it," she told herself. "You don't cry, that's not a part of you."

David said, "I would like this place in the summer."

"I like plants, gardens and hedges. I've worked on this property for a long time."

"It's nice."

"I know."

There was a silence again. Mary Louise looked over at David, at Sean. Her son, not dead, not a monster. And relief suddenly overwhelmed her. It wasn't David who had been threatening her. Never David.

David said, "I wish I knew why we were both locked in here."

Mary Louise thought. "Maybe I know. Let me tell you who your grandfather is, let me tell you about things that have been happening to me, then maybe together we can figure out why we're here."

"My grandfather?"

"Your grandfather. My father was Dr. Sterling Jonas."

"The evangelist? The one who was murdered?" He stared at her, his eyes wide.

"That's him."

He shook his head back and forth. "I don't believe it!"

"Believe it. I shouldn't have told you. Your heritage isn't all that noble."

David asked, "What does that crazy guy who tied us up in here have to do with Jonas?"

"I don't know but maybe if I told you the rest of what's been happening we can figure out what's going on."

"You've been threatened. The police told me that. They picked me up. They thought I was the one doing it. But I was just parked in front of your house...."

"They told you I was threatened?"

"Something about puppets. I didn't get it. I didn't know what they were talking about."

"Puppets. I thought it was you."

"Me?"

"I thought it was you who was threatening me with puppets. But now I know it was our Mr. Rabbit friend."

"Me? But why? Why would I threaten you?"

She shook her head and interrupted him. "I was thinking crazy thoughts. Nothing made sense. Nothing makes sense now."

Again there was a pause. There were lots of these quiet spaces that they were having trouble filling.

He asked, "You married?"

"No. And what about you?"

"No, I'm not married. Don't even have a girlfriend."

She smiled. "That's not what I meant. I mean—tell me about you, your life."

"I have two parents, two wonderful people who told me about you from the very beginning. They gave me the cross that you left with me. I've been a Christian since I was little. Sometimes when I've wanted to falter or to move away from my faith, my birthmother's cross has held me fast."

She looked away. What was happening to her lately? First Carolyn, now her own son. She moved slightly away from him, and continued to rub the rope against the buckle on her boot. "I've almost got this," she said. "As soon as I get this loose, we'll get out of here."

"Yeah," he said.

CHAPTER 53

Kate wasn't the only one that Roger was snapping at. Roberta, Roy Laird, Dennis, Duane and a couple of unnamed constables from Calgary, all found their way in front of his foul mood. Finally Laird took him aside, "Get a grip man," he told him, placing an arm on his shoulder and leading Roger into his office. "This whole case doesn't revolve around you and you can't be six places at once. We're all doing our jobs. We'll find that puppeteer."

"But we don't have him. Nor can we find Mary Jones. Excuse me Mary Louise Jones, nor can we find that David Brackett character, although how he fits into this I have no idea...."

"We'll *find* him, Corporal! Now go home!"

"Go home?"

"Yeah, go home. How long has it been since you've seen your wife?"

"A few hours ago at a teacher's meeting for Sara."

"Sara? I didn't know they had teacher's meetings for university kids."

"I meant Becky. Give me a break."

"Go home, take Kate out for supper, then go home and get a good night's sleep. You're no use to us here like you are."

"Can't sleep tonight. Tonight's the night we find the guy."

"If we're lucky."

"Go home. You're a wreck."

Roger left. Laird was right, of course. Fatigue had stripped him of his senses. Kate was his wife but he had hurt her. He was hurting his whole family. Becky. Sara. Moving. And when was the last time he had read the Bible and prayed? Last Sunday he hadn't even gone to church, so busy was he on "the case." He was reflecting on these thoughts as he wound his car home. Part way home he veered his car right, rather than left. A few minutes later he found himself driving down the ravine road. It was plowed only part way and he drove down as far as he could and parked. He put his head in his hands then and all he could say was "Oh God." And as he sat there, head in hands, tears of fatigue at the edges of his eyes, questions of why: Why the move now? Would the house sell? Why the continuing problems with Becky? Why Sara's choice of boyfriend?

It didn't happen all of a sudden. It wasn't like a vision from the depths, an angel visitation walking up the creek toward him; but from somewhere deep within him, a peace began to surround him, a peace which he recognized as the Holy Spirit ministering to him. He bowed his head and prayed. He didn't know how long he was there, but when he rose and started the car he made a decision.

On the road to home, Roger called Kate on the cellular.

"Hello." Her voice was dull.

"Have you had supper?"

"Not yet, I was going to make something for the girls and me."

"How about going out with me? I'm on my way home to take you out."

"Out for supper?"

"Don't sound so surprised."

"You have time for this?"

"I'm going to make time. Besides, I have to tell you about something."

At home, Roger showered and changed into regular clothes in a record seven minutes.

Supper was Italian food at Anthony's, one of the few very good restaurants in Chester. Most of the tables were taken when Roger and Kate arrived, and he sincerely hoped that none of the reporters from places beyond who were staying in Chester would recognize him. Being out of uniform helped.

They followed their waitress to a private table in the back, specially requested by Roger when he had made reservations from the car.

Steak and mushrooms and a Diet Coke for Roger and clam fetuccine and herbal tea for Kate.

"I'm trying to develop my seafood taste buds for when we move east," she explained after the waitress left.

He leaned forward. "That's something I want to talk to you about." He paused and she looked at him. "I've made a decision. I've decided not to go," he said simply.

"No!" and then, "Why?"

"There are a couple of reasons. Hear me out. I've been thinking about this a lot. The first one is, that I guess I've been selfish. I came home and basically *told* my family we were moving east. The promotion's something I wanted, and that was that. I didn't say 'What do you think of this?' or 'How would you feel about this?' I just come storming in like I always do and say, "Hey guys, we're moving, and you'll never guess where?' No wonder Becky's bent out shape. And I never even asked you. You have a career here, too, and Sara, what would she do? Stay here by herself and go to university?"

"Sara says she wants to move, and Becky will be okay, and you didn't come storming in. That's not how I remember it. And we'd talked about it before. When you wrote the sergeant's exam we knew it would mean a move."

"Yeah, but I never thought it would be so far."

"But you said so yourself, there's so much opportunity there, special training and such." Kate was getting flustered and she was talking fast.

"There's another reason, too."

"What other reason?"

"I won't be a good sergeant."

"Don't say idiotic things."

"No, it's true, Kate. I take things too personally, too seriously."

"You have to take police work seriously."

"No, what I mean is—right now we're on the verge with this whole Jonas thing and I'm a basket case."

"You're tired, that's all."

"Yeah, but if I am tired I shouldn't *act* tired."

"Yeah, and you can wear red tights with a big 'S' on your shirt."

"I'm serious, Kate."

"So am I, Roger. You're the best police officer they have up there, *because* you take things so seriously. How many times have you told me that certain people, witnesses and such only want to talk to you. That they ask specifically for you. And you're not a basket case."

Roger shrugged. "I lose my focus too often."

"I don't know what you're talking about."

"Sometimes I lose what and who I'm doing this for. I was praying earlier, before I called you. The Bible says that I'm a minister of God, ordained so people can live peacefully and quietly, and not fear their neighbors. But so often I get just like Jonas, intoxicated with my own power. I was driving home and thinking about these things, Kate. So that's why I've decided not to go to New Brunswick. Being sergeant would give me more power, and right now I just don't think I can handle it."

"Roger, don't say no. Sleep on it please."

He promised he would.

CHAPTER 54

Roger dropped Kate off and promised he would be home, the minute he checked in at the detachment. When he arrived, there was an inordinate amount of activity. He saw in Laird's office two people swathed in blankets. The woman, Mary Jones, had one leg up on another chair. The young man he recognized as David Brackett sat next to her. Laird called him over.

"We found these two," he said, "just a little while ago. Our suspect both in the Jonas murder, the puppet incident, and possibly the Philpott murder tied these two up in a shed in Mary's property."

"How'd you find them?"

Laird snorted. "That was the easy part. We went to Mary Jones' house. Her car was there so we thought, bingo, and all we did is follow the tracks through the snow and there they are, the two of them, tied up in the shed. They started yelling as soon as we closed the door on our car."

"No puppet master yet?"

"No, but we got a full ID. He's a small man, walks with a limp, wears a khaki jacket and seemed to...."

"Hold it!" Said Roger putting his hand up. "That sounds like Howard Becker. The guy in the place where the Philpott lady was killed. Get a car over there right now! Any idea what's behind all this?"

"Not yet. Neither one of them in there has any idea why he went after them. Oh, by the way the two in there are mother and son."

"Excuse me?"

"Mother and son. Mary Louise Jones," he emphasized the Louise part, "is the biological mother of David Brackett. David came looking for his birth mother and winds up involved in the murder of, get this, his grandfather."

"Something wrong with her leg?"

"Sprained ankle."

Roberta called in from the hallway, "We're on our way to his apartment now. The guy comes home, he gets nailed. Don't think he'll get too far though. The two in there say he's pretty sick."

Roger rubbed his chin. "But what's his connection with Jonas?"

"That's the one missing link. Only he'll be able to tell us that. He's lived here all his life. Never even been to Oregon. Doesn't know that Fiona Stone person, or Muriel Ames. No one."

He remembered the words of Dr. Mosaic then, *"It could be as simple as someone holding a grudge because Sterling didn't heal their mother like he promised he would."*

Roger said, "Maybe Jonas was supposed to heal him and it didn't take."

Laird shrugged.

CHAPTER 55

His stomach was hurting worse now. He lay on the concrete floor and pressed his belly against the cool of the cement wall. He wouldn't go back to his apartment. Mrs. Philpott was going to call the Mounties on him.

But why didn't Paula come? He was calling and calling for her and still she didn't come. And there was another thing that confused him. His trunk wasn't where he had left it. It was out in the main part of the basement. He couldn't remember putting it there. He began to cry then, but the coolness of the cement was not enough to quench the burning in his stomach. "Why don't you come, Paula, why did you have to go?" He lay down and hugged the soft rabbit to his face. It even smelled like Paula. But there was something hard inside its body. He reached in and pulled out a black gun. He stared confusedly at it. Where had it come from? There was something in his memory about two people in a shed, tied up; he hadn't shot them, had he? So many people had to die because of Paula. His stomach was burning, but thankfully the voices weren't bothering him. Maybe they would be quiet for a minute and let him rest.

He heard a voice then, a whispery voice and an arm on his shoulder. He didn't shrug it off. He let it lay there. "Paula?" he asked. He was too tired to move, to look over at the person who was touching him.

"Howard." The voice was familiar. But it didn't sound like Paula.

"Paula, it hurts so much."

"I know, Howard. But this isn't Paula. It's Father Graeme. Do you remember me?"

And all Howard felt was the stroking on his shoulder. Methodically, back and forth, he looked up at the hand, wrinkled, white and veiny. It wasn't Paula's hand. "Howard, you're sick. We're going to get you to a hospital."

"No hospital."

"They can help you in the hospital."

"NO HOSPITAL!" His voice was increasing in strength. Still the hand was rubbing his shoulder, back and forth, gently. Hypnotically. It stilled him.

"Howard, we're going to get help for you." And then the hand stopped in mid-stroke and he was aware of another person in the room. Maybe this was Paula, but no, someone was putting a blanket on him, spreading it out on him.

"No!" he yelled. He didn't want blankets! Especially not that blanket that made it impossible for him to move his arms. But this blanket was just covering him gently, not wrapping him and the voice kept talking gently, very gently, the hand stroking back and forth. He heard the voice whisper something, and then the other person was gone.

"We're going to get you some help, Howard. There are people who can help you. God loves you, Howard. God loves you." And those words went into and out of his mind and were intermingled with dreams. Sometimes he was a young boy again tromping through the farm chasing after the cats and his mother yelling, *"Howie, you're no good like your father. You ain't never gonna amount to nothin' but a hill of beans; why can't you be more like your brother?"*

And then there was Paula, with her long red hair and her smile. She loved him, loved him just the way he was, and they had a dog named Walter. And Paula was telling him everything is going to be all right. All right. All right. And then she was in the wheel chair. Still smiling. Smiling. Smiling. *"It's going to be all right, Howard, you'll see. God will heal me. You'll see, and it will be a miracle!."* But Paula went away.

And that's when the voices began.

"Howard, they're here to help you, to take you to the hospital where they can help you. And I'm going to pray for you. God loves you, Howard, and He always has."

"No hospital!" But as the ambulance attendants carefully moved him onto the stretcher, with an entire contingent of RCMP officers looking on, he was too weak to protest.

CHAPTER 56

"As near as we can figure it," said Roger to Kate a week later, "is Howard's wife Paula went to see Sterling Jonas, who promptly told her to get rid of all her 'worldly' medicines because she was healed."

"But she was a diabetic! Childhood diabetes! Getting rid of her insulin would be like committing suicide!"

"Exactly."

She said quietly, "How many other people have died because they followed his advice?"

Roger shook his head sadly. "Howard himself was a schizophrenic, able to lead a normal life with medication. Jonas told him to throw his away, too."

Kate shook her head in disbelief. The two of them were on an evening walk. It had warmed somewhat since the deep freeze of a week ago. The full moon shone like a giant illuminated disk in the night sky.

"So this Sterling Jonas actually told her to throw away all of her prescriptions? That is so sad."

"Apparently... and by the time she arrived at the hospital she was already dead."

"And her husband held a grudge all this time?"

"According to the psychiatric reports he was always emotionally fragile. When his wife finally died, he went off the deep end. He was in a psychiatric facility for a year."

"And two people died because of this."

"Three, actually if you count Paula Becker."

Roger thought back over the events of the previous week. Howard Becker had been brought in that night a week ago, but not to the detachment, to the hospital, where he still was suffering from some sort of bowel disease. He was still undergoing tests. It would be some time before he would be well enough to stand trial for the murders of Maureen Philpott and Sterling Jonas.

The most surprising factor in the whole thing was that David visited Howard Becker almost every day. RCMP who were guarding his door reported seeing him there sometimes two, three times a day.

Kate was saying, "It was so neat to see Mary Louise and her son at our church on Sunday."

Roger nodded, "I understand he's staying at Mary Louise's house for a while."

"He leaves soon for Israel. That's what he told me in church. And I wouldn't be surprised if she goes out there to see him in the summer. She also told me she'll be flying down to see her aunt Muriel in Seattle for Christmas. She travels a lot, I understand."

"Boy, you guys chatted a lot."

"Speaking of travel...."

"What a nice segue."

"Well, guy," she said putting her arm around his waist and leaning her head on his shoulder, "We've got to start getting you packed."

Roger smiled. He was leaving in a week for New Brunswick.

Other books available
in the RCMP series by Linda Hall:

AUGUST GAMBLE